BREAKAWAY

A.M. JOHNSON

Editing and Formatting by Elaine York,
Allusion Graphics, LLC/Publishing & Book Formatting
www.allusiongraphics.com
Proofreading by Payne Proofing
Cover Design is Bex Harper Designs

BREAKAWAY

To those who dream...
find what gives you passion,
light that match and ignite your soul.

For Kathleen

Head Coach Extraordinaire.

"Risk something, or forever sit with your dreams."

Herb Brooks

BREAKAWAY

(Ice hockey)

Definition: When an offensive player has no defensive players between himself and the goalie, therefore, giving him a chance to skate and shoot the puck at will. Usually, a lapse in the opposing team's defense.

MARK

The familiar sounds of the game, the whistle, the roaring crowd, the jeers, they should've been enough to haul my ass out of this bar. But I kept my nose down and my eyes on the half-empty pint of beer as the commentators tore us apart from the safety of the big screen television hanging to the left of where I sat. Their perfect run-down of our epic fuck-up was almost verbatim, as if Coach sent them a script of how he chewed us out in the locker room while we watched tonight's game tape. Home game. Opening night. We'd had our asses handed to us. Four to one. At least I made that goal. At least I had that.

The rich flavor of the beer did nothing to cover the bitter taste of this loss on my tongue. I should've gone home. It was what I had planned on doing. We were leaving in two days for a stretch of road games, and I needed to regroup—the whole team needed to regroup—but despite Coach's threats, the guys had gone to Channelside, as usual. Partying in numbers generally took the edge off. Girls and

1

booze, anything to drown their sorrows after the disaster we couldn't even really call a game. The thought of going home, alone, lying in my bed, staring at the damn ceiling, trying to figure out how everything had gone to shit tonight was depressing. Though I'd rather suffer in silence, torture myself until I ran every play, every mistake through my head at least five hundred times, I preferred to do it at Mavericks. The small, also my favorite, sports bar on the other side of town. It was closer to where I lived and was always filled with these private college kids too drunk or hopped up on football to give a fuck about hockey. About the fucking letdown of an opener we'd served up.

I drained my beer and stood, dropping a twenty on the bar. Danny gave me a sad smile as I shoved my wallet into my back pocket.

"Don't beat yourself up too much, Melo. You were the only one who showed up to play tonight."

I tried to hide the irritation in my voice but failed miserably. "Nah, man. They just found better holes."

"Your D-men... were they sleeping?" Danny's chuckle reminded me how much he loved to talk shit, especially after we'd lost. He was a Dallas fan. Maybe he should move his ass back to Dallas.

"Don't poke the bear. Not tonight." I gave him a half-hearted smirk.

He raised his eyebrows and shook his head. "It's the new guy on your line, you guys played like you're fighting against each other. He hogged the puck like he had something to prove."

I exhaled a long breath. Everything that happens on the ice stays in the locker room. It was my rule. It was the only way I'd ever been able to co-exist. NHL star and real life.

They couldn't blend, and Danny was screwing that up. Even if he was right, I didn't want to talk about it.

"Maybe you can get a job with those idiots since you have so much to say." I nodded my chin to the television blaring ESPN. "Turn that shit off and put some music on. It's midnight, people want to party, not listen to old dudes talk about how they could've done it better back in the day."

"No way!" The excited voice had my shoulders sagging. "Mark. Mark Carmelo? Holy shit, bro, it's—"

"Keep it down," Danny barked in a harsh whisper and the kid paled.

I chuckled to myself. The kid—he was probably twenty-one or twenty-two—not much younger than me. I was twenty-six, but I felt like I was going on thirty-six. My bones ached more than they should. My whole body did.

"Oh my God, I'm sorry, man, but... it's you."

"It's me." I held out my hand and he took it eagerly.

My smile was sincere as I watched his eyes light with that fire I loved. Our fans were fucking spectacular. I was lucky. Blessed to be able to do what I do. My father strapped skates to my feet the minute I could walk. Hockey, cider, and Monday night football were what my dad had touted as his "religious practices." Growing up in the small town of Redding, just a car ride away from Manchester, New Hampshire, hockey was the culture. My father played and his father played and his father's father played, basically, my blood was made of ice and fury, and the moment my blades hit the rink, I felt the call.

"You were second round draft pick, didn't even get to graduate from The University of Maine before they scooped you up. Best center the college had seen in years. First of your family to play for the NHL." The kid rattled off my life like it was a homework assignment, his eyes going wide. "Fuck, dude, you must get laid constantly."

A real laugh erupted past my lips. It lifted the weight, the feeling I'd been harboring since I'd left the locker room. I loved hockey. That ice in my veins, it was what I lived for. I loved that unique cold smell of the arena, that shiver that trickled down my spine as I made my way down the chute, scented with sweat and anticipation, to the rink. I loved this damn kid and his enthusiasm for the game. It was why I'd stopped partying with my teammates. It was why I'd had to find my way out of the clouds and back to the ice.

Hockey was my dream and I was living it.

"I'm saving myself for marriage." I joked and dropped the kid's hand with a laugh.

Danny's raised brows did little to stifle my laugh. I was who I was, and I didn't hide it. I wasn't into plastic chicks who only wanted me because of my NHL contract. They could pretend all damn day they loved the game, loved my talent, loved the "man," but in the end, I saw right through it. Their eyes only held hunger. They were hungry, thirsty for my money, my apartment, and my dick, regardless of who I was, or what I had to offer. I figured that out pretty fast my rookie year and swore off puck bunnies for life. My teammates used to let me get away with it when I was with Mia, but we'd split two years ago, and the fact I was single and not eating up all that attention, all that pussy being thrown at me, had the rumor mill churning. I never paid it any mind. The media, and their theories, didn't matter one fucking bit to me once I stepped off the ice. After how they treated me when Mia and I split... if it wasn't for my coach and the PR department breathing down my neck, I'd never do another interview ever again.

The fan's name was Kyle, and after I signed his wallet, and every stray piece of paper he could find in his pocket, he finally let me be. Danny's scowl and threat that he'd kick him out if he didn't lay off might've helped. I was grateful his friends had kept to themselves in the back of the bar. It was then, as I turned to watch him leave, that I saw *her*.

"Holy fuck," I whispered to myself.

Apparently not quietly enough because Danny chimed in, "What?"

I ignored him and took a few tentative steps away from the bar to get a better look. She was surrounded by guys in stiff white button-downs and loosened ties. Her long, thick, chocolate-colored hair fell around her heart-shaped face and framed her full, rose-colored cheeks.

It was definitely her. Right?

My eyes remembered those bashful lips, those pert and pink fucking lips I'd wanted to consume the first night I'd met her, as they parted in a smile. It was barbaric, but I was jealous of the guy who'd just made her laugh. She was all shy smiles and looked almost the same as when I'd met her around this same time last year. Except for the dark-rimmed glasses and silky office-ready shirt, she looked exactly the same. It was sick how my body reacted, how my legs dared to move me even closer, how my heart thundered just as fast as it would've on the ice when I was about to score.

Holy God, it *was* her.

My feet wouldn't stop moving, no matter how hard I tried to find the will to make them. Danny's confused questions became white noise as I neared the table. Her head was down, her eyes, those funny-colored brown eyes with that burst of blue around the pupil, were focused, intent as her fingers trailed over the screen of her phone.

5

It was irrational, but the hair on the back of my neck stood at attention, the memory of what her hand felt like in mine, the way she'd smelled like fruit-scented soap and summer, all of it came rushing back, and the need to taste her made my mouth water. I didn't get the chance last time, and as if a year had never passed, I felt her skin, the heat of her cheek just like it had scorched my palm and never healed.

She was right there, sitting at a table with three men, one of them could be her husband, and yet, each step I took came quicker than the last.

"Stevie?" Her name dripped from my mouth in a hungry question.

It was an out-of-body experience. Her name on my lips felt both foreign and familiar at the same time. Why was she in town? Had things changed since the last time I'd seen her? I swallowed past the fear and the narrowing of my throat. When her eyes met mine and widened, sparking with the flame I'd remembered so clearly, a big, victorious smile spread across my face.

You'd think I'd just scored on a breakaway.

"M-Mark?" She fumbled and her left hand raised to her full lips in shock.

The movement guided my gaze to her hand. Her left finger was bare of the diamond that used to adorn it. She could've taken it off for the night. Maybe it didn't fit, or was being cleaned. I could've told myself this shit all night, and it wouldn't have stopped the progression of my steps, or the drum in my heart and how it consumed me with every beat. The adrenaline spiked in my chest, like it did in the rink when that lamp lit, when I skated faster, harder, and changed the game for the night with a winning goal. She had my heart sprinting, my muscles celebrating, and the other guys at the table, they were insignificant. There was nothing stopping me this time, no one defending, no obstacles between me and her. When her shock faded and her eyes fell to my mouth, I knew I had an open shot.

STEVIE
ONE YEAR EARLIER

"Can you have liquor after drinking wine? Or should you have liquor first?" I asked.

"Liquor before beer—"

"I know the saying, Reagan, but I don't think you can count wine as beer."

She smiled and raised her shot of Jack as she cheered, "You'll be hungover regardless. So who cares?"

She tipped the glass to her lips, and I watched in awe as the dark amber liquid disappeared in less than one second flat. My laugh, the wine, the heavy bass of the bar, made me smile. "I'm glad I came."

She set the shot glass down and leaned across the table with a serious gleam lighting her dark green eyes. "It's been three years, punk, I don't care that Ben thinks he's too busy to come home and visit, I expected more from you."

The guilt Reagan was too good at brandishing sliced through my armor. I'd tried to keep everything wrapped up tight since I'd landed less than twenty-four hours ago, but being back home, seeing Reagan with her pink hair, living life, breathing, with a pulse I envied—her little barb shattered through my weak exterior and tears filled my eyes.

"Ben... Ben and I... I'm so lonely, Ray."

Her smile evaporated. "I can tell."

"You can?" I held her all-knowing stare.

"He was never the one."

My breath came quick and fast as I tried, unsuccessfully, to dislodge the boulder in my throat. "He's been good to me."

"He's lucky to have you," she said with a familiar edge as she raised her hand, waving to the server. She held up two fingers and the server nodded. "What's going on?"

I felt so selfish even thinking about leaving Ben. He made good money. He didn't hit me. He didn't cheat. He helped clean the house, and really, most women I knew told me their husbands didn't even put the seat down after they peed. Ben always did. He was neat and orderly...and utterly lifeless. Reagan had always thought he was controlling, but I'd felt so removed for so long, I hadn't been able to see it.

"I feel like I'm losing who I am... who I was. Who we used to be."

"You married the captain of the chess team, Stevie. What did you expect?"

"That was high school." I rolled my eyes and took a deep sip of my Cabernet.

"Yeah, I know, and you've never been with anyone but him."

"That's a good thing."

She pursed her lips. "Then what's the problem? Why are you here? And more importantly, why isn't Ben?"

"He had a really—"

"Important thing, yeah, you said that already."

The server dropped two shot glasses of whiskey at our table with a smile and hurried to the back with an almost full tray of booze. There were about twenty guys in the other room being rowdy as hell. The music, combined with the banter coming from the tables around us was loud enough on its own, but those guys must've been celebrating something with the amount of alcohol I'd watched the servers haul back there tonight.

"Be straight with me, Stevie. You two have been married for what, thirteen years? You used to be attached at the hip, why wouldn't he come home with you? You guys haven't visited since—"

"Gary's funeral."

Reagan's eyes glassed over, and she brought the fresh shot of whiskey to her lips, but not before pushing the other one in front of me. "To Gary," she said in a strained voice, and we both gulped down the fire water.

Gary was a high school friend of ours who passed away three years ago in a motorcycle crash. No wife. No kids. He'd preferred things that way, but I still felt terrible for his parents. He'd been their only child. Gary's name sucked the wind out of me and pulled my life into perspective. I had a husband who loved me. Well, used to love me. Well, loved who he thought I could've been. But, I had my health. I was breathing. I had a nice house in Richmond, Virginia. A great job as a CPA. Even if it was for Ben's company, and maybe I was more like his assistant, I was still my own person. I did my own thing.

My own thing.

I didn't really know what that was anymore.

I eyed Reagan's pink hair and twirled a boring brown wave of my own through my fingers, evading her original question.

"I'm jealous of your locks."

"I can do your hair this color, too. Or anything really. I'll cancel some appointments for you, fit you in before you go. I used to love it when you sported that fire engine red, it was sexy as hell."

I snorted. "I was sixteen... and Ben would go postal. I told him I wanted to get that tattoo—"

"The phases of the moon?"

"Yeah."

"Oh my God, let's get it done before you go." Her excitement bubbled and brewed in her green eyes.

"Ben flipped when I suggested it. Said tats are trashy."

"Trashy?" She was appalled.

My gaze scanned the half sleeve of ink on her left arm. "He's different, Ray. He's changed."

But I was still me. Still not good enough.

I finished the last sip of wine and set my glass on the table, avoiding Ray's shrewd stare. I lifted my hair off my neck, letting the cool air of the bar tickle away the humidity on my skin. I closed my eyes and breathed in the deep scent of the south, and the beer and sweat of the bar. I let the loud punk music rage in my ears and remembered whom I'd once been.

"Um... Stevie, the guy to your six is seriously digging on you right now. And sweet Jesus, he's hot."

My eyes popped opened but I kept my gaze on my friend. "Stop. No one is looking—"

"Hey." The deep caramel tone of his voice painted my cheeks with heat. Reagan's Cheshire grin made it worse.

It was an epic feat, but I somehow managed to keep my eyes on her. His clean scent. Ocean water and something masculine filled the air around me. Smothered me, begged me to turn and give him one look.

"Hey." Reagan's sweet voice had my eyes narrowing.

I suddenly wished my wine glass was full so I had a reason to grip it and still my shaking fingers. Men made me nervous, in general. I'd only ever been with Ben. I never got hit on and the heat from this guy's body was drowning me. It didn't help that I was able to see from my peripheral vision, the large size of his arm and how it was covered in ink as it rested on the table.

Reagan held out her hand. "I'm Reagan and my very rude friend over there is Stevie."

His chuckle warmed my belly.

"My name's Mark, it's nice to meet you."

My eyes hadn't strayed from their forward position. They were good little girls and stayed right on Ray's, but I could feel him, feel him assessing me. Goose bumps trailed along my neck and shoulders.

"Stevie... that's a different name."

"Her mom named her after the singer of Fleetwood Mac."

Silence.

"As in Stevie Nicks... you know... *Go Your Own Way....* *Landslide... Rhiannon.*" Reagan was incredulous.

"Not ringing a bell."

"Awe... that's cute. How old *are* you, sweetheart?" she asked, and I had to stifle my giggle.

His laugh was palpable in the space between us and for some reason, its open candor finally broke my resolve.

I wished I hadn't looked.

Maybe if I'd ignored him. Played the uptight bitch I'd gotten so good at portraying, I wouldn't have ever felt it.

The shift.

The weight that held my heart broke free and fell into my gut, raising every last one of the butterflies from the dead.

"Twenty-five."

"You should know who Fleetwood Mac is, I don't give a fuck if you're twelve." Reagan's smile was teasing and his was—beautiful.

He was tall and formed from lean muscle. The faded gray, short-sleeve shirt he had on hugged his broad shoulders and chest, exposing strong arms covered in full sleeves of ink and powerful muscles. His brown hair was on the lighter side of chocolate and needed to be cut. It curled over his ears and flopped across his forehead. His structured jaw was smattered with stubble like he'd decided a few days ago he wanted to grow a beard. I liked the way his upper lip was bigger than the bottom and I'd bet a million dollars they'd feel just as soft as they looked. They stretched into a broad smile, revealing straight white teeth. The front top two teeth were slightly parted with an endearing gap. He was charm and power and as he laughed, I wished I would've shaken his hand when he offered, at least then I could've said I touched him.

Cinnamon-colored eyes held me captive. "Hi," he said again, this time just for me and without my permission, without any warning, I smiled just for him. "Looks like you need another glass of wine." Before I could protest, he raised his hand to the server passing by. "Can I get a glass of..."

He let the request dangle in the air waiting for me.

"Cabernet."

"Cab for the lady, and..." He nodded his head to Reagan.

"Whiskey, Jack, if you don't mind?" she asked and gave me a private grin.

"And for you?" I didn't miss how the blonde bombshell of a server batted her lashes for Mister Wonderful as she asked.

"Grab me your favorite IPA."

He didn't spare her a second glance after she nodded with a flirty smile, giving me his full attention. "You should come sit with me."

He pointed over his shoulder to the group of noisy men I'd noticed earlier in the back room.

"Um, I think—"

"Sure." Reagan answered for me and shot me a glare that said, "Comply or die."

I was already on glass number four, and I'd come home for the weekend to relax with my friends, hadn't I? The whole purpose for this trip down memory lane, to my hometown, was to figure out what I wanted. To decide if Ben was really it for me. It wasn't a coincidence I'd chosen the weekend Ben had a conference he couldn't miss to come back home for a visit.

Somewhere down the line, the girl I used to be was kicking up a fuss, wondering when I'd finally let her out of timeout. My husband and I had spent the last three months in counseling, and I swear to God, he had no idea who he married. Or maybe he'd changed and I didn't? I couldn't help that I wanted more than sex once a week, or romantic dates, and maybe a few adventures. Sometime during the last thirteen years, the late nights at the office, the lackluster life we'd slid into, became a noose around my neck. We had no children and that was fine with me. But we never reaped the benefits of being on our own, either. Hell, we didn't even have a dog. We didn't travel; we didn't do anything.

There were no midnight skinny dips in our heated saltwater pool. No fucking on the back porch, there was no fucking, period. Ben even hated the word. It was always that way. Ben was form and function, and like he liked his food—white bread and bland—was how he liked his sex. Ben had succeeded in his dream. He owned his own accounting firm. He was all-American handsome, but he was as cold as the gray stone surrounding our seemingly perfect fireplace. In high school, he'd been youthful and fun, but we got married too fast, and I think we both resigned ourselves to stick with it because it was easier than the alternative. And besides, divorce meant failure, and Ben West did not fail.

I stood and found my balance by gripping the table. The wine hit me harder than I would've expected, and Reagan giggled as she watched Mark watch me.

"You alright?" he asked and reached out to steady me.

My stupid smile trembled at his touch.

The heat of his palm on my exposed arm melted my sensibilities. I had no words for this guy, and I felt like a twitterpated asshole.

I was married.

I purposely ran my left hand through my hair, not missing how his eyes zeroed in on the rock sitting on my ring finger. I couldn't be sure, and maybe it was vain to think it, but it almost looked like disappointment flashed in his light brown eyes. Regardless, the pressure of his grip on my arm remained, and I didn't like how nice it felt.

I regretted listening to Reagan about wearing this stupid sleeveless dress. Sure, it was all soft and jersey cotton. And maybe the dark green color did make my eyes pop. But my boobs were practically falling out of the top, and she knew I hated my so-called curves.

Calling a girl curvy was a nice way of saying she was chubby, or as I liked to say, fluffy. I was too soft and in all the wrong places. My thighs touched, my stomach was smooshy, and I had an ass for days. One nice thing about this dress was that it flowed out from my only good feature, my small-ish waist, hiding all the "curves" I loathed. My mom used to say my height helped with my "full-figure," I guess it was kind of a break that I was five-six and not five-one. I'd look like a roly-poly if I was that short.

"You sure you're okay?" He smiled at me like he could tell his presence made my knees weak. Or maybe he thought I was stupid. A guy like him, a guy who could make a girl dizzy just by smiling, was probably used to this kind of reaction.

I finally managed a strangled, "I'm fine."

The back room roared with a chorus of 'hell yeahs' as we were about to head to his table.

Mark eyed me nervously, as if I might change my mind, and he was probably right, going back to a room full of boisterous boys was not what I'd signed up for tonight.

"Maybe I could just join you guys?" His brow dipped and his dimpled smile turned into an actual blush that had me sitting back down on my chair without an official yes or no.

He pulled out the chair next to Reagan, but she'd lost interest about two minutes ago. Her eyes were glued to her phone.

"I'm meeting Pete. I'm going to grab an Uber, want me to drop you at your mom's?" Reagan asked without even looking at me.

"Now?" I asked, and the squeak of dismay I'd let slip made me internally smack myself. I was only here until Sunday, and she could see her on-again, off-again boyfriend whenever. Me... I hadn't seen her in three years.

Reagan finally looked up and met my glare. She switched her gaze back and forth between Mark and me twice, before she finally said, "Stay."

Mark's smile tipped up at the corners and I shook my head. "Um, no," I whispered like he wasn't sitting right there.

The waitress chose that moment to bring our drinks. Reagan swallowed down her whiskey faster than I could have said 'check, please'.

"You came home for a reason. Remember who you are." She gave me a wink and it was obvious she was feeling the effects of the Jack Daniels.

"You don't have to stay if you'd rather leave." He placed a twenty on the table and started to stand.

I was married, but not dead. I could sit here, have a glass of wine, and talk with a handsome stranger. I didn't have to do anything. It was only eleven, and I wasn't ready to go moping back to my mother's place.

"I'll stay, but you're paying for my Uber." It was a joke, but his laugh drove away any remaining hesitation.

That charming-as-hell smile made my heart skip. "Deal."

Reagan gathered her bag, and me, into a hug. Before she left, she whispered into my ear, "Be careful and don't let him buy you any more drinks. Keep your glass in sight at all times and call me if you need anything."

I squeezed her as I spoke softly, "I'm thirty-two, babe. I can handle myself."

She stepped away and let her eyes scour my body. "I know you can, but I don't know if he can, especially with you in that dress."

His eyes were eating up every inch of me when she backed away. There was a small part of me that didn't want him to ever stop. I was a junkie. A girl placed in a sterile jar, and even though this fabulous dress hid my flaws, I'd take the compliment of having his eyes on me.

She turned and raised her phone in one swift movement. The sound of her camera click made me laugh. "I now have your picture in my phone. If my girl doesn't show up in one piece, I have your mug as evidence."

"You're thorough." His grin was devious.

Reagan smirked, "Last name, please."

My laugh was light as his smile darkened with anxiety. She *was* pretty intense when she wanted to be.

I thought I imagined it, but as he spoke, his body leaned in almost protectively, private, like he didn't want anyone to hear. "Carmelo."

"Well, then, Mark Carmelo, keep my girl safe or it's your ass." She kissed me on the cheek. "See you tomorrow after I get off work, okay?"

"Okay."

MARK
STILL ONE YEAR EARLIER

Eyes like fire met mine only for one fleeting moment before they dropped to the fresh glass of red wine sitting in front of her. *Stevie*. Her silence only increased the color of her round cheeks. This chick was soft everywhere. The kind of soft you wanted to sink into and never stop touching.

"It's a little intimidating..." She raised her eyes. The color, pupils rimmed with a blue burst that bled into a rich brown, threw me off my game, and I had to swallow the `holy shit' that tried to trip from my over-eager mouth. "And not to mention, kind of rude to stare."

Her smile pulled her kissable lips into quiet dimples. It was a good thing the guys hadn't noticed my departure yet, because if they got one look at me, doe-eyed and struck dumb by this woman, I'd never hear the end of it.

"It's hard not to."

"Be polite?"

I chuckled. "To stare. You're pretty amazing to look at."

19

I took a swig from my bottle of beer. All confidence, high from the win of our game, high from the fact this beautiful creature had no idea who the fuck I was. I was used to girls throwing themselves at me. Women who wanted me only for the gossip of it, or the dollars in my wallet. She had no clue, and if I hadn't already fallen for her curvy-as-fuck figure, or those damn eyes, that alone would have been a turn on.

Her eyes lost their flirtatious challenge and glazed with skepticism. "I'm serious," I pressed and won a smile. Making her smile felt better than it should have.

Her gaze heated my features as she took me in from across the table. "I'm sure," she said with a bite I felt all the way down to my groin. She raised her wine glass to take another sip, and the vulnerability I'd hoped to capitalize on faded into poise. That sexy confidence radiated. "You probably do this every weekend. Am I right?" She nodded her glass toward the back of the bar where my teammates were partying. "You're young, a player, I bet... definitely a player. You give some poor girl your attention with your brooding eyes, and sexy tattoos—" She paused when she realized her slip.

My smile turned from interested to triumphant. "You think I'm sexy?"

"You know you're beautiful," she said with a flash of irritation and a sweet sigh. Fuck, she was cute. When I shrugged, she ran her long fingers through her hair and regrouped. "I'm married."

"I noticed." I took another pull from the beer bottle but kept my eyes on her.

I'd caught her off guard, flattered her, but she was unavailable. A better man would have bowed out when he saw the ring, if anyone knew the damage an affair could do to a person it was me, but I'd rattled her and it made me curious. The ring was a symbol I should heed, but her body language was a glaring contradiction. Digging deeper couldn't hurt.

Tiny white and blue shreds of paper littered the countertop as she took her nerves out on her cocktail napkin. I was about to ask her where her husband was, ask her what her friend meant when she'd said Stevie was home for a reason, but my idiot friends started to chant again. The televisions in the back had been replaying our winning goal, my winning goal, all damn night. She cringed at the noise.

"You do realize you're in a sports bar?" I asked, and she turned her head to look around the room. It was slow and deliberate, as if she hadn't even cared to notice where her friend had brought her. "Tampa Bay won. Opening night. It's a big celebration."

"Opening night?" Her brows dipped. "I thought baseball—"

"Hockey," I barked the word around a laugh.

"In Tampa?"

I choked on my beer. "For twenty-four years."

"Huh."

My brows lifted to the ceiling. "I think I love you."

"Why, because I didn't know Tampa had a hockey team?"

"It's precisely why. I'm used to..." I stopped myself.

It was a rare and beautiful thing. Her ignorance of the game. I didn't want her to care that she was sitting with the star center for Tampa Bay. The silicone girls, with their painted-on smiles—the bunnies—had been circling me all damn night. It would be nice to actually have a girl like me, just for being me. I'd only found relief from all the fake bullshit when I excused myself from the party to grab a beer up front. Best decision of the night, because fuck, she was perfect. Married, maybe. Seven years older than me, whatever. She was perfect, nonetheless.

"You're used to what?"

"This place is usually crawling with college chicks, and that shit gets old."

Bold laughter tipped her head back, exposing a wide expanse of flawless skin. She was cream and silk. My eyes wandered down her smooth neck, the path of her pulse and dipped to her full tits.

Married.

"There's nothing holding you back. You can do as you please." Her eyes searched mine and the color faded from her lips as she whispered, "You're lucky."

Lucky? The rock on her finger caught the light as she lifted her glass to her mouth once more. The mood changed from easy to heavy. *Steer away from it, Melo.* My conscience agreed with the devil on my shoulder. Her earlier assurance wilted away, and the good boy my mother raised was telling me this girl was sinking, that she needed me to stay in the deep water with her in this moment. The slant of her shoulders gave me a clue that not all was well for the home team. That slight frown creasing the delicate skin around her eyes, she was defeated. I'd seen that look on my opponents' faces, hell, on my own teammates, so many times. The ache of knowing there was nothing you could do to turn the loss into a win. I had to know why this stunning woman was sitting with me, without her husband, on a Friday night.

"What's holding you back, Stevie?"

The air sizzled and thickened, and each breath she took was marked by the hard rise and fall of her chest. Those wicked eyes shimmered and the blue burst was eclipsed by the black of her pupils. I could've kept it light, flirted a little more, sent her on her way, closed this place down with my boys, but my ass wasn't moving from this chair. And the pressure building was almost unbearable as I watched her war with herself.

She let out a breathy sigh, and I had the urge to kiss away the sadness from her lips. Kiss her until my hands sank into the curve of her hips and...

"Have you ever been in love?"

Her question cleared my head. "Nah."

That wasn't the truth and I wasn't sure why I lied. But it seemed she ignored my answer anyway as she continued without pause.

"I married the first guy I loved. And over time, I think we've both fallen away from each other. We're so different."

"You changed?"

"No..." She was thoughtful, looking through me when she said, "He did."

"How so?"

Her laugh was gentle. "Do you really care?"

"I'm still sitting here, aren't I?"

She ran the tip of her finger around the top of her glass. "He doesn't like me anymore."

"I doubt that."

"No, I mean..." She stumbled over her words and took a deep breath. "I mean, I'm still me. I'm still the same girl he fell in love with. The girl who loves bad punk rock music, and trashy novels. I binge watch shows when I should be cleaning. I still want to get the tattoo I've always wanted, but he gets angry if I talk about it, if I talk about the past. I want to be spontaneous again, travel—do something risky. He's happy in his tiny, complacent, little life. He tells me I need to grow up, be serious all the time, but I'm only thirty-two, and I feel older than I should. I feel so stagnant."

"If you were married to me you could do whatever you wanted."

Her vacant eyes flared and locked me to my seat. I shouldn't have said that, but what she said next floored me.

"Time is what binds me."

"How long…"

"Thirteen years. We've been married for thirteen years."

I coughed. "Whoa, that's a long ass time."

"Too long to throw away."

"Kids?"

"No."

Time wasn't enough to hold a person. Time was fragile, and loyalty could only get you so far. I'd learned that for myself the hard way. It didn't matter how much you loved a person, it wouldn't make them love you back.

"Where is he tonight?"

"Back home in Richmond for a work thing. I'm here to visit with my family. I needed to get away… missed being here. I was raised east of Tampa, but moved years ago when we had the opportunity to build our accounting firm with his best friend from college."

"You're an accountant?" Thinking about her in a tight blouse with the top four buttons popped opened, her hair pulled up into a bun, turned my grin into something scandalous.

I had her blushing as she laughed through her next sentence. The woman had read my mind. "It's not that exciting."

"I'd like to see you behind a desk." My tone was coated with innuendo.

"So charming, did you pull that fantasy from the latest issue of *Playboy*?"

My chuckle shook my shoulders. "Nope, just my own dirty mind."

The rim of the glass rested against her bottom lip as she smiled at me. It was easy to make her smile, to make her happy. I wondered how, in thirteen years, her husband hadn't realized that. Then again, I didn't really know her at all, did I? For all I knew, it could be the wine that pulled out those pretty smiles and brushed those soft cheeks with a glow.

When the server came by the table, I thought for sure Stevie would ask for the check, but she surprised me and ordered another glass. She was more than tipsy when we'd decided to take off. I paid our bill even when she tried to kick me under the table in an attempt to stop me. Apparently, she was a feisty drunk. I let myself imagine she was feisty when it came to other things, too. This girl was bottled up and I wanted to set her free. We'd spent the last hour talking about her life in Richmond. She was bored at her job and hated that she hadn't made any real solid friendships over the years. All her friends were his friends, and after she'd had her last glass of wine, her truths had become a faucet. I wanted to drown in them for her. Her husband had put her on the bottom shelf and, from how she portrayed it, he'd forgotten she existed beyond the office and the normal good mornings and good nights of their marriage.

She never once asked me about my life, and it didn't offend me at all. She needed a sounding board and allowing her to vent was a hell of a lot better than listening to some broad tell me how great I was, when she didn't even know me beyond the rink. Only once did I have to deal with one of my teammates. He'd stopped by the table on the way back from the bathroom and asked if I was heading out with them to the strip club. Stevie had gotten a good laugh at that and, when I said no, Bryson shrugged his shoulders and went about his business.

The usual humid air clung to the fabric of my shirt as I held the bar door open for her. I felt disappointed that she was ready to leave, and almost wanted to ask her back to my apartment, which was a quick car ride away. But I didn't want to be that guy. I didn't want to capitalize on her misery. She was married and confused and needed to figure her shit out. And I certainly didn't need to open the new season with another cheating scandal.

"Thanks," she said as we walked a few steps away from the crowd of people smoking outside the building.

"For what? The wine? It was—"

"No. For listening." She took a step closer, and holy fuck, I wanted to reach out, wrap my arms around her waist and pull her body against mine.

She didn't seem fragile anymore under the light of the moon. She was taller than most girls, but small compared to my six-foot-one frame. The table we'd sat at had hidden her lower body for the most part, but standing in front of me was a full-on hourglass. Those hips and that ass. She was thick, but in a good way. Like I wanted to bite her *thick*, hold her down *thick*, explore every inch of her and not have to be gentle kind of *thick*. Goddamn it, she was married.

"Your husband is an idiot," I blurted without thinking, and she giggled.

The sound of it was like fog in the dense October, Florida air. Warm and soothing.

"I'll make sure and tell him you said so."

The breeze was salted as it stirred from the bay, whipping strands of her long chocolate waves across her cheeks. She lifted her fingers to her face to move the stray pieces, and laughed as if she hadn't a care in the world. Her eyes closed and her nostrils flared as she breathed in. My hand itched to touch her, to feel the flesh of her cheeks, but I kept my arms planted at my sides.

"I'll find us a ride."

I reached into my pocket, disappointment filling my chest again when she spoke so quietly I almost missed it. "I don't think I can go home yet."

All my restraint got stuck in my throat when her wide eyes pleaded with mine. I didn't want to use her. She was drunk and I wasn't about to take advantage. Not after everything she told me. She wasn't the type of woman I wanted to use for a quick, messy fuck. In another lifetime, she would've been the type of woman I would've tried to keep.

"Let's walk around, sober you up," I offered, and as if to prove my point, she took a misstep and laughed.

"Good idea."

It was late enough that the usual crowds had dispersed. The bars were still open but the sidewalks were empty.

"Ready?" I asked and let myself take one small token as I threaded our fingers together. She paused, tipping her chin, her eyes examining my hand in hers. "Am I overstepping?"

"No." She lingered on the connection briefly before tilting her gaze to my mouth.

Her hand was hot in mine and I let it sear through me. I licked my lips and stared down into hooded eyes. The static in the air fed the erratic beat of my heart. Want. Want.

Want. The sound of my pulse thundered in my ears. My free hand cupped her cheek, and her lids fluttered closed. We were both breathing too fast, sucking down each other's air like it was precious. My thumb dusted the high arch of her cheekbone and her lashes tickled the tip. She was gorgeous and scared and felt perfect under my palm.

"Hey." My voice was rough with suppressed need as I lowered my hand from her face. Her eyes opened and that fear I sensed shadowed her irises. "Tell me to stop."

"Stop." The way she said it though... she couldn't lie if she tried.

"We shouldn't do this, right?"

"Right."

But her hand remained in mine.

I couldn't stand still or I'd break down and kiss her.

"Come on," I said and led her along the walkway.

I kept my nose down as we made our way through a group of guys sporting Tampa Bay jerseys. We walked about a block before I tested her again. "What if someone found out?"

"They wouldn't." She stopped and shook her head. "I mean... nothing is going to happen." She let go of my hand and I didn't fight it.

"Would you feel guilty?"

I wasn't sure why I asked. She'd clearly stated nothing was going to happen. But my heart was a fucking battering ram, and I could see my need reflected in her eyes. Her blush had spread all the way down to those spectacular tits, and the alcohol I'd consumed blurred the line. I stepped in, leaving little room for her to breathe anything other than me.

"I'd feel terrible." Her admission was real and I backed off.

I knew better.

She cleared her throat and left my eyes cold as she turned and walked away from me. I let her get a few feet in front of me, but she stumbled again and I grabbed her hand. It was more selfish than valiant, but she held onto me, and I smiled even though I shouldn't have.

That hot silence covered us as Stevie kept pace with me. Seconds, maybe minutes, passed before she said, "Tell me something, Mark... I talked all night, it's your turn."

"What do you want to know?"

"I don't know. What do you do for a living? Where did you go to college, did you even go to college..." She playfully bumped into my shoulder. "Oh God, are you still in college?"

My laughter brought us back to that pleasant little bubble we had going at the bar. Where it was safe.

"I'm twenty-five, not eighteen."

She glared at me and I laughed harder. I hadn't laughed this much in a long time.

"I grew up in New Hampshire, went to The University of Maine."

"Major?"

We both stopped on the corner as we waited for the light to change. I had no clue where we were going. But things felt easy, so I ran with it. I just hoped she didn't ask me what I did for a living again.

"Education."

That got her attention and a slow smile spread across her face. "Like a teacher?"

"Yeah, well, more like a coach."

"You're a coach?"

"Not yet, maybe someday." I had my dream job already, but being a coach, watching kids succeed, reach their goals, help them live out their hockey dreams, when I retired from the NHL, coaching college hockey was all I wanted to do.

The light changed and before she could ask me another question, I gently pulled her into the crosswalk. We'd walked farther than I had intended and if we kept going, eventually, I'd have to tell her the truth about who I was, and I didn't want to watch her change from this unassuming woman to some fangirl. Maybe she wouldn't, but my past experiences proved otherwise.

We got to the other side of the street and I released my grip on her hand. I reached into my pocket and pulled out my phone. "It's getting late, can we share a ride? I live on the other side of town."

"Sure."

My phone felt heavy in my hand, and I had to make myself not look at her as I found the closest ride with the app on my cell. "The car will be here in two minutes."

"Great." She didn't sound like she thought that was great.

The awkward moment didn't last long, thank God. The ride arrived faster than I thought it would and, before I knew it, I was tucked away in the back seat asking Stevie for her address.

"I live kind of far away, you should get dropped off first."

"Are you sure?" I asked.

"Yeah."

I gave the driver my address, and without any guilt, I took her hand in mine. She scooted closer, and I forgot I wasn't supposed to want this, want her. Her hair smelled like the salted air of the bay mixed with something fruity. She melted nicely against my side and I wanted to pull her even closer, but I kept my hand in hers and my arm as the barrier.

"Who's Atlas?" she asked and caught me staring.

"My dog, I got him last month."

Her free hand traced the letters of ink on my forearm. I didn't give a damn that my skin broke out in goose bumps, and that she could see, plain as day, how her touch affected me.

"Great Dane, cutest fucking puppy on the planet."

She bit back her smile. Her teeth pressing into the pink of her bottom lip.

"You're kind of adorable." She giggled and tapped my shoulder again with hers.

"What? Atlas is like my kid."

She smirked. "I bet."

The driver stopped outside of my apartment building, and I exhaled an unsure gust of air. This was it. My last shot on goal. I shouldn't take it. It'd be a sloppy shot, but maybe this was what she needed to remember who she was, just like her friend had said.

"Come up and meet him?"

The seconds that ticked by were agonizing. The emotions flew past her eyes as she struggled with her own conscience.

"Yeah?"

I gripped her chin between my fingers, letting my thumb explore the outer line of her bottom lip. "Is that what you want?"

She swallowed. "I should go home."

I let go of her hand and chin at the same time.

"You should." I smiled before I turned to open the door. Even though I felt like I was letting something amazing slip through my fingers, this was the right thing to do. Nothing ever good came from lies or deceit. I sucked down a sobering breath. I'd been the victim once, and I never wanted to be the one to inflict that pain on another person. I'd let Stevie's eyes, her lips, the cloud of beer, and the sweet smell of her skin get the better of me. "Thanks for chilling with me tonight," I said once I was out of the car.

"Thanks for keeping me company."

I leaned down like a masochist stealing another greedy breath of her scent. "Take care of yourself, Stevie."

I didn't wait for a reply, or a goodbye. I shut the door and tapped the roof of the car twice. I took the loss like a man, and as the car drove away, I pretended I didn't see the regret in her eyes as she turned for one last look.

MARK
PRESENT DAY

A quiet tension had fallen across the table, but I hadn't noticed it at first. Typically, I was good at that sort of thing. Feeling out the dynamic, seeing a play before it happens, tuning in to the opponent's line and realizing the weak link and taking advantage, but I was too busy trying to hear above the pounding of my own pulse, too drawn into her eyes to realize I might've made a huge fucking mistake approaching her.

"Wow." Her smile faltered as the guy sitting next to her draped his arm possessively behind her chair. "I never thought—"

"I'd see you again." I finished the sentence for her, hiding the nervous candor of my voice behind my grin. I kept my focus though and rested my hand on the high-top table. "You look good."

Stevie's lips lifted at the corners as her gaze lingered, at first on my face, my mouth, and then lazily down my body as if she couldn't believe I was standing here. The feeling was mutual.

"Who's your friend?" the guy sitting next to her asked, regarding me in a way that if we'd been on the ice I would've thought about punching his teeth in. All condescension and bravado.

One of the other suits almost spit his beer all over the table at the question. Fuck, he recognized me. "You have to be kidding. Ben, you're not that out of the loop, are you?"

Ben.

Shit.

That possessiveness made sense, and I felt a twinge of guilt. She'd only said his name a few times the night I'd met her, but I'd never forgotten it. He was the reason I hadn't taken what I wanted. The reason that drum in my heart stopped beating and that familiar feeling of loss, the feeling I got when I was sure I had the win but shot too wide. She was *his*.

Stevie's eyes fell to her friends across the table. Confusion cinching her brows together. "What are you talking about, Alec? Out of the loop?"

I clenched my jaw waiting for the hammer to drop, or maybe my heart. I hated the fucker who was about to unveil me, show me off, and ruin everything. The third guy, not Alec, not the whistleblower, kept his head down avoiding my stare as his friend plowed along. Alec's excitement, his inner fan, started to unravel. Most people tried to pretend not to be affected by the "stardom" of a celebrity or an athlete. It wasn't arrogance, it was a fact. Eventually, the cool exterior people held onto cracked and faded and exposed their intentions.

"You guys..." Alec sent a glare around the table before giving me an apologetic smile. "Mark Carmelo..." Stevie's eyes widened when he said my name.

Her face blanched. I could almost hear the question in her eyes. Why did her friend know my name? Several emotions played across her features. Anxiety, confusion, and finally as he said, "He's a starting forward for Tampa Bay." Something akin to mortification settled inside her eyes.

"And I'm supposed to know what—"

She cut Ben off with a whispered, "Hockey?"

Her face—that fear and wonder swirling in her stormy eyes—was precisely why I'd never wanted Stevie to know when I'd first met her who I was. I'd wanted our moment to be pure of that infectious expectation. I'd been just a guy in a bar, hitting on a beautiful woman, and it had been hands down one of the most bittersweet nights of my life. I couldn't lie and say I hadn't thought about her, about the what-ifs, over the past year. It was like the whole thing had been some sort of dream. Like I'd conjured her from my winning-night high.

Stevie sitting at that table—she was the most stunning woman I'd ever seen.

Her husband's shrewd eyes judged me as he asked her, "Since when do you watch hockey?" He took stock of my six-foot-one, two-hundred-plus-pound frame, my lean muscle, my easy-going smile, my ink. I was his polar opposite with his clean cut, starched shirt. If everything Stevie had told me was true about him, he wouldn't know I was more her type than he was. Then again, Ben had known her for almost half of their lives, and I was just some punk jock who'd stolen a moment, and it would appear he was a lot smarter than she gave him credit for. I'd jumped the gun. I should've never stepped foot at this table.

She shook her head. Her eyes on mine. Her mouth opening and then closing, unable to give him an answer.

I jumped in and saved her. "No, if I remember correctly you didn't even know Tampa had a hockey team," I said with a smirk and my blood thrummed as she blushed.

Her friends laughed, but it was Alec who chimed in, his star-struck eyes fully exposed. "Now that you've moved back, we'll have to catch a game."

"You moved back?" I asked without tamping down my enthusiasm. Unfortunately, her husband keyed into that, too.

Ben's voice pitched an octave higher as he asked, "*How* do you guys know each other?"

"Last year, when I came to visit." She spoke softly only for him and that quiet tension became a loud thunder.

"I hit on her friend, shit, what was her name?" The lie felt wrong, but I had the urge to protect our short amount of time together. It was ours and nothing had happened. No point in putting her in front of the firing squad.

"Reagan?" Ben smiled and his shoulders relaxed.

"Yeah, her. She blew me off," I joked, but Stevie's stare held the truth of that night and it nearly knocked me on my ass. All that desire, it was still there in her eyes.

"This is surreal. I'm a huge fan." Alec's friend finally spoke up.

I held out my hand trying to regain some footing and my manners. "If I have everyone's names correct, it's Ben, Alec, and—"

"Oh, sorry." Stevie's confidence thrilled me as she straightened her spine and commanded the table's attention. "This is my new boss, Trenton—"

"Just Trent." He held out his hand and I shook it. "Trenton sounds—"

"Pompous," Alec's jab made Trent chuckle.

I offered my hand to Alec next and he took his turn.

"I have to admit, I'm not a huge hockey fan, but it's cool as hell to meet you." Alec's grip was firmer than I figured it to be. "Grab a seat, you should join us, have a beer—"

"I was actually about to take off, early morning practice, but I wanted to say hi to Stevie."

She glanced up at me from under her lashes. We were stuck inside that bubble from a year ago. The electricity she fed me through that one look was enough to tell me if we had our chance, I'd never get her out of my fucking system. Her husband's arm no longer lingered across the back of her chair. His attention not as pin-point after my little fib. I didn't miss that he never offered me his hand, though. Maybe he wasn't that gullible after all.

"You have to leave?" she asked, and I internally cheered at her disappointment.

I rubbed the back of my neck. "I do. It was good to see you, though." I wasn't sure if that was true. My temptation, in the same city, and fucking married.

"It really was." Her smile felt private, and God, I needed to touch her face, her cheeks were burning and I wanted to see if they felt warm. My fingers twitched so I slid them into my pockets. She took the last sip of her wine and pushed back from the table, her chair grating against the floor. "I'm going to grab another glass."

"I can—"

"I got it, Ben." Her tone lost the soft edge it'd held for me. "Walk with me?"

I shrugged despite my rising surprise. "Sure."

I gave the guys a wave and a nice to meet you, ignoring the way Ben ignored me.

Stevie led me to the front of the bar and I followed behind, loving the way her hips swayed in her form-fitting skirt. My fantasy of her behind a desk played loud and clear in my head. I had to snap the hell out of it. This chick was married. Unavailable. Unobtainable.

She stopped abruptly and turned to face me once we were no longer in the line of sight of her table. She was breathing fast and the flush in her cheeks bled into her lips. "You're a professional hockey player?"

"Does it matter?"

"Yes!" Her tone was petulant and kind of cute.

"Why?" My lips broke into a playful grin as I toyed with a few stray pieces of her hair. It was stupid, but I had to touch her, it might be the only time I'd ever have the chance to again. "You don't even like hockey." She bit her lip, and I let the strands of her hair slide from between my thumb and forefinger. I expelled a long breath, a wakeup call, and slipped my hands back into my pockets.

"I dumped my life in your lap, Mark." My name sounded way too good on her tongue. "I feel stupid that I didn't—"

"You needed to vent and it was nice not having to deal with the whole—"

"I'm a famous person thing."

I chuckled. "Yeah. It can be a pain in the ass."

She puffed out a nervous laugh. "I guess it could be."

My smile fell as the laughter from her table drifted over to where we were standing, reminding me we were not alone. "You guys worked things out? Moved back?"

"No." Her eyes were filled with something I couldn't read. The blue burst was alive when she said, "We got divorced." *Divorced.* The word was that first drop of water after an hour on the treadmill. Relief. And I felt terrible for thinking that way. "We've literally been in town for four days, he's only here because I needed help moving. He convinced

Trenton to hire me on temporarily until I can find another firm to work for, or prove I know what I'm doing."

"How long?"

"Have we been separated?" She dropped her eyes to the floor. "About a month after I met you, actually. Divorce was finalized three months ago."

My body gravitated toward hers. "Are you okay with everything?"

"It's been a long year." Her smile was sad, but as she raised her head, her eyes shimmered. "I'm happier than I was, that's a good thing. I'm finding my way. Stevie West rises again." Her laugh was sweet and I wanted to taste it.

Stevie West.

She was finding new ground, and I should let her be, but I took another step closer. "Nothing to hold you back?" I handed her the same words from a year ago and she laughed.

"I guess not."

"I want to call you."

"You do?" She sucked in an anxious breath.

I nodded, keeping my cool when all I wanted to do was say, fuck yeah. "I'm leaving in a couple days. We have three road games but I'll be back next Friday and I want to see you."

I'd only met her once, spent one night getting to know her, and now she was free to get to know me. Hell if I didn't want that more than the win we'd lost tonight. It could've been that my bed had been cold more often than not these days. The start of the season made it difficult to have a personal life. It also made it hard to avoid my ex, and generally put me in a fuck-off kind of mood. My apartment, my bed, was an inhospitable environment. But Stevie, with those lips I wanted to touch, and hips I wanted to lose myself in... yeah, for her, I'd make an exception.

She hesitated, and I waited as the beat of her pulse became visible in the slight crook of her neck. She stepped back an inch giving herself room to breathe. The physical pull we shared was something I hadn't encountered with anyone else, and I was glad that it hadn't been there only because she'd been off limits. Stevie wet her lips, and the sexy curve of her mouth sent a jolt of anticipation down my spine as she smiled and said, "I think I'd really like to see you, too."

STEVIE

Spinning.

It was the only word that came to mind as I watched Mark walk out of the bar. My body was a puddle, my cheeks burning, my knees were actually weak. There was about a pound of cotton in my head. I hadn't been back in the city for more than four days, and I'd run into the one man I hadn't stopped thinking about since last year. I had to pull myself together before I went back to the table. I took a few deep breaths and lifted the hair off my neck, letting the cool air kiss my skin. A shiver had goose bumps rising across the surface of my neck and arms as I remembered what it felt like to have him touch me, to have Mark's hand on my cheek. His touch was a breath and I needed to inhale it. It was the argument happening a few feet away at another table, college guys adamantly debating how Tampa's loss could've been worse if it hadn't been for Carmelo's goal that brought everything back into perspective. He was a professional athlete. A hockey player. What planet was I on?

Over the last year, Mark, and our almost affair, had never left the recesses of my mind. I'd realized so much about myself that night. Mostly, that I was done being married to Ben. I'd fallen out of love with him, and I hadn't been able to hide from myself anymore. I'd wanted Mark's mouth on me, his hands in my hair. I wanted more. I'd wanted to say yes when he asked me to come up to his apartment. That desire, if I had been a truly happily married woman, would have never surfaced like it had. I'd been engulfed in a dangerous flame. If my marriage had been solid, I would've never dreamed of even saying more than hello. Mark's imprint never faded and that was the most telling thing of all. My moment of clarity. I told Ben I wanted a divorce the minute I'd walked through the doors after my trip.

One month later, I'd moved out of our house and into a small one-bedroom apartment. It was weird being on my own. I'd become a single dish cookbook. A shopping for one grocery list. There were times when I had to remind myself not to buy his favorite deodorant, or that chocolate almond milk he liked. It was lonely, and we'd already been separated for a few months when Ben had finally decided he might want to fight for me. I had to remind myself it was too little, too late. Ben had been my best friend for so long, but he'd turned into a roommate with benefits, and after a while, a silent partner. Ben thought he could pick and choose when he wanted to "need me" but I had already moved on.

I ordered a glass of wine from the bartender and closed out my tab before I made my way back to the table. The guys were all smiling and laughing as I approached.

"What did I miss?" I asked as I slipped onto my chair.

Trenton's grin was infectious. "I was just telling Ben about this morning."

My face heated all over again. "Oh my God, that was so embarrassing."

"How did you not know Trent was gay?" Ben asked through a laugh and it kind of irritated me.

How would I have known? Ben's friends were *his* friends. I couldn't blame Ben completely. It had been my choice to blend too seamlessly into his side of our "us." I'd depended on him and he liked it, and to my recent chagrin, I'd needed to depend on him one last time. At least for a little while. Our relationship had become very precarious. Almost parasitic. Without his recommendations, I would basically look like a glorified secretary. The firm he owned with his friend in Richmond was just that, *his* firm. I hardly ever had the opportunity to take on accounts, falling more into an assistant role. Trent, another connection he'd made in college, was nice enough to hire me on Ben's recommendation. In charge of the smaller accounts until I could build a better resume, until I could prove myself, I was stuck. I was smart, had my degree, and I knew what I was doing, but on paper, I looked like a new grad. Ben was being the good guy that he always was by asking his friend to help me. Most men would've signed the divorce papers and said, "see ya."

"I just met him. It was a little bit of a shock. I'd have been the same way if he was making out with a woman in his office. I'm not used to interoffice shenanigans." I meant it to be playful, but Ben's smile fell enough that I noticed.

I'd always teased him about having sex at the office. *Totally unprofessional.* His words, not mine.

"My boyfriend thinks you're adorable." Trent raised his glass and I did, as well. Leaving Ben's mood change behind. "Welcome to Byron & Elm."

There was a small chorus of cheers and I smiled. They may be Ben's friends, but they were making me theirs, guiding me to the ledge of freedom, and I was so ready to jump.

"I can't believe you know Mark Carmelo," Alec said, bringing my mind right to where it shouldn't. Sitting this close to Ben, he'd read me like an open book if he hadn't already. It didn't matter. We were divorced. But I never wanted to hurt him.

"I wouldn't say I—"

"I guess the gay rumors were false?" Trent raised his eyebrows.

"I wouldn't know." I sipped from my glass a little too deeply and his keen eyes assessed me. I cleared my throat. "There were gay rumors?"

"He had a terrible break-up a few years ago. One of his teammates was banging his girl. Media spun it like she was a prop to cover that he was gay. Hasn't been spotted with a chick in a while, I guess." Alec's depiction sounded like a tabloid article.

I rolled my eyes. "Why do they even care?"

Alec's laugh was incredulous. "Because most of those guys are fucking a new chick every night. He's either really good at keeping things private or..."

"Or he's gay?" I snorted, trying my best to ignore the "new chick every night" statement. "Has he been spotted with a man?" That shut him up. "I didn't think so. Maybe he's not a man whore. Gay or not."

"He used to be, that's for sure. When he first got drafted."

Trent shoved Alec's shoulder. "For someone who isn't a *huge fan*, you sure do know a lot about him."

"I was trying to play it cool, man. He's one of the top fucking centers in the league."

"Tell me something I don't know."

Top center. I had no idea what that meant, but it sounded important. And now I wanted to throw up. I liked it better when he was just Mark and I'd almost kissed him. Now he was real, and had my number, and he was famous. My heart was doing this weird fish-out-of-water flop. The swarm stirring in my belly remembered what he smelled like, clean and masculine, and took flight. I'd been off the market for too long. What were the rules? When would he call? I was lost in my internal meltdown when I heard my name.

"W-what?" I asked a little breathless. A little in lust with a certain tall, sexy, inked, hockey player.

"I said, I can't believe your friend turned him down." Alec finished his beer and set it on the table, pulling his wallet from his pocket.

"She didn't know him, and she was with Pete at the time, her boyfriend." It was a white-lie I told myself. I kept the shame I felt for that night on a tight leash. What had happened wasn't right, but I tried to remember I hadn't given in.

"Well, he had his eye on you tonight, that's for damn sure."

"I'm sitting right here, Trent." Ben's voice was cold and Trent frowned.

"Sorry, I didn't think. My mouth has a mind of its own sometimes."

The atmosphere at the table burned to ash at the edges. Ben's eyes found mine, and my guilt had screws burrowing into my sternum.

I don't belong to you, Ben.

The words were a whispered plea skating on the tip of my tongue. But I swallowed them down. "We should get going. It's really late."

Trent and Alec were already standing, settling their checks, and I left my glass of wine half-full on the table, standing as well.

"See you in the office tomorrow." Trent wrapped me neatly into a side hug.

"Tell David I'm glad he thinks I'm adorable," I said as I pulled away. To my surprise, my very good-looking boss blushed. He was shorter than most guys, just an inch or two taller than me, but traditionally handsome with blond hair and blue eyes.

"Much more professional tomorrow. I promise."

I laughed. "I think it's great. Don't stop kissing your secretary on my account."

Alec shook my hand with a promise to show me the ropes. He was a junior accountant, still making his way, but he'd been assigned to help me adjust. "It's good to have you on board, Stevie." He smiled at me, letting those piercing green eyes of his scan my body from head to toe like he had this morning.

Those eyes and his sharp features probably won him favor with the ladies for most of his life. Too bad he was arrogant as hell.

"Did you want me to drop you at your place?" Ben asked as he pulled his rental car keys from his pocket.

His light eyes were glazed and the flush in his cheeks told me he drank more than he'd intended, but he'd never be too drunk to drive. He was too controlled to ever risk it.

"You don't have to do that...I can call for a ride."

"I want to." He raised his hand and I stopped breathing as he placed a stray piece of my hair behind my ear.

"Your hotel is by the airport, Ben. It's out of the—"

"Let me take you home, Stevie."

"No."

He let out an exasperated breath. "Why? You meeting that guy?"

I laughed without humor. "That's not your business."

"I hate that."

"Hate what?" I couldn't hold back my frustration. Where was jealous Ben a year ago? Two years ago, three years ago, for that matter.

"That it's not my business anymore." His jaw flexed and tears seared the corners of my eyes.

"A little over a year ago, we sat on that tiny couch in the therapist's office and I told you I was drowning. You didn't care then and you don't care now. I love you, Ben. You're one of my best friends, but we stopped being *in love* a long time ago and you know it."

I took a step back, relieving myself of his familiar scent, his heat. We were each other's comfort food. The ice cream that was really bad for you, and you only needed as a crutch to get over whatever life was throwing at you.

"I should've been a better husband."

I gave him a small smile and a teasing push to the shoulder. "Remember that. Treat her right, Ben. When you find her, treat her as if you can't breathe without her."

"You were always such a romantic."

And you weren't.

"I know, I'm hopeless," I admitted and his smile reached his eyes.

"You sure you don't want to ride with me?"

"Go. I'll be fine."

Ben took a half-step toward me and hesitated as if he thought better of it. His throat bobbed and he rubbed the back of his neck. "Bye, Stevie."

I gave him a small smile, the embers of anticipation lighting my skin, as I watched my past walk away through the same bar door that my future had left only moments before.

Never Google search the hot guy who asked for your number, before nine in the morning. I was knee deep in Mark Carmelo and I'd only had one cup of coffee. It was all Alec's fault really. He'd fed me all that intel last night and I got curious. Curious was harmless, right? A quick little search and I'd be fine. Forty-five minutes later, and I was well-versed in Mark's stats, how much he made each year, which by the way, made me nauseous, to what underwear he preferred. And I might've watched a few video interviews where he avoided topics about a girl named Mia, and his less-than-stellar behavior when he was a rookie. I never intended to snoop, and now I was wide-eyed, staring at my computer screen feeling awful, like I'd invaded his privacy.

"Stevie?" Alec's voice had me shutting my laptop faster than I could say stalker.

"Good morning," I said, hoping my tone was more casual and less hand caught in the Carmelo cookie jar.

"Hey, pull up that file I sent you yesterday and meet Trent and me in the conference room."

"Bruin Brothers Construction?"

"That's the one. Small contractor, but a great account for you to start with." His eyes fell to my laptop. "You ready to roll?"

"Sure, let me grab everything. I'll be there in five."

"Want me to have David get you a coffee?"

Maybe I liked Alec more than I thought I did. "Yes, thank you."

He left without a nod, and I locked my desktop and grabbed the paperwork I'd printed out earlier. I stood and smoothed my hands down the front of my pencil skirt. This was it. My first account. I could do this. Excitement bubbled in my chest and I couldn't contain my smile. I straightened the hem of my blouse making sure I was presentable. I was readying to leave when my phone vibrated against the desk.

Mark: *How's your morning?*

Slowly, I sank back into my chair, a giddy smile creeping across my face.

ME: *At work, only one cup of coffee. It's ugly. You?*

Mark: *About to skate. Are you sitting at your desk?*

I let out a quiet laugh at his odd question.

ME: *About to go into a meeting.*

Mark: *Please tell me you're wearing those sexy-as-fuck glasses you had on last night.*

My cheeks flushed with heat. At the compliment. At the word fuck. My fingers lightly touched the rims of my glasses and I bit my lip.

ME: *It's a possibility.*

Mark: *Hair up or down?*

My eyes darted to the open door of my office. I was sure my face was red. My hand shook as I typed the next message.

ME: *Up*

Mark: *Jesus Christ, I'm going to skate for shit today.*

My laugh sounded more like a giggle, and I lost my grown woman card for the day.

ME: *Why?*

Mark: *Because I'm going to be picturing you behind that desk, looking like a sexy fucking librarian, and I'll be VERY distracted.*

A pool of warmth poured over my body.

ME: *I hear you have a pretty good shooting percentage, best in the league, I'm sure you'll be fine.*

After I hit send I regretted it immediately. He hadn't told me who he was at first for a reason and I just quoted the Internet like a fangirl.

David walked by the door with a tray of Starbucks and I stood. "Better hurry, Mama, don't be late. Trent gets cranky."

Anxiety had me scrambling to make sure I had everything, but thirty seconds later my phone vibrated again, and I couldn't contain the smile on my face.

Mark: *Don't believe everything you read on the Internet. ;)*

ME: *So you didn't streak through the parking lot of your alma mater when you won your first playoff game as a freshman?*

His response this time was immediate.

Mark: *Oh, hell yes, that's totally true. One of my best nights.*

My smile was borderline star struck.

ME: *I'd pay good money for that footage.*

Mark: *Good luck with that.*

I exhaled a nervous laugh, grabbed the things I needed for my meeting, and headed down the hall. Trent and Alec were talking and setting up their own computers... luckily, the client hadn't arrived.

"Sorry, had to get everything organized," I stammered, thinking about how my face was most likely blotched with red.

"No problem. Have a seat, we'll get started as soon as they get here." Trent nodded to where David had set a huge cup of coffee next to Alec's computer.

David was officially my favorite person in Tampa. Well, almost.

I opened my computer, setting the paperwork to the side for Alec to go over. Once I was in my seat, I chanced a peek at my phone and had a text waiting.

Mark: *I fly out tomorrow, and should be back pretty late next Thursday night. That Friday still work for you?*

My colleagues were busy in their own conversation so I risked sending him an answer.

ME: *Friday works.*

Mark: *I'll text you when I get in Thursday if it's not too late.*

ME: *Sounds good.*

The memory of his skin, the heat of it on my cheek, had my heart pounding in my chest. There were so many things I should've been worrying about. For one, I'd bought a house. I was starting over, and wasn't it weird that I was seven years older than him? He was a young, crazy-talented athlete with a schedule that made me tired just thinking about it. How was this going to work? Should it even matter at this point?

Mark: *Gotta skate. Thanks again for the mental image.*

I had to stifle my laugh.

ME: *Any time.*

Mark: *Hope so. Talk soon.*

This little exchange of words had me tripping over the beat of my own heart. Messy and hot. I closed my eyes for only a second and I could picture his smile. It made my belly feel full and whole. "Talk soon." God I hated how much I really needed that to happen. I was humming from the inside out.

"You ready to get started, Stevie?" Trent's question opened my eyes.

"Sure," I replied.

In more ways than one.

MARK

Heading into a three-game road trip after losing our first and only game wasn't ideal. In fact, the team's confidence had been waning since yesterday's morning practice. Coach had messed with the lines, experimenting with the chemistry of the team, but inevitably left the roster as it was. I leaned my head back into the cool leather of my seat and exhaled a long breath. The atmosphere on the plane seemed hopeful, as I slipped on my earbuds in an effort to drown out the loud laughter of my teammates. I loaded up the music app on my phone. My eyes closed, letting the bass fill my head and my shoulders relaxed. We could do this, our team, we'd been so close last year to winning the Cup. We had the chemistry Coach wanted, we had all the fucking tools. We just needed to pull our heads out of our asses and use them.

I was about to doze off when someone shoved me in the shoulder. "The hell, Jensen?" I muttered as I pulled one of my earbuds down only to hear my team Captain laughing like an asshole.

"Bro, we still have two hours before we get to Detroit, and you're already falling asleep."

"I always sleep," I said as I pressed pause, silencing the music.

He shrugged his shoulders and shoved me again. Bryson's smile dipped as he settled into the seat next to me. He let his eyes dart around the cabin. The guys were all awake, talking shit, and flirting with the flight attendants as usual. Bryson's speculative gaze landed on me.

"What?" I asked with a slip of irritation.

"You gonna be on point in Columbus?"

Fuck that.

"I'm always on point, maybe ask Rasmussen if he's figured out how to tape his own damn stick."

Rasmussen was a rookie left winger picked up from a small private college in Michigan this past June. He'd showed up to play this summer at camp, and hell, he had skills. Too much attitude and ego, though. The small amount of time he'd spent on the ice this last game was a disaster, but Coach had high expectations for him, placing him on our starting line.

"Rasmussen can handle his shit, Melo... I'm asking you... you got Columbus handled? If not—"

"Fuck off, Jensen. Yes, I have it handled." His narrowed eyes begged to differ. "Yes, goddamn it, alright. Lynch isn't gonna fuck with my head." I pinched the bridge of my nose and exhaled a noisy breath. "It's been two years."

"Yeah, and every time we play them one of your asses ends up in the box and this game is too important to—"

"I have it handled. Mia... Lynch—old fucking news."

He watched me cautiously for a second before he let out a short huff and leaned back into the seat. "Good, 'cause I want to destroy those fuckers."

"They have it coming."

He smiled. "Fuck yeah, they do. They've won their first two games. They look tight, Melo."

"Let's get through Detroit and New Jersey before we worry about Columbus."

I was about to pop my earpiece in again when he said, "You good?"

Bryson was being a good team Captain. He looked out for me, for all of us. Mia was a mental game I lost every damn time I played it. Mia and I had been together a little over two years. I'd met her the summer after I'd turned twenty-one. She'd been hired on as our skate coach. Once a top figure skater in her prime, she'd become the perfect addition to the team. It didn't help though that she was drop dead gorgeous and had all the guys tripping over their own skates trying to get dibs and into her pants. Mia was the type of girl who knew what she wanted and never took no for an answer. At the time, she wanted me, and I'd felt like I'd hit the fucking lottery.

She was fit, smart, funny. Mia loved the game as much as she loved to skate, and the fact that she was unaffected by any of our stardom bullshit made her even more tempting. It was like she was one of us. Back then, I never thought I was ready to be a one-woman guy. I'd been just two seasons from my rookie year, my own star growing and building a strong foundation. She'd liked what she saw in me, and man, I fell for all her bullshit.

"I'm good." I swallowed twice before I said, "It's been a long time, and yeah, she fucking burned me, Bryson, but I'm over it. I'm not going to give the media something to chew on for the entire season, okay."

"Tyler Lynch has always had your number, bro, and even if you're over Mia, you're not over *it*. When was the last time you got laid?"

Training camp. This summer. But hell, it wasn't his business.

"You keeping tabs, Jensen? Why? You want a ride?"

His laugh rumbled in his chest. "If I was in to guys..."

My eyebrows hit the cabin roof as I chuckled. "I think you'd be in to it no matter what."

He smirked. "I'm not too picky."

His grin made me laugh and I shook my head. "No... no, you're really not."

Bryson's tendencies to bang whatever bunny got to him first made us all cringe. The guy could have the pick of the litter but his whole, "first come—first serve" policy made us all question his sanity.

His laughter died down. "For what it's worth, Melo... if I had to play against a guy who fucked my girlfriend... if I ever had a girlfriend, I'd want to bash his teeth in, too. But we need your head in the game. What that chick did to you, and the fact she's still our damn skate coach... it sucks, but if you end up in the box against Columbus, we'll lose and you know it."

He was right. Columbus was known for capitalizing on the penalty. Christ, they'd led the league last year in power play goals. And after their first two games of this season, it seemed they wanted to hold on tight to that title.

"I'll keep my head straight."

The thing was... Mia screwing Lynch wasn't necessarily the reason I still harbored such hatred for both of them. It was how I'd put my whole heart into something I had no idea was so damn fragile. When I'd met Mia, I thought I was done playing around with phonies and liars. I thought Mia was the real deal. She became part of my entire world. She'd met my family. Spent time with my sister and my niece, Poppy. The same niece who had inspired me to help fund a bankrupt ice hockey camp in Toronto for special needs children on the autistic spectrum. I'd invited Mia to come with me to the camp in Toronto that spring after the season ended, and she'd said she couldn't go because her fucking dad was sick. Turns out that her dad being sick really meant she'd made plans to stay at home and fuck my teammate while I was gone. Apparently, their affair had started right under my nose during playoffs. Lynch had played like shit for too long. The asshole had known all along he was going to get traded that July, so he figured he'd screw over our team in more ways than one before he left. Lynch was a piece of shit, but Mia was the one who'd betrayed me. She'd made it hard for me to trust another woman... another person, for such a long time.

"I've got your back man, we all do... remember that when he starts talking shit." Bryson gave my knee a sharp slap before he stood. "Get some rest, I know how much you need your beauty sleep, especially when you're turning away pussy like it's the plague." His grin tipped up on one side as I flicked him off. "Just saying, Mark... I have a list of girls—"

"Keep your fucking list, I've got my own thing going, alright?"

Stevie's bright eyes flickered through my head.

"I'll believe it when I see it." Bryson nodded his chin with an ear-to-ear grin and turned toward the aisle.

Ignoring him, I placed my earbud back in and pressed play. My fingers lingered over the screen of my phone. Technically, we weren't supposed to use our cell service while in flight, but my smile spread too deliberately, too sure across my face as I thought about her. Stevie's flushed cheeks, the nervous way she bit her lip, the way she summoned her confidence and knocked me on my ass the first time I'd met her. But what I liked most about her was that she'd said no. She'd had a chance to cheat on her husband with me, and she took the high road instead. She'd chosen loyalty over lust even though her husband didn't exactly deserve it. Trust was a hard fought thing with me. Very few people in my life had my faith. A few of the guys on the team, maybe, my family—my coach. I wanted to let myself trust her, know her.

I quickly typed out a text and uploaded the short clip I had saved on my phone.

ME: *Enjoy.*

I was about to flip my phone back into airplane mode when her text came through.

Stevie: *I just choked on my coffee.*

Stevie: *Your ass is so white.*

I barked out a laugh and took a quick glance around the plane. No one gave a shit about what I was doing.

ME: *I was eighteen, and way too proud. A first playoff win will do that to a guy. And it's cold as fuck in Maine.*

Stevie: *Definitely not the Sunshine State.*

My jaw ached as my smile pulled wider. I wondered if she was smiling, too. Probably laughing at my naked ass running across the parking lot.

ME: *Twenty-bucks says you're going to watch that video at least fifty times today.*

Stevie: *Um... I already sent it to all my friends and maybe uploaded it to Facebook.*

This time my laugh garnered some attention. Bryson stared at me from across the plane. I raised my eyebrows and shrugged.

Stevie: *Just kidding. I should send it to Alec, though, I think he has a man crush on you. Talked about your stats all morning the other day.*

I rolled my eyes.

ME: *Oh, yeah. What did he say?*

Stevie: *Something about plus minus, I don't know, he lost me about three minutes into the conversation.*

I fucking loved that she knew nothing about hockey. When I lifted my gaze, I noticed the flight attendant was a few rows from mine handing Harris a drink.

ME: *Gotta go. Shouldn't be texting while in flight. Talk to you when I can.*

Stevie: *Good luck in...*

ME: *Detroit.*

Stevie: *Good luck in Detroit. Maybe I'll watch the game.*

A warm feeling stirred inside my chest making it hard to breathe. It made me a total pussy, but I felt like a teenager again. Thoughts of Stevie at the arena, in my jersey, wearing my number, cheering even though she had no clue what she was cheering for, actually had all the blood in my body pumping toward my groin. I shifted in my seat as I typed.

ME: *Yeah?*

Stevie: *I'll send all the positive juju.*

We're going to need it.

ME: *I'll text you after the game if we win.*

Stevie: *And if you don't win?*

ME: *I'm blaming you.*

I chuckled as I read her fast response.

Stevie: *No pressure.*

ME: *Bye, Stevie.*

Stevie: *Bye, Mark.*

I switched back into airplane mode and turned up the volume. One of my favorite hip-hop songs thumped its perfect beat, and I tried not to read into the moment. I'd let myself fall for Mia's little nuances, all her well-laid traps. I had to pace myself. Stevie wasn't Mia, but she had the power to hurt me, and I'd spent a very long time making sure that'd never happen to me again. Regardless, my smile couldn't be contained as I let the visions of her run wild in my head. Those sexy glasses. Full hips. Tight blouse. Her ass pressed against the edge of a desk in some nondescript office. I licked my lips as I closed my eyes. Drifting, letting my worries about the outcome of this road trip dissipate into that decadent beat streaming from my headphones, fade into the blue burst that surrounded her pupils, and dissolve into the phantom feeling of her lips on mine.

I couldn't even look at myself in the fucking mirror. The only thing bringing me any sort of peace was Atlas as he nudged my hand with his nose. He licked my palm a few times, and I let the heat from the shower that lingered in the bathroom pull deep into my lungs as I sucked down a ragged breath.

"I fucked up," I said and he looked at me, his ears perking up when I met his eyes.

I ran a towel through my hair before I hung it on the rack and walked out into my bedroom, trying not to think about the flight home and how not even Bryson was smiling.

I grabbed my underwear and sweatpants out of the drawer and pulled them on. Atlas's collar jingled as he strutted from the bathroom, his muzzle wet from licking up stray pools of water from the shower floor.

I flopped down on my bed and patted it. He didn't hesitate and jumped up next to me. Atlas wasn't usually allowed on my bed, but after the fucking horror show of the last twenty-four hours, I didn't really give a shit. I caught my reflection in the glass of one of the framed jerseys on the wall, the black and blue surrounding my left eye was getting worse.

Cocksucker.

Atlas nudged my elbow with his nose, bullying his way into my lap. He rested his head on my thigh, and I scratched behind his ears. I almost left him overnight at the boarding place, but I wanted to come home and sleep, not have to worry about anything other than my fuck up and how I was going to apologize to the team. Our flight had been delayed, and when we finally landed back in Tampa it was almost midnight. I called the owner and used my celebrity, which I rarely did, to get Atlas out tonight.

I sighed when my cell phone started to vibrate. It was a little after one in the morning, but she wouldn't let it go. She never did.

I leaned over, ignoring Atlas's groan as I grabbed my phone and answered, "Shouldn't you be sleeping?"

"I wanted to make sure—"

"I'm fine."

She hummed. "You're fine. That's what I say to Dax when I'm ready to implode."

"How's Poppy?" I evaded.

"Worried about you. You took a big hit."

"Fuck, she saw it?" I ran my hand through my wet hair and winced.

"She couldn't stop talking about it. She asked me six times if Uncle Mark was going to be okay before I made her go to sleep. I guess the blood freaked her out."

"It was mostly his. I think I broke his nose."

"Good."

"No, Molly. I could've gotten ejected. Suspended."

I heard her sharp intake of breath. "But you didn't."

"But we lost because of me."

"No, you lost because your *team* fell apart in the third."

My sister always called me after every loss. She was like my post-game therapist. But tonight nothing she could say would change how I felt. I let him get to me, I let Lynch draw me out and got a major penalty called. They scored twice on the fucking power play and our tied game became a crushing loss. We'd won both games previously. And my stupid fucking ego killed our streak.

"Mol, I let him talk shit... get in my head and left my guys short."

"Your team was in the box all night. The penalty kill wasn't the problem. It's always the third for you guys, your coach tried that new line and—"

"Lynch talked shit about Poppy, about the camp. He was fucking laughing at us, Mol, and I lost my mind."

"Poppy?" Her voice cracked.

"Yeah. Called her retarded and I—"

"I hope you broke more than his nose."

A sad chuckle rattled in my throat. "He looks worse than I do, that's for sure."

"I can't believe they didn't call a penalty on him, too."

"I threw the first punch."

"They let the fight go on too long."

Anger spurred inside my stomach, twisting and turning. "Not fucking long enough."

I would have never stopped.

"Try to remember… this is not all your fault."

"You sound like Maddox."

"Well your coach knows his team. Yeah, you messed up, but it was a group effort." She let out a yawn. "Now go to sleep and no more pity party."

"I'm not—"

"You are, God, I could hear your man tears hitting the pillow all the way in Manchester. It's why I called." There was a smile in her voice and it made my lips twitch, too.

"Man tears?"

"Just don't blame yourself. Any one of those guys would've done the same thing."

That's what Bryson had said.

"I'm gonna go. I've got an early day at the gym tomorrow, and I'm sure Coach will make us watch a few game tapes before we get the day off."

"You push yourself too hard. Do something fun tomorrow, get your mind off everything."

It was then I remembered I was supposed to call Stevie when I'd landed. *Fuck.* I was so far gone to my piss poor mood I totally forgot. I hadn't had a chance to text or call her since that one time on my way to Detroit.

"Yeah, stop *Mom-ing* me, love you, Molly."

"Love you, too. I'll tell Poppy you asked about her."

"Tell her I love her more than pucks and beer."

My sister's soft laugh had an actual smile stretching across my lips.

"I will."

I ended the call and stared at my phone debating whether or not I should send Stevie a quick text. I had a sick feeling growing. I hoped she hadn't watched that game. I never fought, that wasn't my thing, and I didn't want her to think I was some crazy ass hothead.

Atlas jumped down and snuggled into his oversized dog bed in the corner of the room. I situated the covers and comforter to the side feeling overly warm. I set my phone down on the bedside table and lay back onto the mattress, annoyed at how our winning road trip turned to shit, restless and not in the mood to chat, I resolved to call Stevie in the morning.

MARK

It took me a second to catch my breath as the treadmill slowed to a stop. My muscles burned and stretched as I leaned over and braced my hands on my knees. Nausea rolled in my stomach; the stench of the gym, and a mixture of body odor and sweaty socks, wasn't helping as I sucked it down with each desperate breath. I could feel Bryson staring at me from his own machine. Most likely judging how much I would let this latest loss affect me, affect them.

"Why do you torture yourself?" he asked.

Heaving in precious bits of air, I glanced at him with a grim smile. "I'm not, sprints, Jensen... it's good cardio."

"You look like you're about to fucking puke."

I stood to my full height ignoring the way my head spun. "I think I might." I laughed but he saw through my bullshit.

His brows dipped into a severe line. "Too hard, man... you push like that and you'll wind up on the IR list."

"If I end up on the injured list doing fucking sprints, then I don't deserve to play."

I stepped off the treadmill and the ache in my quads intensified.

"I know you, Melo. You're punishing yourself. Knock that shit off, get laid, and move the fuck on. Leave all that shit in Columbus and bring it on Monday." Bryson stepped down in front of me, shoving my shoulder with a smirk. "Come out with us tonight... Karlsson found this strip club and—"

"Of course, he did." I chuckled. "I've got plans." I lifted my shirt and wiped the sweat from my face. The air felt less thin as each breath came easier than the last.

"Yeah? Does it involve your hand and your dick, because I'm pretty sure that's all the action you're seeing these days."

"Why are you always so interested in *my* dick? Need a better mental picture when you're having *you* time in the shower."

His laugh echoed in the empty gym. "Nah, man. I have enough spank material to last me a lifetime."

"Jesus, you're so mature."

"Says the guy who still makes fun of the fact that my initials are B.J."

"It's not my fault your parents hate you." I shrugged, but my lips started to tic up at the corners.

"You're an ass—" His smile fell along with his insult. "Shit."

I didn't have to turn around to know someone had walked into the gym. The door banging shut was indicator enough, but by the look on Bryson's face, I had a feeling it could only be one person. I really wasn't in the fucking mood to deal with her brand of shit today.

Bryson's eyes met mine and he dipped his head with a rough whisper, "Five minutes. That's all she gets. Get your ass in the locker room."

"Hey, Bryson." Mia's sickly sweet voice set my teeth on edge.

He nodded his chin at her. Not really a warm welcome, but keeping the peace, nonetheless.

"Can I talk to you for a second?" Mia asked me and I allowed my eyes to find hers.

I'd gotten good at ignoring her. Only tuning in when necessary during skate practice. Business, never personal.

"I've got tape to watch," I said with as little emotion as possible.

Bryson and I started for the locker room, but Mia reached out and touched my arm. "Mark." My name sounded like a reprimand.

I shrugged off her touch and snapped, "What?"

Bryson clapped his hand on my shoulder. "Don't be long."

Mia and I stood in silence as he walked away. She ran her hand through her blonde hair, her smile feigning an innocence I'd learned not to buy into anymore. My irritation gained speed as my pulse increased.

"Make it quick." I nearly barked as I shifted into defense mode.

Her gaze lingered on the purple crescent forming below my left eye. She boldly raised her hand as if she was about to touch my face and I took a step back.

"Don't."

She lowered her hand, letting it fall to her side. Her fingers curling into a fist. "Mark, you have to stop fighting over me, it's been too long and—"

"It's not about you."

She raised her eyebrows and pursed her lips. "Really? You felt like breaking Tyler's nose for fun."

"Welcome to hockey."

"Don't be a dick."

"Why? Isn't that what you like?" The words held more anger than sarcasm, and she narrowed her eyes.

"I know I hurt you and I'm sorry about that. I never wanted to, but things happen, and people change, you need to get over it."

"I'm over it." I made an attempt to leave, but Mia always loved the drama, the attention, and couldn't leave well enough alone to save her own damn life.

"The black eye you're sporting clearly shows how over it you are."

"It's. Not. About. You. *Christ, Mia.* I know that's hard for you to fucking understand, but truly..." I laughed without humor. "It's not. I stopped caring about you a long ass time ago."

I hated the sad slant of her head. The way she assessed me as if at any moment I'd fall apart and tell her how much I missed her, how much I needed her. This chick was delusional.

"If you didn't care, then why fight Tyler?"

"Last time I checked, you lost the right to know my business the day you decided to fuck Lynch behind my back."

Her mask faltered. I'd gotten to her and I couldn't help my silent celebration.

"Don't look so proud, Mark. That fight cost us the game."

"Us?" I balked. "There is no *us*, Mia. You're just an employee. *My* team... they know who the fuck you are. And if you want to know why I served that piece of shit a well-deserved beat down, ask him."

There wasn't anything left to say, and if I stuck around I'd end up saying something I'd regret, but I refused to feel sorry for the shock on her face. For the past two years I'd played nice, and even though I harbored guilt for fighting in Columbus, for giving them the win, she had no damn right to point fingers. None.

"I've got tape to watch."

I didn't wait for a response as I turned, leaving her behind, and headed to the locker room.

My anger poured down my spine along with the hot water. The pressure of the shower on my neck and back relieved the remaining tension. I'd spent a long time avoiding conflict with Mia, but today, I felt actual goddamn relief. I was done hiding from her. This was my team, my life, and she was just an incidental. I lowered my head and rested my palm against the tile, allowing the steam and heat to envelop me, let the water soak through my hair, run down my face, wash away the shitty road loss and the fucking argument with Mia. I concentrated on each breath and let it all go. All I wanted to do was watch the footage Coach wanted us to see, get the fuck out of here, and call Stevie. I'd texted her this morning before I'd left for the gym, and the last time I'd checked she hadn't responded.

I hurried through my shower after Bryson yelled through the locker room at the top of his lungs that they were all "waiting on my sorry ass." After I dried off and threw on a pair of jeans, I grabbed my phone from my locker. I had a text from my sister, but still nothing from Stevie. I debated texting her again, but decided I probably should give her a call like I was supposed to do last night. The guys could wait a few more minutes.

The phone rang three times, and when she answered, her voice was a husky whispered hello. Sexy as hell. I smiled the first real smile I'd had since I planted my fist in that asshole's face.

"Are you busy?" I asked.

"I am. Just heading into a meeting." No longer whispering, she said, "I was just walking back into my office."

"I was going to text you last night, but I got in late."

"I know. I read your text this morning." Her tone was distant, nonchalant. Almost like she'd thrown up a wall and wasn't going to let me past it. "I've only got a few minutes."

I switched the phone from my left ear to my right as I exhaled a long breath. "I should've called."

"You had a bad night, I understand." Her voice was gentle, less clipped, and it gave me hope I was still on her good side.

I chuckled. "Please tell me you didn't watch that tragedy of a game."

Her laugh was warm, and fuck if I didn't feel it in my stomach. "You have quite the temper."

This was the exact reason I'd hoped she hadn't watched.

"I'm not usually so hotheaded. I never fight."

"That's what Trent said." Her voice was soft, low again, almost a whisper. "He said for you to throw a punch, the guy must've really said something bad."

"He's a dick."

She laughed and the lump in my throat dissipated. "So, he had it coming?"

"Yeah... he did." More than she would ever know. "Have dinner with me tonight?" I asked.

"I think I could be persuaded."

"Ever been to White Tail?"

"Never heard of it."

"It's a new place off South Howard and it happens to be my favorite."

"Sounds promising."

"Then I'll pick you up at seven-thirty."

"I can meet you there," she offered. Her hesitation was resurfacing.

"I think I'd rather pick you up. You know, the whole chivalry isn't dead thing, I'm a big advocate."

"Seven-thirty?" she asked with a smile in her tone this time.

"Text me your address."

"I will. See you tonight."

I said goodbye and let the calm of having our plans put in place settle over me. I messed up in Columbus. I messed up when I let the bullshit in my head distract me from calling Stevie. Seeing her again at the bar, it hadn't erased all the shit Mia had poisoned me with, but it made it less visible on the surface. My walls were less daunting... scalable... when I looked into Stevie's eyes, when her scent surrounded me and knocked down my defenses. When all I wanted to do was touch her, there was no room for uncertainty or anxiety. She was fuel and I was the match begging to catch her on fire. I could deny it, the feelings I had, but what would be the point? I'd let myself wade in the cold of Mia's shadow long enough. And I craved heat. I wanted skin and lips. The sound of Stevie's voice, the picture of her full-figure, her curves, and smile, it flashed, branding me. There was no perfect explanation as to why Stevie made me feel the way she did. We had a connection, a chemistry, and that was undeniable.

"Let's roll, Melo." Maddox's deep voice dragged me from my thoughts.

"Coming."

I pulled on my shirt, slipped my phone into my pocket, and headed into the media room with a smile. Ready to face the shit talk I was sure I'd have to endure for the next sixty minutes.

STEVIE

If you asked my ex-husband, he'd tell you I was a level-headed, easy-going, never-let-anything-get-to-me, type of woman. In reality, I was the total opposite. With Ben, I was able to hide behind the mundane, find a home in the cozy comfort of ease and predictability. The everyday, the same ol', same ol', I hated it. In this moment, though, I'd give anything for it. Almost twenty-four hours had passed since I'd watched that game, but I was still filtering through the images in my head. Trying to reconcile the man I'd only met the two times, with the savage I'd seen on the bar's television screen. Reconcile that handsome, sweet face to the brute covered in armor and sweat. I'd tried to concentrate on the memory of his sexy voice making plans for dinner, instead of the way he'd violently beat another man into the ice of the rink.

The guys I worked with said it was normal. "It's hockey," they'd said.

Maybe I wasn't cut out for hockey.

Perhaps I'd been slightly delusional, thinking I could handle the tall, hot, tattooed, hockey player who most likely had a long line of groupies waiting and willing to fluff his ego. It shouldn't have bothered me that he didn't call Thursday night like he'd said he would. He had a bad night, and he was probably nursing his wounds, and I wasn't some naïve twenty-something, sitting on my bed, pining for the guy I knew very little about. But it *had* bothered me. I hadn't been with anyone other than Ben. I was a thirty-three-year-old with absolutely no idea how to date.

I exhaled a tremulous breath and stared at the laptop opened on my dresser. Reagan was supposed to video chat with me via Skype. Help talk me off the first-date ledge, but she hadn't called yet. I stood in my bedroom, wearing black slacks and a cute black and white polka dot blouse awaiting the predate approval call she'd insisted that we have.

"I'm not cut out for this," I repeated to myself.

I puffed out an irritated breath and a few strands of hair on my forehead shifted. It hadn't helped my insecurities either when the post-game wrap-up announcers had discussed his rocky relations with his skate coach. They'd made it sound like the fight he'd gotten into was related to her, to a woman named Mia Sokolov. His estranged ex-girlfriend. The woman he'd been with for two years. The woman who "broke the star's heart," the same woman who currently worked for his team. Blonde hair, light exotic-looking eyes. Athletic, tiny—everything I wasn't. I stared at the computer willing Ray to call already. I was falling into the pit of self-doubt with no rope to get me the hell out.

I closed and reopened my Skype app again and caught the reflection of chaos in the mirror above my dresser. I stared at the boxes strewn around my bedroom floor, some not yet opened, and the way my pale gray and green duvet was only unmade on one side. Single girl. The shelf left of the door was empty waiting for me to fill it with new books, new knickknacks—new memories.

As if the powers that be knew I was in a downward spiral, my laptop sang the familiar ring, and I accepted the call with a quick press on the touchpad.

"What the hell are you wearing?" Reagan's confusion dipped into the creases around her eyes.

I smoothed my palm over the silky fabric of my blouse. "What's wrong with what I'm wearing?" I tipped the screen of my laptop back to remove the glare.

"You look like you're going to the fucking library."

"I like polka dots."

"Yeah, and I'm sure Mark's grandmother does, too. Take that shit off." Reagan turned and looked over her shoulder, distracted. She was at work tonight and the noise of the salon sifted through the speakers.

"I think it's classy?"

"Classy?" she asked, facing the camera again. "I know he's ten years younger than you, but—"

"Seven."

She rolled her eyes. "Whatever. You look like his kindergarten teacher."

I ignored her comment and glanced at myself in the mirror. My hair was down and I'd managed to tame my wayward strands into soft waves. And, okay, the outfit was stuffy, but I'd found the restaurant he was taking me to online and it was swanky.

"What about those cute black skinny jeans I saw hanging in the back of your closet and the sexy, flowy, V-neck tank top you wore when we went to lunch the other day? Pair those together and let me see."

"You don't think that top is too... I don't know, Ray, revealing?"

She glared at me from the computer screen. "You're going on a first date with a hot, younger guy who happens to be a famous millionaire hockey player. Revealing is good."

"I refuse to be someone I'm not just because he's a professional hockey player."

"Stevie..." She said my name as if it hurt her to say it. "That get-up you have on... that's not you either, that's Ben."

I shuddered. Shit, she was right. I ignored the heaviness in my chest and the tightening of my throat as I nodded. My voice was thin when I said, "Give me a second."

Reagan's smile had a sad edge to it. She knew me too well.

It hadn't taken me long to change after I'd found the pair of jeans she was talking about. The top had been recently dry cleaned and was still hanging on the back of my bedroom door. Once I was dressed, and put back together, I presented myself to her majesty.

"My work here is done." She laughed as she ran her fingers through her purple hair.

"I feel too chubby for these jeans." I tugged at the bottom of the tank trying to hide my stomach and stared at my full-figure in the mirror.

"You look sexy, Stevie. He's gonna die."

I huffed out a laugh. "You think?"

"I know."

The jeans hugged my hips and ass like a second skin. My curves were outlined in what seemed like high definition, and my top dipped low enough to showcase some cleavage. Despite the large size of my breasts, the blouse wasn't too indecent. My arms puckered with goose bumps and I wondered if I should throw on a jacket. It was always warm here compared to Richmond, but Floridians loved to crank the A/C.

"Do you care if I borrow that black leather jacket you left here yesterday?"

"Only if you wear those badass gray boots you bought at Nordstrom."

"Done."

I licked my lips to stop them from trembling, to stop the anxiety from seeping past my smile.

"You look hot, Stevie. He's gonna die."

"You already said that."

"Well, I meant it. Now go burn that fucking polka dot monstrosity or I will."

I shook my head as I laughed. "It's good for work."

"No, not even for work."

"Bye, Ray."

I walked toward the laptop and she held up her hands. "Wait."

I giggled. "What?"

"Please remember to be yourself."

"I will."

She smiled again and the width of it had me smiling, too. "You can do this."

I flicked my gaze to the mirror. My lips were painted pink, my eyeshadow was smokey, and in this outfit I almost didn't recognize myself. I wasn't staring at Stevie West. I was staring at Stevie Baylor and I hadn't seen her since I'd graduated from high school.

The doorbell rang and my heart dove into my stomach. I shrugged into the jacket Reagan had left here and slipped on the gray boots she'd told me to wear. Grabbing my purse, I headed to the front door with a stomach that had twisted itself inside out. My hand hesitated on the doorknob as I caught my breath. I counted to five before I finally opened it, and when I did, I realized there was no number I could've counted to that would've prepared me for the man standing on my front porch.

"Wow."

He chuckled.

"Oh God, I said that out loud, didn't I?" I asked and a few more knots made a home in my belly.

Mark stood in front of me in dark, fitted, expensive looking jeans. His white button-down had the sleeves rolled up, his ink-stained arms etched and lean. The brown leather boots he had on probably cost more than my entire outfit. His beard had grown in while he was away and, as I shamelessly admired the lips that made me feel like I'd die if I never got the chance to kiss them, I noticed the bruising under his left eye. I wanted to run gentle fingertips over his purple skin, soothe any pain that might've remained.

He noticed my scrutiny. "The other guy looks much worse."

"Does it hurt?" I whispered.

"Not anymore." He raised his hand letting a few strands of my hair sift through his fingers. "You look... *fuck*..." His smile was private, for me, as he rubbed the back of his neck. "So sexy."

Mark's eyes wandered the length of my body. Lingering on every curve, kissing them with heat. Blush filled my cheeks, dripped down my chest and settled low inside my stomach. I was terrible with compliments. I wasn't used to the way his eyes devoured me, and it scared me how much I liked it. I hadn't felt sexy in over a decade, maybe even ever, but in less than thirty seconds he had me believing that maybe I was.

I exhaled a shaky breath as I said, "Thank you." My anxious laugh made his smile even brighter. "Who knew hockey players cleaned up so nice?"

His laugh was full-bodied and it poured down my spine. "We have to wear suits all the time. For games... charity events..."

"Really?"

"I have more suits than casual clothes."

Mark in a suit.

"I think I'd like to see that more than you streaking the parking lot."

"What? Me in a suit?" He chuckled. "I'll Google some images for you when we get to the restaurant."

He reached for my hand, his fingers lacing with mine, and my heart climbed its way back into my chest from my stomach. Mark's eyes fell to my mouth, and for a split second, we both stopped breathing. How could I have missed the touch of a man I hardly knew? The static air between us crackled, and I stepped closer seeking relief from the prickling distance that had separated us.

Mark cupped my cheek with his other hand. His thumb resting soft against my skin. His breath was sharp, it hitched and expanded his chest as he lowered his hand from my face. "Should we get going?"

I nodded, giving him a shy smile. The tension I carried vined around my veins, the vessels straining with each hammered beat of my pulse. I felt Mark everywhere, down to the apex of my thighs.

His lips parted into a handsome grin as he squeezed our connected hands. "Let's go then."

Mark's Mercedes G-Wagon sat in my driveway looking out of place and dangerous with its matte finish and heavily tinted windows. I coughed back another nervous giggle as we stepped off the porch at the absurdity of such an expensive vehicle being parked in the driveway of my home. Reality began to sink in again.

"I'm pretty sure this car costs more than my house."

He shrugged. "I like your house. It's cute."

Cute.

"It's old."

"It's vintage."

My head tipped forward as I laughed. "You sound like the realtor."

"I almost bought a place here."

I raised my eyebrows as he opened the door of the SUV for me. "In Seminole Heights?"

"Yeah." He held my hand until I was settled into my seat and then shut the door.

I used the spare moment to catalog his scent. New car mixed with his ocean-scented cologne, creating the perfect masculine yet clean smell. I ran my fingertips over the indulgent black leather seat as I watched him round the front of the car. He slid into the driver side with athletic grace and started the engine. His fingers gripped the steering wheel, his tattoos dancing above his muscles as he stared ahead.

"I'm not a flashy guy, Stevie. I'm low-key on most things, but sometimes I like to splurge. I work hard and every now and then I reward myself. I like what I like." He turned to face me, his eyes serious. "Don't let this shit get to you. I'm just me... just Mark."

I swallowed around the bundle of nerves in my throat, the fear of who he was, what it all represented. Our age difference, the fight he'd gotten into, his money, the feelings he was capable of conjuring, I put it all away for now as he reached across the console, his hand settling on my thigh right above my knee.

I let my eyes fall to the connection.

My smile spread as I met his dark gaze again. Mark could have anything he wanted, anyone he wanted, but he was sitting here—with me.

I nodded, pressing my lips together in an attempt to contain my growing smile. He responded, his confident grin pulling into a dimple on his right cheek as I said, "Just Mark."

MARK

She gave me a shy smile before turning to look out the passenger side window as I backed out of her driveway. The silence afforded me a moment to get my shit together. The sun hadn't completely set and the orange-colored light illuminated her face. She was actually glowing. Stevie was sexy in a way most girls were not. She held herself with a modesty that was in complete opposition to her pouty lips and full curves. She was simply sex on legs and had no damn clue. In the last five minutes, I'd expended a mass amount of energy trying not to look at her tits. I had to admit I underestimated her. All week I'd held onto the vision of her looking like a hot librarian. So when she opened the door wearing tight-as-hell jeans and a low-cut top with a black leather jacket, I was surprised my dick hadn't saluted her immediately.

"Is the restaurant far?" she asked, giving me her attention. She leaned back into the seat, her head resting casually against the leather as she turned to look at me.

I glanced at her briefly before bringing my eyes back to the road. I'd noticed her cheeks were flushed and she was doing that thing with her lip where she nibbled on the left lower corner. She'd done it a few times the night I'd met her. It was distracting, and I'd rather not get into a crash before I had the chance to at least kiss her.

"It's off of South Howard." I lowered my gaze again, this time to the way she was wringing her hands in her lap. She was anxious and it made me chuckle. "You nervous?"

"A little." She laughed softly. "Okay... a lot." She exhaled. "This is a little overwhelming."

"Ask me anything."

Her brows dipped, humor edging at the corners of her mouth as she asked, "Why?"

"Ice breaker." I grinned and she gave me her sweet smile.

"Um..." She laughed and shifted in her seat.

My eyes dipped to the soft slope of her tits and I swallowed. *Pace yourself.*

She finally spoke, breaking me from the dirty thoughts brimming on the fringes of my undersexed brain. "Why hockey?"

"Why hockey?" I repeated and she nodded. I licked my lips letting myself mull over the question. The weight of her stare a pressure on my chest. Why hockey? There wasn't one good answer, it was more a feeling than a reason. And I didn't want to sound like a fucking idiot. "Because when I'm on the ice, the world stops when the puck moves, and everything inside of me comes alive."

Our eyes met, the seconds expanding like the color of her cheeks. Her smile was stunning. "That's a great answer."

"It's the truth."

We came to a stop at a red light and the surrounding traffic became a muted backdrop as I used the time to really look at her. The blush of her cheeks intensified.

"Did you watch all of the games?" I asked, not recognizing the low tone of my own voice and hoping for a yes I never thought I'd want.

"No, just the last one." She dropped her gaze, her smile waning, and I ignored my disappointment.

"Did it scare you? The fight?" My left hand gripped the steering wheel as I rested my right on her knee. She sipped the thick air in small, short breaths, and I wished I'd never laid a hand on that fucker, Lynch.

Stevie lifted her chin, her eyes finding mine. "It was intense to watch. And, yeah, if I'm being honest, it freaked me out a little. But..." She shifted her gaze to where my palm rested on her thigh. "Do you still have feelings for her?"

The muscle in my jaw pulsed. "No."

Fucking media.

"I know what they think, and how the announcers probably speculated, but when it comes to Mia, my ex, they fucking live for that shit, and I couldn't care less. I knocked him on his ass because he talked shit about my family."

"He did?"

My life was pretty private. I never gave the media much, and as far as chicks were concerned, they didn't need to know specifics. My life was mine, and after Mia, and the way she shredded my fucking trust, I was wary of letting anyone in.

The light turned green giving me a reprieve from Stevie's curious stare. Like I'd told her before, I was just a guy, and I might've had expensive shit, and a badass day job, but there was more to me than that. And I'd decided that I wanted her to know me.

I kept my eyes on the road as I said, "My ex cheated on me with the player I got into a fight with, and yes, we've fought over her before, but this time he crossed a line and I couldn't let it go." My knuckles paled as I gripped the steering wheel. That night and what he'd said was fresh in my mind. "My niece has autism. And the fucker only knows that because he and Mia got together the summer I started my hockey camp for special needs kids. He called her retarded, Stevie. And I straight up lost my fucking mind."

I didn't miss her gasp and when I stopped at the next stop light and found her glassy eyes staring at me, my chest tightened.

"He's a terrible person." Her whisper was thick.

I squeezed her knee. "I broke his nose."

"I hope it heals weird and he's horribly disfigured." I chuckled and she laughed. "I'm serious. What an asshole."

I lifted my hand from her knee and rubbed the back of my neck. "Fuck it. I'm over the whole situation." She tilted her head to the side as if assessing my statement for truth. "Mia isn't my problem anymore."

She was quiet for a few heartbeats. A million questions ran wild behind her odd-colored eyes. I waited her out though, the light turning green once again. We passed through the next intersection when she said, "I think it's pretty freaking amazing that you opened up a camp for children with special needs."

"It was already established, but needed more funding. I donated the cash, helped keep it open, and I get to play hockey with some awesome kids every summer." I glanced to the side and caught her smiling. "What?"

She shrugged and pinned her bottom lip with her top teeth, appraising me. "Mark..." She laughed again and the light sound of it relaxed every tense muscle in my body. "Can't I have a moment to hero worship?"

"It's not a big deal. My niece loves hockey. I take her with me every summer. A lot of my teammates have charities and foundations they support."

"I find philanthropy very attractive."

"Yeah?" I couldn't hold back my growing smile.

"Arrogance, not as much."

"But it looks good on me."

She didn't answer, but when I glanced at her she smiled. "I really do love it though. When I retire from the NHL I want to coach."

"You said you wanted to be a coach the night I met you."

My heart rate increased. "You remembered that?"

"I remember everything from that night." I might've imagined the breathless way she spoke, but when I stole a look, the fire had returned to her cheeks. She cleared her throat. "I think you'll be a great coach."

The conviction in her words stirred something primal inside my gut. I didn't need her approval, but I liked that I had it. "Besides playing hockey, it's all I've ever wanted."

"I've only seen you play once, and I have nothing to compare it to, but I was totally impressed. All of you guys are so talented. You run on ice, with skates strapped to your feet, chasing a small black dot. I've never even ice skated and I know what you do is impossible."

I stopped at the red light a little more abruptly than I should have. "Hold up. You've never ice skated?"

"No. Not once."

I tried not to glare at her. "How is that even possible?"

"I grew up in Tampa. The south. Not exactly a winter sports town."

She was right. Kind of. It *hadn't* been a winter sports town. But I decided not to correct her, and when the light changed, I made a U-turn.

"What are you doing?" she asked and I fought my smirk.

"Taking you to the rink."

"What? Why?"

She blanched and I tried not to laugh. "It'll be fun."

Seeing Stevie in skates, her ass in those tight jeans moving across the ice, way too tempting to pass up. I didn't care that the rink was probably packed with families for public skate, or how they'd probably recognize me. Most people didn't approach me when I was at the rink. We practiced at the Ice Sports Forum, and it was a community place as much as it was our practice facility.

"I'm not really dressed for ice skating."

"Sure you are," I said, blatantly ignoring the growing panic in her tone.

"What about dinner, you made reservations and—"

"I promise, after we skate, we can swing by one of my favorite restaurants by the rink."

"I hate you right now."

My laughter shook my shoulders and she narrowed her eyes.

"I won't let you fall."

Her answer was quiet, too mumbled, but I could have sworn I heard her say. "Too late."

"You owe me a serious romantic date night, all my choices." Stevie was practically shaking as I laced up her skate.

Figure skates were easier to balance on so I'd rented a pair of those instead of hockey skates. I knotted the lace and stared at her from where I was kneeling, my skates already on. Her eyes were bright, filled with adrenaline and fear. She rubbed her hands on her jeans while her eyes darted around the room.

The lobby of the Forum was packed like I'd predicted. Families out on a Friday night and several groups of rowdy teens. Mostly guys strutting around vying for the attention of the handful of girls they had with them. It was funny to watch, and crazy to think I'd been one of those idiots once.

"Are you cold?" I asked and she nodded finding my gaze. "Here..." I took both of her small hands in mine, swallowing them with my large palms.

I brought my lips to our joined hands and exhaled a warm breath against our skin. When I looked up again, her kissable lips were parted, and I wanted to place my own against them. Steal her breath.

"Everyone is staring at us," she whispered.

"Ignore it."

When we arrived, I hadn't missed the fervent stolen glances in our direction.

"You're used to this."

"The rink... it's a safe place, Stevie. It's where we practice. The people here know me, they get it, they won't approach me or my teammates most of the time, and the ones who do are really chill about it."

I stood, lacing the fingers of our right hands together.

"God, you're tall in skates," she said and I chuckled.

"Come on."

She exhaled a long breath as she stood and wobbled on unsure legs. She placed her hand on my chest as she fell forward, finding her balance, and I wrapped my arm around her, settling my hand at the small of her back. She smelled like summer, and the sweet scent of her hair trickled down and into my lungs as I breathed her in. I'd stolen a piece of her and I wanted to hold my breath. She squeezed my hand, the death grip causing me to laugh, and I finally exhaled hoping that this wouldn't be the only opportunity I'd have to be this close.

She wet her lips and I nearly groaned when her eyes eagerly found my mouth. We were pressed together and the room was filled with kids and their fucking parents. All I could think about was kissing her, how I wanted to drag my teeth across her bottom lip, see how far I could push her until she bit back.

She broke the heady silence as her hand curled in my shirt. "I'm terrified."

It didn't feel like she was talking about skating anymore.

"I won't let go, not unless you ask me to."

"You promise?"

"Promise."

Her lips trembled, but she managed a smile as we made our way in small steps through the lobby to the rink doors. Once she'd gotten the feel for the skates, each step came faster than the last. She shivered as we passed through the main doors to the rink. The room was kept cold, and the body heat of all the people in the large room did nothing to help the frigid temperature. We hesitated on the threshold of the rink. Stevie was taking it all in. The people, the loud music, the signature sound of blades cutting across the ice. Whenever I was here, my blood pumped harder, warmer, and I wondered if hers did, too. Did she feel it, that pulse? Did the crisp scent of the rink make her a little high like it did me?

She answered my silent questions with a huge smile. "This looks like it might be kind of fun."

I smiled as I zipped up her leather jacket. "Then let's do it."

It wasn't easy at first, and I'd like to say Stevie was a natural, but she wasn't. She'd almost fallen about five times and we'd only made it around the rink once. My favorite part about the entire endeavor was that every time she was about to fall she'd swear like a sailor. The girl was vulgar and it was fucking hot.

"Son of a bitch," she squeaked and stumbled over her skates.

In my attempt to stop us both from going down, I grabbed her hips and involuntarily propelled her into the boards. Her head hit the glass and she winced.

"Shit! Are you okay?" I asked and framed her face with my hands.

"I think so."

I did a quick assessment. My eyes swept across her face and my gaze landed on hers. Everything seemed alright. Her pupils looked even. Holy fuck, I'd checked my date into the boards. *Smooth move, Melo.*

"I'm sorry, I was trying to stop you from falling, I didn't mean to—"

"I'm fine."

The warmth of her body pressed against me, there wasn't an inch separating us, the fog spilling from her lips mingled with mine as we both tried to catch our breath. She smiled and everything came into crystal clear focus.

"You're not hurt?"

She shook her head and I leaned in a fraction. The cold air had charged the room with static, and it painted her cheeks and nose pink. My thumbs stroked gently across the silk of her skin and she tipped her head back. I couldn't stop myself from staring at her mouth. There was a small bow to her upper lip, a little indent begging for me to lick it.

"Fuck, I want to kiss you."

I moved in, driven by the selfish need to consume, each breath she took became mine as she whispered, "Then kiss me."

STEVIE

Every girl has that one moment. Something to put up on a pedestal, something to frame. My moment was right now. Mark's hot hands on my face, his eyes locked on mine, our lips barely inches apart. The sound of the rink disappeared and all I could hear was my own rapid breathing. All I could feel was his hard body caging me—the only thing keeping me upright in a world that had been tipped upside down.

"Fuck, I want to kiss you."

His voice was rough and breathless and I folded, easy and willing for the slight command that edged his request. It was unfamiliar, but I loved it.

"Then kiss me."

My chest ached with anticipation, each breath making my head feel dizzy, like I was on the crest of a hill and the roller coaster was about to plummet down the tracks. The cold air of the rink simmered as he dipped his head and my stomach dropped.

"I'm so fucking into you," he whispered and his lips brushed against mine before he took the final dive.

Those lips were so... so incredibly soft.

My eyes fluttered closed as I melted into his kiss. He tasted like mint as he gently parted my lips. He took more, his tongue sweeping across mine, and a low sound, almost a growl, rumbled in his chest. I wrapped my arms around his neck, held him closer, as my fingers curled into his hair. Mark's thumbs grazed my cheeks as he slid his hands into my hair as well. Heat bloomed between my thighs as he pressed against me. My skates slipped and he dropped his hands to my waist, holding me still. He chuckled against my mouth and left two sweet kisses, one on my upper lip and then one on the bottom. I lowered my hands to his shoulders, and the way he gripped my hips, desperate, aligning our bodies, it made me feel brave. I raked his bottom lip through my teeth. He groaned and pushed me against the side of the rink, devouring my mouth with firm and famished lips.

"Get it, bro!" someone called out and I felt Mark's shoulders vibrate with laughter.

He pressed one more kiss against my lips and then pulled away. Mark's cheeks were filled with blush, his ears pink to the tips.

I grazed my fingers over his cheekbone. "I like this."

"What?" he asked, making no effort to move us into a more public appropriate position.

"You're blushing." I slipped my hand into his hair at the nape.

He clenched his jaw, his eyelids heavy and hooded, as he cupped my cheek. The pad of his thumb drew slowly across my skin as he said, "So are you."

I pressed my teeth into my bottom lip, my smile shy as he watched me. "It was a good kiss."

"Good?" He raised his eyebrows, his smile pulling into sexy dimples.

"As far as first kisses go, yeah."

Mark eliminated any remaining distance between us, leaning in, his breath tickled my overheated skin as he whispered into my ear, "That kiss was fucking epic."

The sentence rolled off his lips, graveled and dirty. His left hand grasped my hip as his teeth grazed the lobe of my ear. Warm kisses dusted the sensitive slope of my neck and I shivered. I leaned my head back, granting him better access, forgetting about the public venue for a few more precious seconds. He released his grip on my hip and placed his hand against the glass. His eyes searched mine before he stole another kiss. This kiss was lazy and indulgent as if he had all the time in the world to discover me.

He finally parted from my lips with a groan, resting his forehead against mine he asked, "Should we get the hell out of here?"

"Not yet."

He held my face between his hands, his lips lifting on one side as he leaned back to look at me. "You still want to skate?"

Did I want to skate? I'd fallen on my ass, racked up years' worth of embarrassment, but there was something about the way Mark's eyes ignited from within as he'd watched me, taught me. This was his house, his home, and even if his kiss had me wanting more one-on-one attention, I was still buzzing on the high he radiated just being on the ice.

"Isn't that why you brought me here," I said giving him my best smile.

He lowered his hand lacing it through mine, his smile spreading so bright I was blinded by it, struck straight in the chest, the afterburn of it would stay with me for the rest of the night.

"Let's skate."

The night so far had felt like a John Hughes movie. Unsuspecting girl gets taken on a date by the hot superstar jock, has the best kiss of her life, and then gets swept away in a fancy car. If it wasn't for the bruise I was sure had begun to form on my butt or the way this burger joint smelled like grease, booze, and stale cigarettes, it would've been the best first date ever. Mark rewarded me with his megawatt smile as he stared at me from across the booth. Actually, he hadn't stopped staring at me since we'd left the rink, beyond what was safe, since he'd been driving.

"I know what you're thinking," I said as I spun the silverware that had been rolled into a white paper napkin in a circle.

"What's that?" he asked his eyes fixed on my mouth.

"That I'll never skate again."

"I'll make you." He chuckled and sipped from the glass of water the waitress had dropped by once we'd gotten here.

I almost snorted. "You can't make me do anything."

He heard the humor in my voice and laughed again. "Stevie, if you spend any amount of time with me, you'll learn that statement is entirely not true."

I didn't miss the innuendo in his low tone. I was about to tell him he was full of shit, but the waitress reappeared. She was young, maybe nineteen, dressed in jeans and a low-cut top.

She had moon-eyes for the star player as she asked, "What'll ya have, Melo?"

"I'm not sure yet, Kara, she's never been here before." He tipped his head in my direction and the girl greeted me with a friendly smile.

"Never, ever?" she asked in her heavy southern drawl, and I instantly wanted to put her in my pocket.

The place was a dive. Wood paneled everything, faded beige linoleum tiles, and pool tables that had seen better days sat to the right of the bar. It smelled weird, and the floors under my feet were sticky, but it had a certain charm.

"No, ma'am." I returned her smile and she shook her head in disbelief. I looked down at the laminated menu and tried not to laugh at the fact it had pictures on it. "I'll have a number seven."

Mark's lips were pressed together, a smile brimming at the corners. He kept his eyes on me as he ordered. "I'll have the same, but bring her a shot of your best tequila."

"Tequila? No, I'll just have—"

"Oh, and two Coronas," Mark interrupted me and slid my menu over to his side of the booth, picked it up and handed both of them to the server.

She winked at me before she turned to walk away.

"I can't drink tequila."

"Sure, you can." He was way too smug, and I couldn't hate how his smirk made all the butterflies in my stomach grab pompoms and cheer.

"You have to drink a shot of tequila and a bottle of Corona if you order a number seven."

"Says who?" I lifted a skeptical brow.

"Willie." His laugh was light, clearly enjoying my irritation.

"Who the hell is Willie?"

"The owner." He reached across the booth and pointed to the paper ring holding my napkin and silverware together.

Fat Willie's Bar and Grill was written in red block lettering across the top, and had a tubby-looking man wearing a red checkered chef's hat below it.

"You ordered a number seven. Which, I'm pretty fucking impressed with, by the way. It's tradition that when you order a number seven or thirteen you have to drink a shot of tequila and have a Corona. Willie is very superstitious. He told me the first time I'd ever eaten here. The man himself had actually brought me the drinks... said I had to drink it or I'd lose a game."

"Then why didn't you order two shots of tequila?"

"I don't drink liquor, typically, during the season."

"But you just said—"

"I'm not superstitious, I'm trying to get you tipsy." His grin was downright pleased and I laughed at his arrogance.

"And there's that charm."

He settled his hand over mine, drawing circles on my skin with his thumb. "You don't have to drink it."

His light brown eyes teased me, challenged, and all I wanted to do was surrender to him. Since I was nineteen, after I'd married Ben, all I'd ever known was quiet nights, calculated moments, and kisses that calmed instead of burned. Mark had me wanting to jump onto the pyre.

"I suppose I should have the full Fat Willie's experience." I bit back my grin and relished in the warmth of his chuckle, of his hand on mine.

"It wouldn't be the same otherwise."

Kara stopped by the table as Mark pulled his hand away. She set down the shot in front of me along with a bottle of beer, and then handed him his drink.

"Y'all's dinner is almost ready," she said with a tap of her serving tray on the table.

Once she walked away, Mark nudged the shot glass in my direction. "Bottoms up, babe."

Babe.

Usually I cringed at stuff like that, pet names, but he blushed as if he realized his slip, and his smile reached those perfect dimples as he shrugged his shoulders. "It's not gonna drink itself."

I brought the shot to my lips, closed my eyes, and gulped it down in one swallow. The burn reached my belly and I opened my eyes. I grabbed the lime that had been wedged into the top of my Corona and popped it between my lips. The tart lime juice dripped down my chin as I sucked on it. I wiped my mouth, proud that I'd completed his little challenge without a wince, and finished with a long pull of my beer before setting it down on the tabletop. Hungry eyes met mine as I glanced across the table. The powerful weight of his stare gathered heat along the lines of my cheeks.

My smile spread across my face as I relaxed into the cracked vinyl of the booth. "You're going to win on Monday."

He wet his lips, his eyes darting to the discarded lime wedge, and then back to my mouth before he asked, "You think so?"

I nodded and his shoulders set into a confident line. His entire presence screaming with strength. The same strength I'd witnessed for myself when I'd watched him play, watched him fight. "*I* am very superstitious so I'm glad I've taken the necessary precautions to assure your win."

His head fell back, and I admired the length of his neck, how his Adam's apple moved as he laughed. "We could really use a win after..."

He let the sentence go unfinished. But before the mood could become awkward, Kara brought our dinner to the table. She placed our plates in front of us with a cheerful "enjoy" and rushed off to the kitchen. The restaurant was busy, and I'd only seen one other server.

"This is a lot of food." My burger was almost too big to fit in my hands. And I had about a half pound of cheese fries, too. At least it would soak up the alcohol.

"Just wait till you taste it." Mark lifted his own burger to his mouth.

Grease dripped unceremoniously from his double cheeseburger onto his plate, and I figured formalities had been forgotten the minute he'd made the U-turn to the rink.

Mark wasn't lying. The food was to die for. We both ate in silence, enjoying the reward after our workout, well, my workout, Mark probably didn't even break a sweat at the rink. We'd made a decent dent in our burgers before we fell into easy conversation again. He'd already hit the basics. Asked me about college and how I'd met Ben. I didn't like talking about Ben, but he'd opened up about Mia earlier. I'd given him the rundown about how Ben and I had met our senior year in high school and married at nineteen. *Young and stupid.*

"What about you? You grew up in New Hampshire, right?" I asked as I downed another chunk of cheese fries.

He chuckled. "I'm curious how much Google informed you about me."

"Not very much. Most of my research consisted of Alec and all of his fangirling." I rolled my eyes.

"Did he tell you I grew up in Redding."

I nodded my head. "What about your family?"

"Still lives there. My parents own the same home they moved into after they got married. My sister lives in Manchester with her husband and my niece."

"Poppy." I remembered.

Her name brought out his smile. "My number one girl."

"Is she the jealous type?"

"Very." His laugh softened his features, and I wanted to lean across the table and kiss him. "What about you, any siblings?"

"My family isn't very complicated. Odd. But not complicated." I took a bite of my fries and pushed the plate to the edge of the table. "I'm an only child... and my mother..." I cringed. "I have no idea who my dad is, my mom's kind of a hippy."

His lips formed a serious line. "Shit, Stevie. I'm sorry."

I laughed. "Don't be. I didn't miss out on anything. My mom is a whacko, but she did the best she could raising me on her own. I had a pretty cool childhood. She let me dye my hair crazy colors, bought me old punk records, allowed me to stay out late with Reagan, but I think because she was such a flake I gravitated toward things I knew would anchor me. Steadfast and simple truths. Math and—"

"Ben."

I swallowed. "And Ben." My eyes fell to the table. Mark's gaze was too much to bear. It wondered and measured. "I love my mom, but I saw how her free-spirited lifestyle affected her. She went through so many guys, and I never wanted that. That heartbreak. Ben was supposed to be a sure thing."

Or I'd wanted him to be.

"What do you want now?"

My mouth felt dry as I answered, "I don't know..." I lifted my eyes to his. "But I'm really excited to have a chance to figure it out."

"You know who you are, Stevie. You've just been hiding too long to remember."

His words were a free fall. A ninety-degree drop. He was so sure, well-worn in his own skin. Mark saw something in me, and I wanted to see it, too.

Disappointment quelled the flutter in my stomach when Kara brought us the check. Mark threw a couple of twenties on the table and asked if I was ready to go. I wasn't. Energy surged through my muscles and the expectant tension found its way into my galloping pulse. It stayed that way the whole ride home.

Mark had turned on music as we drove back to my place, and I lost myself inside the lyrics and bass. It was an effort to drown out the loud thump of my heartbeat, but I'd managed it. He lowered the music and left the car running as he hopped out. I'd almost opened my door, but he'd beat me to it. Mark's hand found a home in my own as we walked up the drive.

"Come to my game on Monday," he said as we stepped onto my porch. "I know the last game was rough, but—"

"I'll be there." I leaned into him, and his inked, powerful arms wrapped around my waist.

He closed the distance, and I liked how I had to tip my head back to see into his eyes. I'd always felt like I was too much woman for Ben. My body had shadowed his, my five-foot-six height not too much shorter than his five-foot-ten. My full-figured curves had never made me feel anything other than chubby, but Mark, he made them feel sexy.

His fingers pressed into the flesh of my hips as he leaned me against the pillar of my porch.

"Thank you for tonight," I whispered as he dipped his head a little lower.

"Did you have fun?" he asked with a cocky smile.

"I did."

The warmth of his breath covered my lips, and the soft curve of his mouth enveloped mine. I raised my arms, draping them around his neck. My right hand gently tugged through his hair. The pillar pushed against my spine as he deepened the kiss, his tongue met mine, drawing out a moan.

He pulled away and his breathing was as frantic as mine.

"I should go. Before I can't."

I bit my lip. Warring with myself.

Invite him in or send him on his way.

He leaned into me again; I felt the hard pressure of his arousal against my stomach. He kissed me once and I nipped his upper lip. My hands fell to his waist and I hooked my fingers through his belt loops. He kissed my jaw, the rough bristles of his beard branded a pathway along the skin to my neck. His fingers tangled in my hair as he brought his mouth to mine again. I rocked against him earning another low groan. We were making out like teenagers on my porch, and all I could think was how I wanted him, needed him to relieve the ache building inside me. A wet heat pooled between my legs as his hands found the curve of my ass and squeezed. My fingers gripped his hair, and our mouths crashed and danced as the kiss became a collision of teeth and skin.

"Stevie…" His voice was sex. "Am I going home?"

The humid night air stole his scent as I sucked in a much-needed breath. It cleared my head as I kissed his neck once and then again, before pulling away completely. His hair was a mess, his cheeks blotched with pink, and I wondered how disheveled I looked to him. God, I wanted him to stay, but everything that was worth anything took time, didn't it?

"I think that might be a good idea." I furrowed my brow, my eyes fixed on his trying to discern if he was disappointed. Instead I was met with soft and understanding brown eyes.

He slid a hand into his pocket, and cradled the back of my head with the other, placing a kiss on my forehead. His lips feathered against my skin. "I'll call you tomorrow."

I reluctantly watched as he pulled out of my driveway and disappeared down the road, taking the sting of his lips with him. I looked through my purse, found my keys, and once I was inside, I leaned against the front door.

I closed my eyes.

Brought my fingers to my lips.

And smiled.

Okay, maybe I squealed and danced in place.

Either way...

In this brief immature display... I wouldn't let myself feel lost, or numb.

I'd just focus on how it felt to be sexy, desired, and how it felt to be with him.

MARK

Searing heat tore down my legs, my quads begging me to stop as I rushed over the blue line. I'd seen the hole. The shot. Karlsson was distracted. He took the bait as I faked the pass to my left winger, Rasmussen. Karlsson dropped to his knees ready to stop the puck from the left, totally unaware I was about to best him. My D-man set up the screen, taking the goalie's sight. I made it look too damn easy as I slid my hand down my stick and scored over his right shoulder with a wrister.

"Fuck yes!" I roared as the puck hit the back of the net.

Nothing could stop me today. I was still high from Friday night. Stevie's taste was a punch of adrenaline every time I thought about it, thought about her. Thought about the way her lips had wrapped around that damn lime.

"Goddamnit!" Karlsson yelled and it echoed throughout the rink, reeling me back from my dirty thoughts.

He smashed his stick down onto the ice and I chuckled at his tantrum. My skates shot a wave of ice over the crease as I came to a sudden stop. "We've come at you with over twenty-plus shots, Mike, and this is the only one you've let by. Don't throw a fucking fit." I smiled and smacked the side of his helmet.

"I know, but a point's a fucking point." I assessed his eyes through his mask. The defeat was already fading.

As he turned and grabbed his bottle of water off the net, I said, "Yeah, but your save percentage against Dallas is stellar. You've got this, man. We've fucking got this."

He nodded and squeezed the bottle, spraying a stream of water into his mouth through a hole in his mask.

"Shit, Melo, you gonna stroke his dick, too?" Bryson's smile was smug as hell as he greeted me with a glove-covered fist bump.

"I thought that was your job." Mike's tone held more humor than it did any real frustration.

I laughed as I said, "Hey, we could all use a little confidence after Columbus."

"Should we run a few more plays?" Mike Karlsson was arguably one of the hardest working goalies in the league. "I want to try to stop your wrist shot again."

"It doesn't count if you know it's coming."

Mike threw his water bottle on top of the net. "Try me."

Mike ended up stopping every attempt we'd had on goal. A few of which were mean-as-fuck slap shots Bryson had landed straight to the logo of Mike's jersey. We all looked really damn good on the ice today, and afterward, in the locker room, the coaching staff had said as much. The loss we'd taken on the road was long gone for most of the team, by most, I mean everyone but me. Mia had been at morning skate, and the silence between us was a loud reminder of how I'd contributed to our team's loss. But I'd wrapped up that shit show in my head and threw it away before I hit the shower.

Everyone was pumped, and I had to admit, despite what had happened with Lynch, I was feeling that energy, too. Music blared throughout the locker room, some crazy ass metal shit with a heavy hip-hop beat that paced my heart. My limbs were light, my muscles itched, ready for a win. Game day. Win or lose. It was an addictive form of anxiety, a rush toward devastation or fucking glory. The anticipation, the hopeful unknown. Nothing beat that.

I could overhear Bryson talking shit to Mike, and I smiled, pulling my shirt over my head. It was their game day ritual. Hockey was a mental game. And the last thing you wanted was for your goalie to lose his shit and become a sieve.

"Set it up, dick. I bet I can get at least three into the net," Bryson taunted, but Mike laughed.

"Three?"

"Fuck yeah, asshole, maybe even four out of five."

Mike shook his head and I laughed.

"What's so fucking funny, Melo? You want in on this little bet?"

I sat down on the bench and leaned over to lace my shoes. "What're the stakes this time?"

"Pride, Melo."

When I glanced up at Bryson he smirked. *Bullshit.*

"Do I even want know?" I asked.

Mike snickered, and I immediately knew these idiots had bet on something that would have me questioning their morality.

"Whoever wins gets to pick the loser's chick for the night." Mike's smile got even wider.

"There is something seriously wrong with both of you." I stood and couldn't help but laugh as they looked at each other with shit-eating grins. "One of these days you guys are going to fuck over the wrong girl, and I hope I'm there to take a picture when all that crazy comes back to bite you both in the ass."

Bryson waved me off. "Nah. These girls use us as much as we use them."

Unfortunately, he was right, and it made me feel that much better I'd left that shit behind ages ago. Stevie's eyes, her mouth as it pulled into a grin, the way it felt to be pressed against her on the boards. It all came flooding past the weak wall I'd tried to raise for practice today, in an attempt to keep my head straight. I'd spoken to Stevie yesterday and given her the details about her tickets, and where to sit. She'd be sitting a few rows up, behind my team's bench. Having her here tonight had something stirring inside me. A potent mixture of nerves, anticipation, and pride. Something I'd never really felt before in regards to a chick. She was fun, and didn't give a fuck about pretenses. She was real, and as Mike and Bryson had reminded me, that shit was hard to find.

"Well? Melo? You in or not?" Mike asked.

"Definitely not."

Mike's six-foot-four frame deflated and he ran his hand through his hair. "I thought I'd have some actual competition this time."

Bryson coughed out a laugh and shoved Mike in the chest. "I let you win, asshole."

The guys were like brothers with how they acted, and it helped they both had dark hair and blue eyes.

Bryson's deep laughter cut off abruptly, and I turned in time to see Coach approaching us.

"You got a minute?" he asked me.

I grabbed my phone and wallet from the stall and put them in my pocket. "Sure."

His forced smile was a red flag. Unease spread in my gut as I followed him to his office. A few of the guys, some of the younger players, went quiet as we walked by. *Shit.* That was never a good sign. I ran all the plays we'd done this morning in my head, every shot I took. Nothing came immediately to mind. I'd crushed it out there today. So when he actually closed his office door, which he never did, my throat contracted.

"Have a seat, Melo."

"What's up?"

He held out his hand, gesturing to the chair, and I reluctantly sat down.

"Nice work today." He took a seat behind his desk. This wasn't about today?

"I'm not going to pussyfoot around this, Melo. Tonight is fucking important. I got some news today, and I need to know it's not going to mess with your game." He exhaled and knocked his fist on the desk lightly, gathering his thoughts. "I need your head with the team."

"Fuck, Coach, what's up?"

"Mia put in her resignation. Looks like she's moving to Columbus."

A laugh tripped past my lips. Relief expelled from my lungs as I exhaled the past two years of toxic air. Her presence here was a curse. And I'd never really felt the full power of it until now. Mia had been my choice, my mistake, and it had affected our team. That one word, resignation, lifted the corners of my lips and the burden of our relationship off my shoulders.

"You okay with this?" His furrowed brows relaxed and he leaned back in his chair. His relief mirroring mine.

"More than okay."

He nodded, his usual stoic and stone face gentled and it surprised me when he said, "We should've fired her, but—"

"But she's a great skate coach."

You couldn't make a decision for a team based on one man's issues. You had to find balance, and balance was Maddox's specialty.

He shrugged his shoulders. "Let's just win tonight."

I stood, letting the news sink in fully, letting that feeling ignite my spine. My smile was sure, steadfast. "Is there any other option?"

Atlas pulled on the leash as we ran up the stairs to my apartment. I should've taken the elevator, but I wanted to get as much of his energy out as I could before I left for the arena.

"Chill, boy."

He answered with a booming bark, paws digging at the threshold. I laughed as I opened my front door and removed his leash. Atlas bounded into the living room and grabbed his rope between his teeth. He was the size of a small horse, and when he ran toward me, skidding on the wood floors, he almost took out one of the bar stools in the kitchen. I set my keys down on the countertop and opened the fridge, grabbing a bottle of water. I had an hour before I had to be back to the rink.

Atlas nudged my ass with his nose and I swatted a playful hand at his muzzle. I turned to grab the rope but he dropped down into a pouncing position. Leaning down, I snagged the side of the rope hanging from his drool-covered lips and tugged. He growled, but I was able to get it free and tossed it across the floor, watching as he barreled toward the damn thing. Instead of rushing back, the click clack of his paws slowed and then disappeared as he made three circles in the oversized dog bed by the couch.

"You're the laziest dog I know. One pass, that's all you got?"

He ignored me, as usual.

My phone buzzed, and as I pulled it from my pocket, it alerted again. The screen flashed with two names. Stevie and Bryson. It was no contest which one I'd read first.

Stevie: *Is it five yet?*

I laughed at the angry, red-faced emoji on the screen and Atlas's ears perked.

"It's Stevie," I said, and his head turned to the side. "We like her."

I tapped out a quick response.

ME: *Bad day at work?*

I switched to Bryson's message and groaned. It was a link to this bullshit gossip website that specialized in sports and fucking lies. I pressed my thumb onto the link, and there it was in big ass bold letters.

Tampa Bay's Star Player Gets Lucky
Who is Mark Carmelo's new Mystery Woman?
Scroll down to get the details.
Holy shit.

The angle was crap, and you couldn't, thank fuck, see her face, but that's mostly because it looked like I was eating it. The picture was fuzzy, someone had probably snagged the shot with their phone while skating by. My heart rate slowed as I stared at the picture. Unless you knew what to look for, most people wouldn't have been able to tell if it was me or not.

Bryson: *Who's the girl?*

ME: *A chick I'm seeing.*

Bryson: *Since when?*

I pinched the bridge of my nose and exhaled.

ME: *Just worry about the game tonight.*

My phone chirped, but this time it was Stevie, and my irritation with Bryson's nosy ass morphed into a nervous knot in my stomach. How would she react? Better yet, would she even want to deal with all this media bullshit? Even on my best days I loathed the media. They'd already misconstrued, contorted, speculated enough about my life. Stevie was level-headed, mature, she'd understand, at least I sure as hell hoped she would. I came with baggage. My life was hockey. And I loved it. I was always training, traveling, and being with me was like living in a fishbowl. The media was a reality I couldn't sweep under the rug.

I opened her text with a heaviness I wasn't ready to deal with.

Stevie: *One of Trent's big clients is getting audited. He's worried he may need to pull in more help.*

ME: *Sounds messy.*

Stevie: *Very.*

Stevie: *I'm excited about tonight though. Thanks for the tickets again.*

I ignored my growing apprehension. I'd have to tell Stevie about this picture, and I promised myself I would some time later tonight. Right now, I'd let myself focus on how she was "excited" about the game. The way she had me feeling like I'd known her longer, beyond the short amount of actual one-on-one time we'd spent together, it was a natural attraction. There was no hesitation. Only that persistent pull. And I couldn't wait to kiss her again, watch her come alive beneath my touch.

ME: *Did you decide who you're going to bring?*

When I'd called her and told her she had two tickets she'd been relieved to not have to sit alone, but her relief had turned quickly into an adorable panic attack. Her boss and business partner were huge fans, and would "kill her" for the tickets.

Stevie: *I never told the guys.*

Stevie: *I'm bringing my friend, Reagan.*

ME: *Good choice.*

Stevie: *Less hurt feelings.*

ME: *I'll get my teammates to sign something for them.*

Stevie: *You'd do that?*

ME: *I'd do just about anything if it means I'll get a repeat of the other night.*

Stevie: *Such a whore.*

My laugh was loud enough Atlas barked and trotted over to where I was leaning against the counter. I wondered if she was blushing, if her bottom lip was trapped between her teeth, a shy smile playing at the corners of her mouth. I could almost hear her light giggle.

ME: *Seriously, it's no big deal. We sign shit all the time.*

Stevie: *They'd love that. Thank you!*

I rubbed Atlas's head, his gray and black-spotted face stared up at me, his big eyes pleading for something.

"What?" I asked and a low grumble sounded in his throat. "Should we send her a picture?"

I leaned down to his level, opened the camera app on my phone and snapped a couple of shameless selfies. There was only one decent picture. My smile was goofy as fuck, but Atlas had his ears up and his eyes right on the camera. I attached it to the next text message.

ME: *Atlas told me he wants to meet you this time.*

She didn't take long to respond.

Stevie: *Does he now?*

I wanted to hear her voice, hear the sexy laughter in her tone. I pressed the call button. It rang barely once.

"Hey," she whispered and I wanted to lose myself in the sultry, almost sleepy quality of it.

"Come over after the game."

"Are you sure you won't be tired?"

"It doesn't matter. I'd rather hang out with you than sleep."

Amongst other things. But I kept that to myself.

"Mark... I..." I heard her softly exhale. I was ready for her to tell me I pushed too hard, that coming over was a bad idea. "Should I meet you there after the game or..."

"Have Reagan take you to Time Out, it's right by the rink. We always go there after the game."

"Time Out?"

"Yeah, it's the same place I met you." My smile stretched wide. "We don't have to stay long, but it will give you and Reagan a place to chill until we wrap up at the rink. I'll text you when I'm about to head over."

"Sounds like a plan," she said and a quiet laugh drifted through the phone and hit me in the chest. "Reagan is going to lose her mind."

"Why?"

"She'll have an entire hockey team to drool over all night, and when she finds out we're having drinks with said hockey hotties she might implode."

"You'll have to keep her away from my captain, Bryson."

"Noted."

"Hey, Stevie?"

"Hey, Mark?"

"Thanks for coming tonight."

She was quiet for three, maybe four, long seconds. Each one marked and etched into the beat of my hungry pulse.

"I wouldn't miss it for the world."

STEVIE

"**S**hit, shit, shit..." The arena was a storm of sound, and I couldn't hear myself think as Reagan and I made our way down to our seats. "We're so late."

"You have to calm down," Reagan teased, clearly enjoying my dismay. "You can't help that he had a game in the middle of rush hour."

I should've left earlier, I thought to myself and practically tripped down three stairs when the crowd exploded. I vaguely heard Reagan's giggle over the announcer's deep boom. He was saying something about a power play when our row finally came into view. It wasn't until we climbed over five or six annoyed fans, their beers spilling onto my Converse, that I allowed the anxiety to ebb.

"The game's barely started." Reagan gave me the 'wide-eyed, you're a crazy person' stare, as we settled into our seats.

I'd been so focused on finding our spot I hadn't realized how close we really were to the rink. Five rows up from Tampa Bay's bench.

"Wow," I whispered but it was swallowed by the roaring cheer of the audience.

Everyone around us suddenly rose to their feet, hands up in the air as a loud horn blared overhead. Streams of swears and violent joy pounded their hands together as they celebrated. We'd been engulfed in a sea of blue jerseys as the announcer hollered, "Goal!"

Reagan and I both stood, and I wondered if she felt as clueless as I did. "Did they score?" I asked and she shrugged.

The announcer started to bellow again, but I couldn't decipher what he was saying until he uttered two words, "Mark Car-mel-o."

The arena echoed back his last name, enunciating every syllable just as the announcer had. Reagan and I turned to look at each other at the same time. An incredulous giggle tickling my throat. Her smile was ear to ear while mine shook a little. My heart pounded staccato beats inside my chest, desperate to get a glimpse of him. Like everyone else, I was in awe, but for a completely different reason. This was his life. Every row of this arena was alive, buzzing, and brimming over with adrenaline because of him. Every single person here knew his name, and I was here because he knew mine.

Reagan screamed, "Go, Mark!" as the crowd stomped their feet, and I stood on my tiptoes to see over the giants standing in front of us. Ray nodded her chin to the large monitors hanging above the rink and I followed her gaze. Mark's stick was raised, his mouth split into a gorgeous smile as he skated past the row of players sitting at the bench bumping fists with each of them. That smile, I wanted to catalog it, remember how it radiated, and how its warmth flooded my chest. I hadn't before witnessed this smile, this side of Mark.

The men in front of us finally sat down, and maybe I should've too, but I was mesmerized, clapping like a mad woman, when his eyes found mine. I was paralyzed by the power of it and how the lights of the arena bounced funny shadows over his sharp features. He didn't look real. For a half of a second, I thought I had dreamed him up entirely. He chuckled, or it looked like he had at least, as he stepped up to the bench. He lifted his glove-covered hand and gave me a small nod of his chin before he sat down.

My cheeks flushed and Reagan bumped her hip into mine. "Jesus, that man is hot."

"Hey..." I laughed as we both sank into our seats.

"I wasn't talking about *your* man." She pointed to number twenty-three. "How do you pronounce that?"

I stared at the man's name on his jersey. "Ra-nan-ow-ski?"

"He's a giant, and your man better introduce me tonight."

"I'll never understand the relationship you have with Pete."

"We have a nice thing going."

"You've been with him for years."

"Friends with benefits," she corrected me. "I prefer it that way. It's less messy."

"You're delusional."

"I'm a genius."

"If you say so." The last word of my sentence faded into a cacophony of jeers. There was a flurry of movement on the bench, and just like that, Mark was on the ice again.

Hockey was an organized chaos. The fans were rabid, and even though I didn't exactly know all the rules, or what was happening, I could feel it. I never liked sports, never liked watching them, if I was being honest. In college, while everyone was at the football game, I was in the library studying with Ben. I wasn't sure how much of it was hockey, or how much of it was the sexy player with the number nineteen stitched into his jersey, but as the clock ticked, and the game went on, the pressure in my lungs stretched past comfortable. My spine felt rigid, and my hands rotated between clenched fists and clapping. I was on the verge, a silent scream queued and ready stuck in my throat, and every time our team looked like they were about to score I would lose my shit. I'd jump or scoot to the edge of my seat. At one point, I might've stood, yelling like a crazed lunatic when some meathead from Dallas smashed Mark into the glass.

My favorite part, and I pocketed away every single one of them, were the private smiles Mark kept sending me every time he came to the bench. Each smile, each subtle nod of his chin was for me. It fed the competitive pulse that thundered inside my ribs, and when he scored again, I got to see it this time, witness the power behind his shot, the skill honed into one defining second. He made it look so easy.

All that pent-up anticipation emptied, as I flew to my feet, my hands at my mouth and shouted, "That's right, baby!"

I stomped my feet with the crowd and high fived Reagan. I actually "wooed" and took pleasure in the way the bass of the arena melted my muscles. When Mark scored a third time in the second period, a hat trick is what I'd overheard the guys in front of us call it, I'd pretty much morphed into the world's craziest cheerleader. My cheeks hurt from smiling. The fans threw their hats into the rink while

Mark's team surrounded him on the ice. It was barbaric the way they punched and shoved each other's shoulders, the way they smacked their helmets, and yet, it was the most adorable group hug I'd ever seen.

Reagan had been so thrilled with my little displays of sports-induced lunacy that during the first intermission she'd bought me a t-shirt from the shop. It was white and had Tampa Bay's logo on the center of it. Carmelo and his number were scrolled across the front, as well, in bold blue. When she'd first handed me the shirt, I had no intention of wearing it, but during the second intermission I'd gone to the bathroom and changed. I wanted to be all in, to belong to this win, to this team—to this man.

Ray and I had taken longer than I'd wanted, and by the time we got back to our seats, beers in hand, the last period had already started. Mark was on the ice and I couldn't tamp down my excitement.

"I love hockey."

Reagan sipped from her beer to hide her smile.

"It's fun," I said and hated the defensive tone of my voice.

"You're all fired up, it's darling. Mark has himself a fangirl."

I looked down at my shirt wondering, if maybe after all, it was a stupid idea to wear it.

"Does this seem too—"

"Groupie?" Reagan interrupted. "Definitely."

"I'm taking it off." I made a move to stand but she held her arm across my chest like my mother used to do when she'd slammed on the brakes too hard while driving.

"He'll love it. You're his own personal groupie, Stevie."

As if to prove her point, when I turned toward the bench he was staring at me. A smirk formed on his lips.

"See." She raised her cup to him.

The pride in his eyes wasn't something I imagined. It was the same thing I was feeling. It was mutual. His gaze held me. The arena disappeared and it was just him, just Mark looking at me like I was the only thing that mattered. My heart sputtered and sprinted and split wide open as I caught my breath. It was only a look, but there was a promise in his light brown eyes, and it made my limbs tingle with its intensity.

"Yup, you're so getting laid tonight." Reagan's immature statement brought the reality of the room rushing back.

"Sometimes, I wonder if you're mentally stuck in high school."

"I'm only stating the obvious."

I exhaled a laugh, and when I turned to the rink again, Mark was talking to one of his teammates.

"It's too soon for that..." Wasn't it?

"Stevie. Who cares about limits? You guys are like the definition of attraction. I'm hot just watching you eye fuck each other. Can you honestly say, without a doubt, that last year, if you hadn't been married, you wouldn't have accepted his invitation that night?"

I let my gaze slide back to the bench and lied, "I don't know."

I would've said yes in a heartbeat and it scared me. There was this wildness blooming inside me every time I thought about him, looked at him, and that night, as much as I wanted to embrace it, it was what I'd been running from when I'd married Ben. That trait was my mother's. I loved her with all of my heart, but I'd seen her loneliness etched into the frown lines of her mouth, the creases that surrounded her eyes, and I'd worried sometimes if I let that wildness take root, if I let feelings like I had for Mark grow, I would end up like her. The negative voice, I was pretty good at keeping at bay for the most part, snuck in a few jabs. How long would a guy like Mark, a guy with options, a guy who was always on the road, stick around?

"Stop overthinking." Reagan laughed. "You're too easy to read, chickadee. Have fun, take your time, whatever. You're a pup all over again. Enjoy it."

She held up her beer and I gently touched the rim of my cup to hers. "Enjoy it," I repeated before I took a sip. The burst of carbonation and hops spilled over my tongue. Ray gave me a knowing smile as I leaned back into my seat, lightly tugging at the hem of my new t-shirt with my free hand. "I think I can do that."

Hundreds of girls were wearing Mark's last name. Okay, maybe a hundred was overly dramatic, but I'd stopped counting at fifteen. Some had on his jersey, which spurred some weird, misplaced adolescent jealousy inside my stomach, and others had shirts like mine. Reagan and I were at the bar and on our third beer when my phone buzzed on the table top.

"God, I hope that's him. It's getting a little claustrophobic in here." Reagan eyed the growing crowd.

Mark: *Walking in. Where are you?*

ME: *In the back.*

I stared at our previous texts. The one I'd sent congratulating him, with the little top hat emojis, seemed juvenile to me now. The palms of my hands began to sweat as I laid my phone down. Nerves I should have gotten over after our first date worked their way up my throat as it contracted. He'd just won a game, he was the only player who scored on his team, and he'd done that hat trick thingy. He was special and I'd sent some stupid emojis.

"Finally," Reagan muttered and I lifted my head.

I'd half expected the room to fill with applause when he walked in. But his fan club was either too enthralled or too used to seeing the guys here. I, on the other hand, couldn't tear my eyes away. Mark's tailored, charcoal gray slacks clung to his muscular thighs as he approached us. He had the sleeves of his navy blue button-down rolled past his elbows displaying his tattoos. The top two buttons were popped, exposing his neck and a slice of his tanned chest. I swallowed as his full lips pulled up at the corners, his white teeth, that cute little gap between the top two, made my heart flop, stop, and then restart again.

"Hey." His husky tone vibrated down my spine as he leaned in and kissed me on the cheek first, and then allowed his lips to hover over mine as he spoke. "Nice shirt."

I crinkled my nose. "Is it too much?"

"Fuck no. I love it."

The heat of his breath tickled my lips as he closed off the small space and kissed me. His mouth was soft and sweet mint as it moved against mine. The fight, the war between hesitation and need flavored his kiss as his fingers slid into my hair. He made all the insecurities I had seem trivial, unnecessary, as we lost ourselves to the taste of us. His thumb pressed against my jaw as he pulled away from my mouth.

Reagan cleared her throat. "Great game."

Mark lowered his hand from my face, only to run it through his damp hair. I liked how it curled and flopped onto his forehead.

His cheeks matched the scarlet flame of my own. "Thanks... Reagan, if I remember correctly?"

"That's me," she said and took the last sip of her beer.

"I'm glad you could make it."

"Ray's a little infatuated with number twenty-three," I said and Reagan's devious smirk made Mark chuckle.

"Rananowski? He's married."

"Well, shit, I waited around for nothing." She looked over Mark's shoulder and a crestfallen expression marred her smart-ass smile.

His head tipped back as he laughed. "The guys will be stuck for a while, I think. Big crowd tonight." His teammates had lingered behind chatting up some of the fangirls.

"I think I'm gonna take off. I have to work tomorrow." Reagan stood and opened her purse.

"I got it." Mark held up his hand.

"Dating a hockey player perk number three hundred and five. He buys drinks for the friend." She pushed a chunk of her hair behind her ear and offered him a friendly smile. "Thank you."

"No problem."

She turned the full weight of her gaze on me. "Text me tomorrow?" But her eyes, they held secrets. The conversation we'd had at the game about tonight, about enjoying it, danced behind her irises.

"I will."

Reagan kissed me on the cheek before she left, and I assured her again I'd text her sometime in the morning. Once she was gone, I assumed Mark would take her seat, but instead he threaded his fingers through mine, pulling me from the bar stool onto dizzy feet. His arms wrapped around my waist as my greedy lungs gathered his scent, soap and ice. I let it crawl down my throat as I breathed deeply, leaning my head back enough that I could see into his eyes.

"Did you have fun tonight?" he asked before pressing his lips to the hollow below my ear.

I shivered. "Yes."

He left kisses on my neck and jaw, trailing a scorching path of heat along my skin as he made his way to my mouth. My heart was thoroughly spent, beating and bucking like a bull stuck in its pen by the time he freed his lips from mine.

He spoke with a smile against my mouth, "I liked having you there."

His fingers eased under the hem of my shirt, brushing indecent lines along my stomach and ribs. His large hands gripped my waist offering me an illusion of fragility. The skin-to-skin contact puckered my flesh into goose bumps as he painted tiny pictures with his thumbs on my hips.

"You ready to leave?" he asked.

"You just got here."

"And?"

His dimples appeared and I shook my head with a laugh.

"Don't you want to celebrate with your team?"

The corners of his mouth twitched with humor and he shook his head. "I see these idiots way too much." He was close enough I could see the different flecks of yellow and ginger that bled into the chestnut color of his eyes. He kissed my forehead, and the gentle confidence of his smile matched the deep and sure sound of his voice. "I want to be alone with you."

STEVIE

A lone.
With me.

It was safe to say my heart had plunged into my stomach, stirring the already frenzied butterflies into mass hysteria.

"You look a little scared." He was teasing me, his smile was more of a half-moon, lifted only on one side. It was more of a boyish grin, sexy regardless, and also, I'd decided, my favorite.

I eased into my own breath as I shouldered the strap of my purse. "I think it's finally hitting me."

"What?" he asked and wrapped his arm around my waist pulling me closer.

There was no distance to hide behind as I admitted the truth. "Tonight... the game... Mark, you're..." I tipped my head back to gauge his expression. His eyes danced with humor, his smile pulled into dimples.

"I'm what?" The whispered question was laced with mirth and confidence.

He brushed his knuckles softly against my cheek. His touch was gentle, but the rough feel of his skin billowed down my spine, covering me in a blanket of warmth. Overcome by the thundered pace of my heart, my voice was unsteady when I answered, "You're amazingly talented, every person was on their feet for you tonight, an entire sold-out arena..." I paused waiting for him to say something, to figure out how mundane I actually was compared to what he could have. But he stared at me, and if I hadn't been looking, I might've missed how his brilliant smile lost a bit of its wattage. "Overwhelming..." I stammered. "It's overwhelming, Mark. I watched that game on television but... it wasn't the same. I had no idea." I laughed and his arm tightened its hold around me. "You're kind of a rock star, and I'm just... an accountant."

He chuckled. "Sexiest accountant I know." My cheeks flushed. "Stevie, remember what I said? I don't want this shit to get to you. I'm a guy who's good with a puck and—"

"A guy who runs after said black dot, on ice, with a stick, and has at least twenty girls waiting for him in a bar, all I might add, wearing his name on their shirts." I shrugged. "No big deal."

"The only girl I care about right now is you." I was sure my face was as red as a tomato based on how hot my cheeks felt. He lowered his arm and rested his hands to my hips. The noise in the bar a distant hum. "I get paid to play a game, and you're right, I fucking slay it. It's in my blood, and I love every minute I'm healthy enough to be on the ice; but I'm also a guy who wants to take you home tonight, introduce you to his dog, and make you a grilled cheese."

I laughed. "A grilled cheese?"

"Fuck yeah, I make a mean grilled cheese."

My laughter shook my shoulders and the nervous energy dissolved as I leaned in. I inhaled the masculine scent of him, and instead of self-doubt, I focused on how those strong fingers sank perfectly into the flesh of my hips. My hands moved lazily up his chest, finding purchase around the back of his neck, and I pressed a quick kiss to his lips.

"I am kind of hungry."

When I dropped my arms, he took my hand in his, lowering his gaze to our linked fingers. "I get it, I really do. It's still surreal to me at times. The fans, the media, and the fact I not only get to do the thing I love every day, but I also get paid damn well to do it. You're the first person in a long ass time who's met me and wants to be with this Mark. Not Mark the famous hockey player. It's refreshing."

My head was in the clouds, watching him breeze across the ice, take hits that would injure any other normal man, make goals that seemed impossible, but his light brown eyes found mine, and I could see the quiet plea inside them. I scanned the bar, watching as the girls moved in on their prey, and even though the guys probably loved it, how would it feel to be wanted for your title, your money, and not your heart?

"Just Mark." I repeated the sentiment I'd promised him on our first date and was rewarded with my favorite smile again. "I do believe you owe me a grilled cheese."

"Let's get out of here."

Mark waved to a few of his teammates, some of them smiled and others regarded me with curious stares. One of the guys, a tall beast of a man with dark hair and a thick and equally dark beard, stood from the bar stool he'd been perched on.

"Wait up, Melo," he shouted over the heads of the small mob of girls he'd been surrounded by.

I heard Mark sigh before he stopped and turned. "What's up, Jensen?"

"You're leaving?"

"Got plans." Mark squeezed my hand.

"A fucking hatty, man, you can't leave until you have three shots." The man gave me a playful smirk.

"No shots." Mark chuckled. "We're taking off."

"I don't mind, Mark. You should celebrate," I said with an encouraging bump of my hip into his.

"I'm Bryson, apparently this rude motherfucker forgot his manners." He held out his hand, well, more like a paw, and I took it.

"Nice to meet you. My name's Stevie."

His smile was impish, and I could see why the congregation of women had flocked to him. He was all bulk and rugged and charm and I'd be lying if I didn't say handsome.

"Stevie." He clapped his hands. "Well, shit, it's nice to put a face to the name. This asshole was just telling me about you today."

My heart stuttered and jumped and took my breath away. He'd told his teammate about me? I lifted my eyes to Mark's and smiled when I noticed the shade of pink that highlighted his cheeks.

"You did?" I asked and Mark's smile split wide across his face.

"Don't listen to him. He's an idiot." Mark punched Bryson in the shoulder.

"Three shots." Bryson raised his hand lifting three fingers. "Then you may be dismissed."

"Don't you have a bunny to corrupt?" Mark asked with a laugh.

"A bunny?"

Bryson's dark blue eyes twinkled. "A puck bunny, you know, a girl—"

"And that's why I never take you anywhere, Captain. As nice as those shots sound, I'll have to take a raincheck."

Bryson chuckled, his eyes sweeping over my body, making me feel kind of dirty, before he knocked his fist into Mark's shoulder.

"You owe me," he promised.

Mark huffed out a short laugh. "Um, okay."

"I'm serious."

Mark turned and tugged on my hand, moving us toward the door.

I heard Bryson laugh before he said, "You might want to take the back door. A couple media trucks have been sitting out there since we arrived."

"Shit," Mark muttered and the word sank in my gut. I wasn't afraid of cameras per se, but I wasn't ready for that kind of attention. "Where did you park?" he asked.

"Right out front."

"You mind riding with me? I'll bring you to your car later."

"I don't mind," I answered him with a calm smile and the strict line of his shoulders relaxed.

Mark kissed my cheek and whispered, "Just stay close, alright?"

"Alright."

He nodded his chin at Bryson before he turned us toward the hallway that led to an exit by the bathrooms. Bryson's jovial mask slipped and I saw actual concern in his eyes. These men were bigger than life, everyone wanted a piece of them, and as Mark snuck us out the back door into the dark, balmy October night, his arm draped over me like armor, I felt grateful for the pieces I'd already had. Parts of him maybe no one else knew about, or might ever see, had been reserved for me.

"Sorry about that." Mark glanced at me as he pulled onto the main road.

"Media is a part of your life," I said, infusing every last drop of nonchalance I could muster into the sentence.

"It doesn't bother you?"

I watched, gathering my thoughts as the street lamps shuttered light across the black dashboard.

"I wouldn't say bother... It's weird, and I can't imagine how intrusive it must feel to be at the end of a lens all the time."

"It's not usually too bad, but..." He looked at me again and swallowed. "Stevie..." He swore under his breath. "Someone took a picture of me kissing you at the rink the other night, and it popped up on a few gossip sites." My stomach lurched and the first thing that came to mind was what if Ben saw it. It was a knee-jerk reaction, a stupid reaction, but Mark read me like a book. "Your face is hidden..." He gave me a sad smile that made me feel like an ass for even caring. "No one will know it was you."

I didn't want him to think I was ashamed, or cared if we were spotted together. If we did become a serious thing, our picture—my face—was bound to end up on the Internet eventually. I inhaled a deep breath and pushed Ben to the far recesses of my mind.

Mark spoke before I had the chance to. "I'm sorry, I should've thought—"

"Don't be sorry." I found a bit of bravery in my pulse as I reached across the console and placed my hand on his thigh. "It's a reality, Mark, and I either have to suck it up if I want to be with you or tap out."

The car rolled to a stop in front of a parking garage gate. Mark pressed a button on his key chain and the gate opened, granting us access.

"I don't want you to feel that way. The media will die down. I haven't been seen with a woman in a while. To them... you're fresh meat." He laughed when my lips tipped into a frown. He pulled into a parking spot and turned off his engine. "They'll sniff around for a bit, speculate, but I ignore it, and most of the time they go away." He rested his hand on the top of mine. "Don't tap out, Stevie."

"I didn't plan on it."

His smile spread slowly as he leaned across the console, his hand holding mine pleasantly hostage against his leg. "Good," he whispered along the curve of my bottom lip. "I wouldn't have let you anyway."

His mouth coaxed me into thinking about all of this later, kissing me into submission. When my limbs felt as if they'd been stuffed with cotton, and the heat between my legs had turned into an unbearable ache, he pulled away with a satisfied smile.

"Ready to meet Atlas?"

My giggle was more of a dazed school girl than that of a thirty-three-year-old woman and, as I opened my eyes, the spark in his own made me melt that much more. "You really love this dog."

He grabbed his keys and opened his car door. "He's family."

We held hands as we rode the elevator up to the tenth floor. Each floor we passed made it harder for me to concentrate on anything other than the feel of his hand in mine, and the electric pulse, organic and alive, between us. The doors finally opened and we stepped out and into the hall. My heartbeat was palpable, thrumming, as he said, "This is me."

A booming bark greeted us as Mark opened the front door. The clatter of heavy paws slapped against the wood floors, matching the irregular beat of my heart. Mark kneeled down in front of me, taking on the full force tackle from the horse he called a dog. His laughter was honey. Thick and sweet, and the light tone of it made a home in my belly.

"Be nice," he warned Atlas as he stood to his full height.

The cutest dog I'd ever seen regarded me with perked gray and white spotted ears. Light blue eyes, surrounded by even more gray polka dots, stared as he took a few guarded steps toward me. I held out my hand and he stuck his wet nose against my palm. He tickled my skin as he sniffed and wagged his tail. Before I was prepared, he hopped up, almost pushing me to the ground. His giant paws rested on my chest as he licked the side of my face.

"*Atlas*. Get down." Mark's command went unheeded.

He groaned as he pulled the oversized dog off of me.

I giggled. "I think your dog just felt me up."

He playfully smacked Atlas on the hip. "Good boy." Mark's eyes raised to mine. "I taught him well."

"Mm-hmm, I bet."

"Make yourself at home, grab a beer if you want, I'm gonna run him outside, it'll only take a few minutes."

Mark grabbed a leash off the hook by the door and kissed me once before leaving me to my own devices. I inhaled a much-needed breath as I took everything in. I'd purchased a small, older home, in a newly renovated, hipster-type area, nothing too fancy. And in Richmond, Ben and I had no children, not even a dog, but we'd rocked that white picket fence. Mark's place though, it was lived in.

It didn't look like a bachelor pad, despite the huge television that hung on the wall above a well-stocked entertainment center. He'd decorated the place, or maybe he'd hired someone to do it. The floor plan was open and painted in homey shades of brown, and crème and beige. Colorful images were framed along his walls. Mostly hockey-related photographs, I noticed, and his family. I lingered over the images of what I assumed were his mom and dad. A few of his sister, I guessed, and her family, too, as I made my way into the kitchen that sat to the right of his living room.

The earth-tone theme of the apartment flowed into the backsplash behind his stove and countertop. A variation of worn brick. My smile spread as I stood in front of the fridge. The stainless steel had been covered on the left side door with a vinyl sticker. The number nineteen. I opened the door and grabbed two beers I'd never heard of, and I might've silently laughed at how empty his fridge was. Bottled water, beer, and a few preplanned meals in Tupperware. I closed the fridge and set the beers on the dark brown granite breakfast bar that separated the kitchen from the dining area. I used the term dining area loosely. Where a dinner table would normally be, he had one of those stand-up foosball tables. But instead of foosball, it was a hockey rink, with goalies and everything.

The front door opened and I jumped when Atlas barked again. Mark gave me a half-smile and hung the dog's leash on the hook by the door. Atlas galloped past me, grabbed a rope from the dog bed that was next to the couch, and dropped it by my feet. Mark laughed at my dubious stare. The rope was a muddied gray color and I had a feeling it hadn't always been that shade.

"I wouldn't touch that. One, he'll never leave you alone, and two—"

"It's disgusting?"

He chuckled as he slid his arms around my waist from behind. "Precisely."

Mark pressed soft lips against the slope of my neck and I shivered. All the hair on my arms stood as he kissed his way up and then back down again. Without overthinking it, I tipped my head to the side and fell into his embrace.

"I can't believe you're here." The rough gravel of his voice scratched at the need building inside me.

I closed my eyes, let my arms lay loose at my sides as his hands moved under the fabric of my t-shirt. Could he feel how fast I was breathing, could he tell I was slowly falling apart as his fingertips grazed the surface of my belly and dipped below the waistline of my jeans? The heat of his breath soothed the chills breaking against my skin as he nipped my earlobe.

He spoke in a rumble, a low pressure that pulsed between my legs. "I thought about you, more than I probably should've this past year... since that first night." He gripped my hips and pulled me closer.

"Me, too." I kept my eyes shut, my quiet admission burning its way down my spine.

I could feel him against the curve of my backside. He was hard and his breath hitched when my back arched, my body seeking friction, a friction I hadn't known I desperately needed until now. Thirteen years I'd been with the same man. A man who never once took the time to discover what made me tick. Mark had found several of my buttons already, and he played them like he'd known me all my life.

The promise of dinner forgotten. My empty stomach filled with anticipation, and raging butterflies as his left hand cupped my lace-covered breast.

He bit my neck and I stuttered his name.

"I want you, Stevie, so fucking much."

He was asking permission. His lips on my skin a persuasive argument. That pulse between us became a drum. It had started a year ago, and tonight I could hardly hear over its resounding beat.

Starting over was about taking chances, letting myself feel and become something more than the drab life I'd made for myself. I turned my head one precious inch and his mouth covered mine. He sipped from my lips and tasted my tongue with long strokes I could feel all the way down to my toes.

His thumb circled the raised peak of my nipple and my soft moan stilled his kiss.

"Tell me to stop." Mark uttered familiar words.

There was no reason to hesitate this time. No barriers. No honorable intention. Just raw and basic need.

"I can't."

His eyes held mine, a hungry smile lifting the corners of his lips, and when he went to unhook the button of my jeans, I let him.

MARK

I can't....
Oh. Fuck.

Neither could I.

My dick was heavy between my legs as she pressed her ass against the hard ridge in my slacks. I let the tips of my fingers linger along the soft curve of her stomach. The light touches I'd been doling out weren't enough for my greedy fingers. I lifted her shirt a little more.

Shit.

I loved this fucking shirt and how it barely fit, looking a size too small stretched across her full tits. Seeing her in this shirt, with my name on it, had given me more gratification than it should have. I was still amped from the win, from scoring three fucking goals in a row, and now—Stevie. I wanted to lay her out on my bed, wearing only that t-shirt, and lose myself between her legs.

I thumbed her nipple with my right hand as my left molded to her waist. The line of her custom-made to fit my palm. Stevie was too touchable as I buried my nose into the crook of her neck. I found it sort of perfect the way she always smelled like summer. The heat of her skin mimicked the rays of the sun. Burning me so fucking slowly. My left hand inched back down to the opening of her jeans, and when she turned her head again, I kissed her. Like this, her plump lips on mine, it was easy to forget that we were standing in the middle of my apartment, easy to slip my hand beyond the flimsy layers of denim and cotton, to sink my fingers inside her. I hissed at how wet she was, how fucking warm. The tips of my fingers circled her clit as I groaned into her mouth. She arched her back, silently asking for more but I wasn't that easy.

"Tell me how far, Stevie. How far do you want to go?"

I pulsed my fingers and she whimpered, "I need you to... keep touching me."

"Like this?"

She answered me with a soft gasp as I pushed deeper.

The quiet sounds of her need pumped the blood through my veins in a furious rush. My dick was throbbing, aching as I tugged her jeans down with my free hand. I took a small step back to admire the way the top of her round ass was exposed.

Closing off the space I'd created, I kissed her neck, my lips resting against her skin. "You have the best ass."

Stevie's pliable posture stiffened.

"It's..." she stuttered.

My hand no longer between her legs, I turned her at the waist to face me. The blush of her cheeks spilled all the way down into the collar of her t-shirt. Her eyes were a little wild, but I could see a hint of fear in the dark depths.

"Too fast?"

Stevie lowered her eyes, pulling at the hem of her shirt. Was she trying to cover up? *Damn*. I'd pushed her too hard, made her nervous.

"We don't have to do anything. I'm sorry I—"

"No..." Her eyes darted to the ceiling, an unsure smile breaking across the delicate features of her face. "It's... maybe a little too bright in here."

A relieved breath exhaled past my lips in the form of a chuckle. "I like the lights on." I held her hips with firm hands. "I want to see you."

Her nose crinkled as her brow furrowed. "I'm not used to lights... I don't know, Mark. You're... you and I'm..."

"Sexy as fuck." I smirked when she finally looked at me again.

"I'm too curvy."

"And that's a bad thing?" I let my hands skate around to the spot where the swell of her ass met her thighs and she hid her face in my chest. "I like how my hands have something to grab." I demonstrated my sentiment by squeezing her ass. It won me a smile, and I continued, "Stevie... there's no such thing as 'too curvy'." My hands were under her t-shirt again, trailing them over her hips and stomach. "I like this." I pressed my fingers into the flesh of her hips, my thumbs sinking into the softness of her belly.

She lifted her gaze, and despite what I'd said, doubt creased her brow. "I feel like I'm too much woman for you."

"Ouch."

She laughed. "I'm serious."

"You just bruised my ego. You think I can't handle you?" I lowered my hands to the back of her thighs. Instead of stealing another squeeze, I flexed my arms, easily lifting her off the ground high enough that she was able to wrap her legs around my waist.

She squeaked and slapped my shoulder. "*Oh my God. Put me down.*"

"I got you."

Too much woman? Fuck that.

"Mark. Put me down before you hurt yourself."

Clutching the side of her thighs, I turned toward my bedroom ignoring her protests. She tried to shimmy her way out of my hold, but it only made me laugh. "Stop, Stevie. You're gonna make me drop you, and I'd rather worship your ass, not break it."

Stevie wound her arms around my neck, letting her fingers glide into my hair at the nape. She locked her eyes on mine, her cheeks crimson as she said, "Kiss me."

The two words rendered me motionless.

Our lips met and moved with a fluid rhythm. Lazy and languid, I wasn't in a hurry. Her self-doubt was in vain. I could hold her like this all fucking night if I wanted to.

I broke our kiss, my voice rough as I spoke, "Like I said... I got you."

She gave me a grin and I headed toward the bedroom. I heard the distinct sound of Atlas's footsteps on the hardwood floor following behind me and she giggled. "I almost forgot he was here."

I turned to look at Atlas from the doorway of my room. He ducked his head, his tail wagging like crazy. No way, cock blocker. "Go lay down." He didn't budge. "Give me a break, dog."

His expression was bored, but he trotted off toward the living room and I bumped the door shut with my foot until it latched. The heat of Stevie's breath warmed my neck as she giggled again. It took me only a few strides before I was at the foot of my king-sized bed. Stevie unhooked her legs from my waist and I lowered her down and onto her back. The humor around her eyes dimmed into something more serious as I stared at the way her shirt had ridden almost all the way up to her perfect tits, and how her jeans had fallen open, exposing a peek of shortly trimmed hair.

The room had lighting built into the back wall and it reflected onto the ceiling, casting very little light into the room. I'd left the runners on before I'd gone to the rink today and the soft glow illuminated Stevie's supple, cream color. She covered her stomach with her hands as I leaned down to grab her hips. I pulled her, not-so-gently, to the edge of the bed.

"We don't have to do anything you don't want to. But you're not allowed to hide, Stevie. I love your fucking body and I want to see it."

She parted her lips, the rise and fall of her chest quickened as she nodded and lowered her hands to the tops of her jeans. My breath caught in my throat as she worked the denim down along with her underwear. They fell to the floor and I kicked them to the side. My hands found a new favorite spot as I kneeled onto the carpet, digging my fingers into the meat of her inner thighs, I spread them open. My mouth watered as I imagined what she'd taste like, how she'd sound.

"Is this okay?"

She exhaled a shaky breath. "Yes."

I explored the arc of her hips, her stomach. Goose bumps scattered under my fingertips. She was exactly how I'd wanted her the first night. Sprawled out on my bed. Meek and needy. I was tall enough, even on my knees I could kiss her stomach, kiss that slight dip along her hip bone. Her body relaxed, her fingers threading into my hair as I inhaled her scent with my first taste. I groaned as the salty flavor flooded my senses. She murmured my name, shamelessly grinding her pussy against my face as I licked slow strokes. I almost chuckled at the cute fucking sound she made when I nipped her clit.

When her thighs started to shake, she sat up, framed my face with her hands and pulled me to her mouth. Stevie's breathing was frantic, uneven, as she kissed my wet lips. I wondered what she thought about her own taste, if she liked it as much as me. My deep growl echoed in the room as her hand fell to the bulge in my pants, rubbing up and down the stone-hard length. Our teeth bumped in an aggressive and hurried kiss as I dropped my hand between her legs. We both tipped our heads and watched as I slid my fingers inside her. She leaned back onto her elbows and, as much as I liked that shirt, I wished I'd taken it off. I wanted to see those fuckable breasts sway as she rolled her hips, as she worked herself against my hand, the motion pulling my fingers in and out.

My jaw clenched. "Fuck yourself with my fingers, Stevie..." Her eyes closed as I curled them inside her. "I want to watch you come on my hand."

I held my hand still and watched as she let herself go. Her hips trembled, her hands fisting the comforter on my bed as her head fell backward. She cried out, the sound of it was almost mournful, exhausted. It filled my lungs with a deep-seated pride as the warmth of her release coated my fingers. I took my hand from between her legs and she sat up, curling her arms around my neck. She cradled my head, pulling me into a kiss.

There was nothing ladylike about the way she kissed me, her teeth on my lips, her nails digging into my skin. She was stealing my breath, and I wanted her to have it. Her fingers relaxed, idly playing with a few strands of my hair as she came down from the high of her climax. Her lips sipping instead of swallowing. The gentle pull and tug thing she did with her mouth made my dick jump. Stevie was the first to break the kiss, bringing her nose to the tip of mine. Our breath mixed into the violent space between our mouths. Her hands were limp on my shoulders as she inched closer to the edge of the bed. She licked her lips as she leaned back, meeting my heated gaze. Her pupils were blown wide open, her hair a little messy, and her cheeks on fire.

I brushed a wayward piece of her hair from her forehead and smiled as I said, "You look unbelievable right now. So damn beautiful."

The right corner of her lip was pinned between her teeth, her eyes flashing down and then up again. A shy smile forming, she brought her hands to my belt. "I'm feeling underdressed."

STEVIE

Fingers shaking, my nerves frayed and raw, I fumbled with his buckle. Gentle eyes grounded me as he cupped my cheek and kissed me. My scent lingered and I craved the way I tasted on his lips. Everything before tonight had been clean and narrowed lines. Sex had been one dimensional. Tonight was messy, fast, and I liked the disorder. My heart was a drum roll, the pressure building inside me, for once there was no set plan, and I didn't care. I wanted him.

His thumb traced softly against my cheek as he stood. His hot eyes held me steady. Mark moved my hands from the clasp of his belt and unlatched it. He unbuttoned his shirt and shrugged it off. My tongue felt thick in my mouth as I admired the smooth muscles of his chest. The tattooed sleeves of his arms stopped at the shoulder. The rigid landscape of his stomach was only interrupted by a set of numbers, 42.995640 and -71.454789, the ink spelling out in sequence along his left lower rib.

I sat there, quiet, the tips of my fingers tracing the numbers, filing away my questions for later as his skin puckered under my touch. And it was only a second, maybe two, but the hairs on the back of my neck stood, goose bumps raging along my limbs when he spoke, "Hey."

He held his hand out, his smile spreading, curling up on the left. The warmth of his palm gave me the courage to do what I wanted. Instead of standing, I lowered myself down to my knees and he released his hold. I heard his rushed breath as I unzipped his pants, and he helped me as I pulled them and his underwear down to the floor. Mark only took a small step backward to push his discarded clothing away. The motion distracted me, and when I raised my eyes, I had to stifle my gasp. Mark fully naked was a shock to the system. The sharp lines of his lean hips poured down into athletic thighs that framed the hard length of his cock. He was perfect, beautiful. I licked my lips, hiding how they trembled. Insecurity flickered through me and my pulse soared until it pounded its way to my temples.

Mark ran the fingers of his left hand through my hair as he tipped my chin up with his right. My hesitant eyes raised inch by gradual inch until I met his vulnerable gaze. "*God*. I..." His jaw was tight. His voice was clipped, strained as he whispered, "Fucking want you." And the sound of it, the way he stared at me like I could ruin his entire world, it gave me power.

I wasn't the only one baring it all. I answered my doubt by wrapping my fingers around his length. He groaned, pushing his fingers into my hair, holding the back of my head. His hand fisted through the strands as I licked the salty bead that had formed on the tip of his dick. His skin was velvet against my tongue, and my eyes fluttered closed as I pulled away. My body was humming for him.

"Do that again." It was more of a plea than a command.

I pressed a kiss to the head and smirked at the pulse in his jaw. "Do what?"

A low sound rumbled in his chest, his grip pinching at my scalp. "Put your mouth on me."

The desperate desire in his eyes begged, and I fell into the sound of his growl as I took him into my mouth.

His control slipped as he groaned. "Fuck, Stevie..." Mark's hips gradually began to move, driving him deeper into my mouth. I felt greedy as I took it all. "Yeah... just like that."

Everything I'd usually worry about displaced into the white noise of the bedroom. There was nothing but the feel of carpet against my knees, Mark's pleasure, and his guttural groans. I stared at him from under my lashes; watched as his eyes closed, and how his bottom lip raked through his teeth as I teased, licked, and sucked. My climax had cooled, but this view, his head tipping backward, his body above me, it fueled the throbbing between my legs and I was wet for him again. I was smoldering, slow and hot, and when he slid his other hand into my hair, his hips jerked. Something more primal than a growl erupted past his lips and his chin dipped. His eyes locked on mine and the bittersweet taste of him flooded my mouth.

Mark held my chin with his left hand as I swallowed and pulled away. He swept his thumb across my lips and then my cheek. His eyes were glazed with spent lust, his touch— tender. The tips of his fingers ran the length of my neck to the top of my spine. The bones of my body felt light, like a sponge, soaking up his affection.

"I want to kiss you," he breathed his wish and I granted it.

His hands grasped the bare cheeks of my ass as I stood, hauling me against him. He kissed me with impatient lips that slowed to an open mouth sizzle. His tongue taking its time teasing mine. I moaned into his mouth when his right hand found its way between my legs and he hummed his approval when he found me ready.

Three orgasms later, and two for him, we were both naked, a mess of limbs on the top of his comforter and we hadn't even had sex yet. Just hands and mouths and fingers. God, he had glorious fingers. My legs were noodles, my lungs on fire as I gasped his name. Mark gently bit one nipple and then the other before dragging his hand from between my thighs.

"I love your tits," he mumbled against my skin as he licked circles around the dusky pink peaks.

I ran my hands into his hair. My fingers combed through the slight curls as I laughed. The man was practically suffocating himself between my breasts. "I think you better come up for air."

He groaned and rested his cheek against my belly. A little over an hour ago, I would've flinched. Having him that close to my biggest insecurity would've freaked me out, but the way he treated me, leaving no curve uncharted, my hang-ups no longer felt valid.

"Can't a man just be content?" His hands were firmly in place on my hips, the rough pads of his thumbs running circuits along my skin.

"You played a hard game, won a hat thing, you should at least eat dinner at some point tonight."

He chuckled and rolled his body. Lying next to me, he propped onto his elbow. "A hat thing?" He raised his brow. "It's awesome that you know nothing about the game."

I didn't think it was "awesome" I had no knowledge about something he was so passionate about. "I wish I knew more. Wouldn't you like me to know what it means when you do something noteworthy?"

"I like that I get to teach you." His broad smile had my own lips spreading across my face.

My heart did a little shimmy. "Teach me something."

He rested his palm on my tummy. "What do you want to know?"

I turned my head to face him, his cinnamon eyes twinkled, and a light laugh parted my lips. "The basics."

"Okay." His fingers traced absentminded S shapes along the curve of my stomach. "Each team has six players on the ice. One goalie, three forward players, and two defensive players."

"Forward... That's you?"

He huffed out a laugh. "Yeah, babe, that's me."

I playfully smacked his cheek. "Don't make fun of me."

He leaned down, his lips less than a millimeter from mine. "I'm sorry." His smile was repentant, kissing me once and then again before he barreled over onto his other side. He opened his bedside table and rummaged around in the drawer.

"What are you doing?" I asked, but too lazy, drunk on three orgasms, to care enough to investigate or move for that matter.

He answered me by moving back to his previous position, holding up a blue Sharpie with a wicked grin on his lips. He pulled the cap off with his teeth and I might've giggled when he spit the cap to the side.

"Mark?" I drew out his name. The long syllable brimmed with caution.

He snuggled in a little closer, his right hand hovering over my stomach. "You wanted to learn, right?"

I closed my eyes, scrunched my nose as the cold tip of the marker touched down below my breasts. His quiet laughter opened my eyes and I lifted onto my elbows.

"Stay still," he teased, and I made a show of holding my breath.

He drew what looked like a sloppy hockey rink across my stomach. Including two goalie nets, one right below and between my breasts, and the other above my pubic bone. He was busy drawing circles, his concentration something to take seriously, and I had to stifle a laugh when his tongue darted and rested on the bow of his lower lip.

"Goalie," he said and drew an X in his makeshift net. He drew another line below it. "This is called the crease and it's where he hangs out, okay?"

"Mm-hmm."

Mark's mouth lifted at the corners, his eyes flashing to mine as he drew an excruciatingly slow line depicting the crease of the other goal. The cool sensation, the gentle pressure of his touch so close to where I wanted him most, the heat crept along the surface of my skin all the way to my cheeks.

He continued his lesson, scrawling groups of letters onto my flesh. LW, RW C, D, D in mirrored patterns on either side of the dark line he'd drawn horizontally across the middle of my tummy. Once he was finished, he placed a kiss on my belly button and said, "Center ice."

He shot me a sweet smile and the excitement in his eyes made it difficult to breathe. I liked his relaxed countenance, and how it bled into everything we'd done tonight. We were natural, and it made the last thirteen years of my life settle like a brick inside my chest. I'd wasted so much time, so much of myself. I blinked a few times, willing the sudden rush of emotion away.

I leaned onto one elbow as I pointed to the letter C. "You play center."

He nodded. Pleased, he said, "Yes..." He pointed to the other letters explaining, "Left wing, right wing, and the center, we're all forwards, and these guys..." He circled the letter D and I squirmed. His chuckle made me laugh. "You're ticklish... I'll have to remember that." A shuddered breath exhaled from my lungs at the promise. "Right wings are in charge of the right side of the rink and –"

"The Left wing is in charge of the left... simple enough."

"Not always, sometimes I play a lot of defense, too, and sometimes the D-men play offensively and score goals."

My brows pulled together. "This hurts my brain."

Mark's head fell forward as he barked out a laugh. "Says the accountant..."

"Math is easy. Math I get. Penalties, power plays, hat-thingies... I'm going to need a tutor."

"Good thing your boyfriend's a hockey player."

Boyfriend. Is that what this was already? I was too green and maybe my confusion was too readily available in my expression because Mark's smile faltered.

"You know what I mean." He recovered his smile, and I chewed the corner of my lip as he stared at my stomach. "The basics, Stevie, get the puck in the net, light the lamp, and do it more than the other guys." He ran a line from the letter C all the way to the goal crease below my breast.

I lay back, sinking into the pillow, and averted my eyes to the ceiling. Here I was, lying naked in a bed with a man I'd been pretty damn intimate with, and all I could think was how stupid I was for liking that word. *Boyfriend.* Wasn't I supposed to be taking it slow? Figuring out what I wanted, who I was?

"I freaked you out, didn't I?"

I turned my head meeting his gaze.

"We're getting to know each other." I hated the sound of my own voice. Everything that I'd allowed to happen tonight was proof I'd moved beyond the simple boundaries of dating.

The hard line of Mark's jaw flexed as he sat up. "If I wanted to get laid, I could. That's not what I want from you." I swallowed and he grinned. "Well, that's not all I want from you."

Despite myself, I smiled back. "What do you want from me?"

He exhaled and rubbed his fingers along the scruff on his chin. His easy smile shifting. "If you're with me, then you're with me. I'm gone too much, I'll probably mess shit up from time to time, but I won't fuck around, Stevie. I like you, and I don't want to waste the downtime I have on a woman who'd rather be with someone else. I've already played that game."

I sat up, hyperaware of my own nakedness. Inside and out. "I'm trying to figure my way into this new life. Hell, Mark, I have boxes I haven't even unpacked yet."

The heat of his fingertips coaxed my chin, turning my gaze to his. He considered me, his lips breaking into a genuine smile. "I'm not trying to rush you into anything. This can be serious or it can be casual, either way, when I'm with you, it's only you. And I hope you'd give me the same respect."

A nervous smile shivered on my lips as I rested my forehead in the perfect crook of his neck. "I don't know the first thing about what it's like to date someone like you, or anyone in this decade really, but I know I like you, and I don't want to waste my downtime with some random either." I leaned back and he framed my face with his hands. "When you said boyfriend, you're right... it freaked me out. But it wasn't because I want to sleep around and sow my wild oats..." Humor glittered inside his irises. "I freaked out because I want you as a boyfriend, probably more than I should. I'm starting over, Mark, I should want to be on my own, fly free, and all that jazz."

"And all that jazz?" He raised his right brow.

I shoved his chest. "Yeah. And. All. That. Jazz."

"Start over. Fly free, do whatever you want, Stevie. You don't have to worry about that shit with me. I'll never censor you."

What he'd said to me the night I'd first met him shimmered at the edges of my memory.

"If you were married to me, you could do whatever you wanted."

I was making things more complicated than they needed to be. We were having fun. I had a hockey rink drawn on my stomach with a Sharpie for crying out loud. It could be serious or it could be casual. I didn't want to date around, and I really hadn't had any intentions to date at all. I'd moved back to Tampa with the sole purpose of finding myself again. Mark was a happy accident. And after my divorce from Ben, I owed it to myself to try. My relationship with men didn't have to define me.

"So... my boyfriend's a hockey player."

His full lips pulled into those sexy dimples I was starting to worship. "Hot hockey player."

He kissed the spot below my ear and my stomach growled. "A hot hockey player who promised me dinner."

He rolled off the bed with agility that somehow, even after I'd watched him play tonight, still astounded me. He bent down, grabbing my shirt and underwear, throwing them onto the bed as I admired the chiseled planes of his chest. The ink on his forearms rippled as he pulled on his boxer-briefs.

"I think I'm enlisting one more rule tonight beyond exclusivity."

"Oh?" I asked as I slipped back into my shirt and panties. I'd worry about finding my bra later. "What's that?"

"No pants at the dinner table."

MARK

Wet. Warm... Kibble.

My eyes, bleary, opened to the gray light leaking through the blinds in my bedroom. Atlas hovered over my face. His hot breath was the last thing I wanted to deal with, I turned to look at the clock, at seven in the morning.

"Jesus, Atlas." I shoved his drool-covered mug and laughed when he barely moved an inch. "Wanna go outside?"

His tail thumped hard onto the mattress, his ears pointing almost to the ceiling. "Can I make coffee first?" His whole body shook and I groaned. "Shit, give me five minutes."

I rolled to the edge of my bed, resting my elbows on my knees as I tried to wipe the sleep from my eyes. Atlas nudged my ass and I chuckled, feeling guilty. "Alright, I'm up." I'd neglected him last night because Stevie had been here.

Stevie.

My lips split into a smile I was sure would get me punched in the locker room.

I stood, stretching my arms over my head. "Come on, let's go take a piss."

After I finished freezing my ass off in the early morning damp air, I ran up the stairs. Atlas's breathing was labored, his feet clomping as he burned off all his extra morning energy. I had practice in thirty minutes and I hated leaving him again. Sometimes I wondered why I'd even gotten a dog. I was never home, and when I was, I was at the rink. I rubbed the top of his head as I hung his leash next to the door. I didn't like to admit it because it made me feel weak, but I didn't like being alone. Never had.

My mom used to joke about how I'd always had a girlfriend. I'd fallen right into that pattern again with Mia. And now Stevie. I'd dropped the word boyfriend more casually than I probably should have. Some, my sister in particular, would say it was too soon to make it "official." But, I didn't harp on the thought too much as I poured myself a cup of coffee. Stevie wasn't Mia or a pattern. It was simple. I wanted what I wanted. I liked her.

"Shit." I nearly growled as searing hot liquid poured down my throat.

Atlas whimpered at my distress and I smiled. I did this every morning. You'd think I'd get up earlier, give myself more time. Maybe I rushed with some things. But with Stevie it felt right, and I hadn't had that in a long time. I set the cup down on the counter, and a memory from last night played in Technicolor inside my head. My face between Stevie's thighs, right here on this very counter. My lips curled up smug at the corners as I thought about how not-so-quiet she'd been when she came. I could eat her pussy every damn day. My dick came to life at the thought, and I closed my eyes with an internal groan. So I'd rushed things, she seemed to be okay with it, and I sure the hell was. If anything, I was ready for more. More time with her.

I'd wanted her to stay over, but she'd put on the brakes around one in the morning. Stevie wanted to take things slow, and I was a fucking bulldozer when it came to her. If I would've had my way, I would've spent the remainder of our evening buried inside her, but I guess there was something to be said for waiting. What made her tick? What made her crazy? Watching her explode with my touch, my lips, I loved it. She was a fucking firecracker. She'd sat too long in the corner gathering dust, and I was the lucky asshole who got to light her up. If I had to wait a little to figure out all her buttons, I could handle that.

Atlas whined and wagged his tail as I lowered myself down to his level. I trapped his big head between my hands, scratched behind his ears as I said more to myself than him, "Let's hope I'm right... she's one of the good ones, yeah?"

It wasn't until I was parked outside the Ice Forum that I'd found a second to text her. I was already running late, and I hoped Maddox hadn't arrived yet. Having a pissed-off coach before a road trip was not ideal. It only made it worse how tired I felt. I'd dropped Stevie off at her car after two a.m., and for a guy who was used to getting at least eight hours of sleep every night, it was safe to say I was dragging ass. Practice had to go well. We were headed out west. A three-game stretch against the Pacific division leaders. Vegas, San Jose, and L.A., we had to be on the top of our game.

ME: *If I get fired it's your fault.*

I cut the engine and exited my SUV with a shit-eating grin on my face. I pocketed my keys as I slammed the door shut. The Florida morning air was already a few degrees warmer than an hour ago. Moisture clung to my skin as I walked at a clipped pace to the rink doors.

My phone vibrated in my palm as I stepped inside the Forum. The rink air tickled my heated skin, sending comforting goose bumps down my limbs as I opened the lock screen with a swipe of my thumb.

Stevie: *Can you even get fired? Is that a thing?*

I coughed out a laugh.

ME: *Yes, that's a thing. But I'd probably get traded instead...*

ME: *And you'd miss me.*

Stevie: *At least then I'd get more sleep. There isn't enough coffee in the world today.*

I pictured her eyes, how they most likely were smiling at this very second, her sexy, smart-ass comment filling her cheeks with color.

ME: *I'd rather come than sleep, just saying.*

I'd twisted the "I'd rather hang with you than sleep" comment I'd said to her the other day.

Stevie: *And now I'm thinking about sex, and I haven't even booted up my computer yet.*

ME: *You're welcome.*

"What's up, Melo?"

I raised my eyes from my phone and my teammate, Carl Smith, nodded his chin in my direction.

"Running late, too?" I asked and slipped my phone into my pocket following alongside him.

"Yeah, fuck, I'm hungover. Coach is gonna chew my ass. You?"

"Didn't sleep great."

Smith gave me a knowing smile. "Me neither, bro, me neither."

We both snickered like teenage idiots as we walked toward the locker room. He opened the door, and sure as shit, Bryson already had his music blaring. It didn't matter how hard that guy partied, he was always the first to practice looking bushy-tailed and ready to go. Today was no different as he sat on the bench pulling on his pads. He sung the lyrics, rocking his head to the beat, and I had to laugh. Dude was fucking happy all the time.

"You're chipper, as always," I said, dropping down onto the bench next to him.

Bryson looked me up and down before he nodded his head. "You look like hell." The corners of his mouth ticked as he stood and grabbed his skates from one of the wooden cubbies that held our equipment. Every guy had his own stall, name placard attached. It was more of a dressing room than a locker room.

"I get laid practically every night. Maybe you should try it... pussy is a cure-all, man."

I lifted my eyes to the ceiling as I kicked off my shoes. I knew without a doubt he was wrong on that one.

"I can think of at least one instance you'd be dead wrong."

"Your problem, Melo..." He sat down and leaned over to put on his skates. "You get too attached."

"Correct me if I'm wrong, Jensen. But I think there's a rule. No relationship advice before nine in the morning." I stood and pulled off my shirt.

"Yeah, and sure as fuck, not in the locker room," Karlsson said and threw a roll of athletic tape at Bryson's head. "Chicks are bad luck."

Bryson dodged it and it hit the wood of his stall with a hard thwack. "If that would've hit me—"

"What?" Karlsson lifted his eyebrows.

"You're an asshole." Bryson shook his head, smiling as he leaned down again to finish lacing his skates.

The room erupted into its usual immature bouts of laughter and shit talk as we all geared up. I'd finished lacing my skates when Bryson leaned toward me and said in a low voice, "Stevie... she's hot."

"Yeah, Jensen. I'm aware." I didn't like the edge I had in my tone. Bryson was a good guy, my best fucking friend, but those old wounds, they healed too damn slowly.

"Don't forget... you still owe me three shots." He gave me a sly grin before he stood. "*Let's go, ladies,*" he hollered and all the guys, including myself, stood and followed our captain to the ice.

Practice had proved to be a brutal battle and we'd lost.

Half the guys had smelled like booze and the other half had been asleep. About forty-five minutes in, after a sloppy show of defense by the opposing side, I'd flown down the rink with my knees bent, my blades digging deep into the ice, eating the distance to the goal. I'd been sucking air as the fatigue set in and my right quad had cramped. Like always, in a game, I'd ignored the pain, but my usual speed had wavered enough that Rasmussen had been able to poke check the puck, forcing a turnover as I crossed over the blue line.

With such little sleep, I'd played like shit, but I hadn't been the only one in the loser pile. The coaching staff had rode us hard, and after the nets were put away, and the Zamboni had cleared the ice, they'd made us watch reel for another hour. The locker room was quiet after Maddox not-so-subtly told us to pull our shit together, to look in the mirror and see whether or not we'd have wins in our pockets after this trip. Coach was known for his stern candor, but I had to say, I loved the way he rallied us. He was never negative. But he put us in our places. Toned down our ego and reminded us, at the end of the period, we were only human. He reminded us, even though we were gifted men, if we wanted to succeed, we had to fucking work for it. Own the shift.

He'd said, "You are not the only talented men on that ice, not the only players hungry for a win... wins will never be handed to you. They will only be earned."

Bryson blamed himself, looking like a sad sack, the total opposite of how he'd been this morning, as he'd stripped off his gear. No one lingered, we were eager to get home, put the practice behind us before we boarded the plane tonight.

I slammed the door to the SUV and stared through the windshield. Hockey was as much of a mental game as it was a physical one. Fear was an infection and heading out west always got our hackles up. Maybe that fear poured a few extra shots last night for some of the guys despite our win. For me, after how I played, I should've wanted to distance myself a little from Stevie, put my head on straight. Focus on the plays, the win, but hell if she wasn't the only person I wanted to talk to. Her blood wasn't ice and steel-bladed like mine. It was warm and real and it reminded me, just like Coach had said, that I was human.

I pulled my phone from my pocket and dialed her number.

"Hi." I could hear the smile in her voice, and the tight knots in my shoulders untwisted.

"You hungry?" My tone held the weight of every shitty shot I'd taken as I looked at the digital display on the dash. It was almost twelve-thirty.

"Bad day?"

"Turns out sleep is kind of important when it comes to being a professional athlete."

Her laugh was fuzzy, almost far away, and it made my empty stomach feel full. "So it seems... I'm sorry I kept you awake last night."

"Bad practice, but still wouldn't change a thing."

"I'm sorry it didn't go well."

"I have to board a plane in four hours, have lunch with me."

She took a second to answer, but when she did, the one word was infused with her sweet smile. "Okay."

She gave me the address to her office and I scribbled it onto an old Starbucks receipt I'd found in my center console.

"I'm about twenty minutes away."

She laughed. "Take your time. I'll have to prepare the guys. They may faint when you walk in."

"They handled themselves alright that night at the bar," I joked as I pushed my key into the ignition.

"They were sitting down. Apparently my boss's boyfriend has 'shipped' us. Whatever the hell that means."

My laugh rumbled in my chest. "I think it means they've combined our last names."

She groaned. "Like a power couple?"

"Yeah, I think so." My laughter faded, but my smile remained. "Stuff like this might happen in the media. You alright with that?"

She paused, her exhale long and shaky. "I want to be."

"It takes time, Stevie... let's focus on lunch... for now."

"Food."

"Is there anything better?"

"I hear sleep..."

I chuckled. "So it seems."

STEVIE

"You didn't stay the night?" David eyed me over his cup of Starbucks.

I avoided his stare, rearranging a few pens on my desk with nervous fingers as I shook my head. The thing was, I'd barely started at Byron & Elm, and yes, they treated me like I'd worked here forever. And David was probably my favorite person in the office, but my relationship status was too public for only having worked here less than two weeks.

David gasped and I lifted my gaze.

"Oh my God," he squeaked.

"What?"

"He didn't kick you out, did he?"

"*No*, I left. I had to work... as you know."

He sipped his coffee again. "Good, I was going to tell Trent he's not allowed to fanboy for that prick if he'd one-timed you."

"We didn't one time anything, and..." I exhaled. "Why am I even talking about this? Go away." I laughed as I said it and David leaned back in his chair getting cozy.

"So you went to his place and... nothing happened?" He narrowed his dubious eyes.

"Just so you know... I find you very nosy." I bit my lip trying to hold back my smirk.

"I'm the secretary." He waved his left hand dramatically in front of him. "I know everything, and I'm fucking the boss...well, one of them."

"So, you're a walking cliché?" I asked, shutting my laptop.

"I earned that role, thank you very much." David's grin was impervious.

I toyed with the corner of my desktop calendar. I hadn't had more than a quick five-minute chat with Reagan today. She'd made me break down what had happened last night into a ninety-second, gory display of details, in which, she'd basically *virtually* high-fived me, and said she had to hustle or she was going to be late for her first appointment of the day. Ray was biased though, and I think if she could, she'd tell me to walk through fire if it meant I'd get to do something I wanted for once. I stared at David. He'd become a fast friend, and he didn't know me well enough to necessarily lead me astray for the greater good of my vagina.

"Hypothetically..." I started, and he inched to the edge of his chair. "How soon is too soon to make a relationship official?"

"Hockey guy that good, huh?"

I laughed. "You're absurd." He shrugged. "Last night, Mark called himself my boyfriend."

"That was fast."

"Right?"

David settled back into his chair. "You don't want to be official? Too soon after..."

I hated that everyone here knew about Ben. I guess it came with the territory when your ex set you up with the job.

"No... I think I like that he wants to be official. I guess I'm—"

"Scared?"

"More... naïve. I've only ever been with my ex, and it all feels really new. I'm thirty-three years old, and I haven't done this since high school. The rules have changed."

David surprised me by laughing. "The man practically wrote them for you the minute he called himself 'the boyfriend'. It's easy now. Exclusivity is so much better than floundering, wondering who's doing who and all that."

I chewed the corner of my lip. I was overthinking again. "You're right."

He hummed his agreement. "And he's gone a lot. He's just protecting his investment while he's away. Smart man. I think I like him already." David's brows dipped. "As long as he behaves on the road."

I couldn't deny the idea hadn't crossed my mind. He's a famous hockey player. I'd looked up the term 'puck bunny' on the Internet this morning and got a little nauseated. Female fans willing to do whatever the athlete was down for. It was all very cheap and sad if I thought about it long enough. Mark didn't seem the type who was into the philosophy of having a different woman every night. No, Mark wasn't into that. I smiled. He was into me.

My phone vibrated on my desk, and when I opened the lock screen, there was a text from Mark letting me know he was parking.

"Is that him?" David asked.

His excitement made me even more nervous.

"Yes, now seriously, go away, and keep the rabid fans on a leash, would you, please?" I offered him my most polite smile.

He chuckled as he stood. "I promise you nothing."

"And I thought you were my favorite."

"Oh, well, in that case..."

David waved over his shoulder as he left my office. The room was too empty without him sitting across from me, and my heart was practically flying as I stood. I wiped my hands down the front of my gray pencil skirt. Smoothing away invisible lines. Licking my lips, I cinched my loose bun, causing a few strands to fall around my face. Silently cursing my nerves, I pushed my glasses up the bridge of my nose. Most of the time I wore contacts, but after a night with hardly any sleep, my eyes had already been burning. Without my contacts, I was less confident, but before my hands had a chance to start shaking, he strolled into my office with purpose.

"Hey," I spoke as my lips broke into a smile, and my fingers picked at the hem of my dark purple blouse.

His hair was damp, flopping over his forehead, and it curled around his ears and the nape of his neck. He wore distressed jeans and a white and gray, long-sleeved Tampa Bay t-shirt that fit snug across his chest and biceps. The sleeves were pushed up to his elbows, and my eyes traced all the ink on his forearms before trailing them back to his cinnamon-colored eyes.

His smile was sewn into his dimples as he rubbed his hand along his beard-covered chin. He watched me from the doorway, his eyes touching every inch of my body, and I tried not to remember what that beard had felt like along the soft skin of my thighs.

He chuckled as heat filled my cheeks. "Anyway I can talk you into letting me live out my librarian fantasy, instead of having lunch?"

I pressed my lips together, hiding my growing smile, and my eyes flicked to the open door. "Unlike you, I can't be traded to another company. I would simply get fired."

He took three large steps toward the desk and the empty feeling from earlier disappeared. "Maybe next time, or after you've figured out the office politics? The comings and goings..."

"Maybe."

I could feel the weight of his gaze as I grabbed my keys. Willing away my insecurities, I dropped them into my purse and pulled the strap over my shoulder.

"Ready?" he asked when I stepped from behind the desk.

"I should be asking you that question." I nodded my head to the small window next to my office door. The blinds were open and most of the staff were pretending, quite poorly, to mill about in the lobby. "Looks like someone alerted the fans."

He turned and his shoulders shook with humor. I exhaled a deep breath and laced my fingers through his. Mark squeezed my hand and kissed me softly on the mouth once, twice, and the third time his tongue swept across my lips. Everyone in my office was getting a show, but the mint flavor of his mouth, the warmth of his kiss, in that very un-private moment, I remembered what it was like to be me, who I'd once been. Mark had the uncanny ability of making me feel at home in my own skin. Even if I was on fire and smattered with a million goose bumps.

When he pulled away, his smile was all challenge and mischief as he said, "Let's make a run for it."

Chatter and steam, the smell of bacon and maple syrup saturated the space of the small diner. Crashing pans, the clicking of silverware and glasses, the bustled energy of Six Spoons made it hard to hear myself think. I liked it. No time for any useless head talk. The place was fashioned after a train car. The narrowed room hardly had space for the ten tables and a long breakfast bar that ran the length of it. Everything was stainless steel and red-glittered vinyl. Old records were hung on the walls between framed autographed pictures of famous singers from the fifties and sixties. This was the kind of place where they yelled your order to the guy working the open grill, and the waitresses all had big hair, too much eye shadow, and pink lipstick that smudged their teeth. It had character, and you were guaranteed to gain at least five pounds by walking in.

I moaned as I took a bite of my crepe and spoke around a mouthful of Nutella, peanut butter, mascarpone, and strawberries. "When I die, I think my heaven will be created with these crepes."

"S'good," he mumbled around a huge bite of his veggie and cheese omelet. He took a gulp of his orange juice before he said, "I found this place right after I moved here. It reminds me of the restaurant I used to go to with my parents for Sunday breakfast back in Redding."

"Do you miss New Hampshire?"

"Every day. I miss the seasons. Here, it's hot, hot as fuck, and then chilly. You haven't seen a real fall until you've spent the season in New Hampshire." He chewed on another bite of his omelet before he continued. "More than anything, I miss my family, mostly my niece."

"Awe." I smirked and his smile lightened his eyes. "I didn't have much of a family-oriented culture growing up." I laughed. "It's cute how much you love your family... your niece."

"She's my soft spot." He pointed to his ribs. "I have the coordinates for Manchester tattooed right along here. It's a reminder, when everything feels too far gone, so I won't lose my head. It's a reminder of where she is... where home is."

"I'm kind of in love with that."

His eyes were a warm shade of amber as his smile tickled his lashes. "I'm kind of in love with her."

I never wanted kids. Never thought I would have the time to give them the attention they needed, and I wondered if he wanted kids. If our age difference, if this became something truly serious, would that become an unyielding wedge between us.

"Do..." My heart fluttered. "Do you want kids of your own?"

I kept my eyes on my plate, my fork picking at a strawberry when he answered, "Not really, no. I'm gone all the time, I barely have time for my dog."

"What about when you retire? You're only twenty-six, you may change your mind over time."

"Hockey has always been my life, and I've dedicated myself to that ideal. I love my niece, the kids who come to camp every summer... but I never really pictured it for myself. Being a father. I don't think time will change that." The thrumming of my heart ebbed as I looked at him from under my lashes. Mark was watching me carefully, too. "Do you? Want kids?"

He seemed younger, a little naïve himself in this moment. He was worried, too. Worried about what I wanted, what I might expect, and a nervous giggle escaped as I said, "No. Is that weird?"

"I don't think so."

"For a while, I thought maybe I just didn't want to have kids with Ben. Honestly, over the years... I think I became more selfish with my time. I'm an only child. I'd be a terrible parent."

He laughed and playfully knocked his foot into mine under the table. "I think if you wanted it, you'd be a great mom."

"I should try a dog... or a cat first."

"Atlas definitely liked you. I think you're a natural dog person."

He was trying to simplify the mood, but my mind went straight to the gutter. The mention of Atlas conjured up all sorts of memories from last night, and I blushed again. Mark leaned in, his hand reaching across the small table. He touched the tip of his thumb to the top of my hand, drawing gentle lines along my skin.

"That blush is fucking killing me," he whispered. "The glasses, your hair is up in a bun..." His eyes darkened with need and I fidgeted in my seat. One look. The ache built, pulsing, pooling between my legs. "I hate that I have to leave."

"Five days?"

He exhaled a harsh breath and leaned back. "Yeah. We have a back to back Wednesday and Thursday. A couple days off and finish the trip with a game on Sunday against L.A."

"I don't know how you do it."

His jaw clenched and he stared over my shoulder for a few ticks before giving me eye contact again. His gaze swept over my face and his posture relaxed. "This trip is rough. These teams are some of the top in the league. We were shit at practice today."

"Do you think you can beat them?"

The hard line of his jaw faded into a crooked, prideful smile. "Hell yeah. If we keep our heads on straight."

"Anything I can do?" I teased, and his lips parted over perfect, straight, white teeth. He was flawless.

"Send me dirty pictures before the game to wish me luck."

I laughed hard, my orange juice almost shooting from my nostrils as I swallowed down my sip. "Not likely."

"It could mean the difference between a win and a loss. Hockey players are very superstitious." His tone was comically serious.

"How dirty?"

His smile radiated, his eyes locked on mine, his grin painted across his face in triumph.

"I'll leave that up to you."

I secretly smiled as I thought about sending him pictures of my toilet and used dishes.

"I think I'll pass on the porn pics and send you a 'good luck', or an 'attaboy'."

His lips only spread farther, reaching well past his dimples as he said, "We'll see."

STEVIE

The mood at my mother's house hadn't changed over the years. The air was tinged with tobacco and vanilla as my mom exhaled an intricate looking gray cloud from her lips, dashing the two-inch ash of her cigarillo into the tray that sat on her lap. I smiled at how long she'd let it go this time. Her hair was fashioned into her signature salt and pepper side braid. She'd worn her hair like that for as long as I could remember, only ever taking it down right before bed. Music played quietly from the radio that sat on the breakfast bar, the same classic rock station she'd always listened to, and as I leaned back into the worn, rose-colored upholstery of the hand-me-down couch we'd had since I was ten, I soaked myself in all of the nostalgia. The wallpaper was still some crazy seventies floral pattern, and the only upgrade she'd done to the place had been to rip out the rugs for tile. Shelves of books, books I'd loved to get lost in when I was a kid, were overflowing now. Pictures of me, a few with Ben, as well, were scattered throughout the small living room. I was in a time capsule. This house held parts of me I didn't recognize anymore, and the parts I wanted to forget.

"Are you settled?" she asked, bringing the butt of her cigarillo to her lips.

Her mouth crinkled and mine spread into a bright smile. I missed my mom's easy spirit, missed how easy it was to sink into her soft features and relax. She was a balm to my soul sometimes. Even if she'd made poor life choices, and had carted my childhood around for the ride, she was all the family I'd ever have.

"Almost. I haven't finished unpacking all the way. I've been... busy." I curled my jean-clad legs under my body and shimmied into my favorite corner of the couch.

"That firm you're working for, it's better than the one you worked at in Richmond?" she asked, blowing smoke from her nostrils like a dragon.

"Much better. It feels good to be on my own."

"I could have told you that." She winked and I fought the urge to frown.

My mother hadn't been happy when I ran off and got married at nineteen. She'd told me I was throwing away "valuable life experience" and, at the time, my only thought had been how life with Ben was stable, and how we'd save money living in married student housing on campus. Virginia Commonwealth University hadn't been cheap, and the old me, Ben's wife, worried more about pragmatism and less about hearts and romance.

I chose my words carefully as I spoke, "It was important, Mom. For me to find my own way. I'm not like you... or at least that's what I always told myself. I married Ben because I needed something sure, and he was my sure thing, but..."

My eyes collided with hers. The pale brown of her irises sparkled with unshed tears. The cigarette between her fingers almost burnt down to the filter. "I was afraid of the unknown, of getting hurt. I've watched you get hurt so many times."

"That's the thing, I got hurt, but I got to bounce back. I got to experience love on both sides of the coin, bad and good, and the line between passion and self-preservation, I crossed it and I'll never regret it."

"Love and passion were both variables I chose to sacrifice..." My voice was stretched tight. "And I lost myself... I've wasted too much time."

My mom shook her head as she stamped the smoking butt into the tray. "Stevie, time is never wasted. With Ben... you learned something, right?" I nodded as she wiped away a few stray tears from under her eyes and smiled. "You learned what you can't live without. It takes most people a long time to figure out what they want from life. You're young, lucky to be getting another chance, so listen to your crazy mom this time when she tells you never settle."

I laughed as my lips parted into a watery smile. "Mom, there's never going to be one perfect person. You, of all people, should know that."

She winced and the guilt churned in my stomach. I hadn't meant it to be a barb, but it was true. My mother's list of lovers was a mile, maybe a few miles long, and she hadn't found her "soul mate" yet.

"I didn't mean—"

"Don't worry about it." She stood, placing the ashtray on the coffee table. "I don't mind, you know. Being alone, I like my life. I like who I am and where I've been, and that's all I want for you. Be happy with you, Stevie."

I was happy. And it wasn't entirely true to say I hadn't been happy with Ben. We had a decent run at first, but it fizzled and I stayed too long.

"I'm getting there, Mom." Starting over felt right, and I didn't want to think about how much of that had to do with Mark. I'd like to think I was making my own way into the next phase of me, and Mark was a side effect of letting myself live a little.

She leaned down and kissed my forehead, her breath a mixture of mint and tobacco. "I'm glad to hear it, baby. You look good," she said lifting the remote from the coffee table and handing it to me. "Watch whatever you want. I'm going to order a pizza. Ray still coming by?"

"Yeah." Reagan had texted me about twenty minutes ago, letting me know she was on her way from the salon. "She already ate dinner though."

"I'll order enough for her, just in case." She switched off the radio. "She fooling around with Pete again?"

I huffed out a laugh. My mom's penchant for details never wavered over the years.

"Who knows anymore, I feel sorry for the guy."

My mom snorted. "He's a man, Stevie. If he wanted to be serious with her, he would."

"I think it's Ray who can't commit."

"Yeah, but he keeps coming back for more." She nodded like she'd said the most profound thing in the universe.

I hummed in agreement and flipped on the big screen television, a new addition since my last visit, and scrolled through the channels until I found what I was looking for. A familiar whistle blew through the speakers, and my heart expanded inside my chest. The heavy pulse warmed my veins as I listened to the announcers' low voices. The game was well underway, and I found myself leaning forward, my spine buzzing with anticipation as I watched number nineteen skate toward one of the dots on the rink. He hunched over, his stick resting on his knees as he stared at his opponent. My eyes flicked to the score. Neither team had made a goal yet. I swore under my breath and then giggled at my own anxiety as Mark lowered his stick and the ref dropped the puck.

Mayhem.

It was the only word I could use to describe what happened when the puck hit the ice. He was playing against Vegas, and the swirl of jerseys, the yelling, and sheer aggression flashing on the screen had my feet rooted to the floor, my bottom lip pinned between my teeth, and a litany of curses running through my head every time the other team stole the puck from one of Mark's teammates. I'd spoken to him earlier today, after his morning skate. He'd told me he felt good about tonight, and that the funk his team had been in the previous practice was no longer a problem.

"We skated like we'd already fucking won," he'd said, and I remembered the gruff sound of his voice and how, even over two-thousand miles away, I'd felt its heat trickle over my skin.

Mark's confidence was a huge turn on. Amongst other things. The sound of another whistle blowing pulled me from my mental nose dive into some of our dirtier moments. He was on the ice again. Hovering over the dot left of the opposing team's goalie. Again the referee dropped the puck and the game continued. Mark and his team struggled to get the puck, letting one of the Vegas guys successfully steal away with it, but Bryson, the guy I'd met at the bar, stole it right back, passing it to Mark. Time stood still as Mark drew back his stick, hitting the puck hard enough I heard the sound of metal ringing as it bounced down and into the net. His team erupted into cheers and the crowd booed as red lights lit up the glass behind the goal. Mark skated behind the net and jumped, chest first into the plexiglass, his fist pounding it in celebration. All at once, his teammates swarmed him with giant bear hugs.

I was on my feet screaming, jumping up and down when my mother shouted, "Since when do you like hockey?"

"Since she started dating one of the players," Reagan said with a smirk as she shut the front door behind her.

"You're dating a hockey player?" My mom's eyebrows disappeared into her hairline.

"Umm..." I stumbled.

"He's hot, Ms. Baylor." Reagan dropped her purse on the sofa before walking over to my mom and kissing her on the cheek.

I had to restrain myself from physically silencing Ray's big mouth. It wasn't that I didn't want my mom to know, but I'd wanted to present it to her in a way that didn't have her looking at me with those "I know what's better for you" eyes.

My mom stared at me, humor hinting at the corners of her lips. "You haven't been in town two weeks..."

I exhaled and groaned like a teenager as I sank back into the couch. My eyes flicked to the screen as the clock ran out. The first period was over. I wished I was at home and away from the prying eyes of my mother. I wanted to text him. Congratulate him on his goal. I figured his phone was in the locker room, but I wasn't sure if he'd even have it on. My mom cleared her throat, obviously waiting for some type of explanation.

"It's a long story."

She sat down in her chair, and Reagan made herself comfortable on the other end of the couch. "I'm all ears."

Lucky for me, Reagan was intrusive and had no boundaries whatsoever. She'd basically given my mother the lowdown on how her daughter had almost become an adulterer, and how Mark had sparked the match I'd needed to finally see what I'd always known, but had been too afraid to face. It was interesting hearing Ray's interpretation of my misdeeds and choices. My "new" life sounded way more fabulous the way Reagan had painted it, but that was because I knew Mark, and who he was had nothing to do with his status or money.

My mom's eyes fell to the screen of the television. The second period had started about three minutes ago, and all I wanted was for the pizza to get here and for this conversation to be over.

"He's the opposite of Ben," Reagan said as she gave me a smile. "I think you'll like him."

Not that she was going to meet him anytime soon.

Mom turned her head slowly as if lost in thought. Her eyes met mine, and she stared at me for what felt like an eternity. "You didn't give yourself much time, Stevie."

I couldn't argue with her on that one.

"I know." My gaze followed Mark across the screen as he skated toward his team's bench. "But... I jumped in, Mom. I didn't calculate every detail like I would've done in the past. I said, screw it, and went with what my gut was telling me." Her smile spread wide and into her eyes. "Isn't that what you've been preaching to me my whole life?" She nodded and I took a deep breath. "I want messy, Mom. Even if it hurts. Mark makes me feel... I don't know... a little reckless, but he makes me feel safe, too. I don't have a plan... I just like him."

The doorbell rang, and Reagan jumped up to answer it, leaving me alone with my mom.

"You like him?"

"I do."

"Then that's all that matters. A hockey player...huh," she mused, and her smile unknotted the ball of tension that had coiled in my belly.

"He's really good, too," I said as Reagan set the pizza boxes down onto the coffee table. "Well, I think he is. I'm trying to figure out all the rules."

"All you have to know is most of them are hot as hell." Reagan giggled as she plopped down onto the floor and lifted the lid of the pizza box.

The smell of parmesan and oregano filled the air and made my mouth water.

My mom's laughter made me grin. "That's all I have to know? Hockey seems brutal to me."

As if on cue, a fight started to break out in front of Mark's goalie. A few of the players were pushing each other while two of the referees attempted to pry Mark's teammate, number ninety, a guy named Rasmussen, apart from a Vegas player he'd pinned to the ice. I cringed as another Vegas player took a swing at one of the refs. Tampa was still up by one, and it appeared Vegas didn't like being scoreless.

"This is only the third game I've watched. I can already tell I sort of like it. I might have a heart attack watching Mark play, though."

"Hockey has always confused me. I dated a guy once who loved it, but he could never explain to me the freaking point." My mom laughed as she leaned over and grabbed a slice of pizza.

"The point..." Reagan smirked. "Hot guys... in skates.... Like I said... what else is there to know?"

"The point, Mom, is to get the puck in the net."

"Score points," Reagan agreed.

The fighting I could do without. But the game itself, was addictive. I loved the fast pace and how everything could go terribly wrong or terribly right in a matter of seconds. The skill alone had my eyes glued to the rink. I had a feeling once you fell in love with hockey there was no turning back. My heart stuttered over a few beats as I thought about how that same line of reasoning could be applied to the players as well.

I pulled my phone from my pocket as Reagan schooled my mom on a few of the rules we'd learned Monday night at the game. I opened my messaging app and thumbed down to Mark's name. My cheeks ached with a smile as my fingers swept across the screen without caution.

ME: *CONGRATS!*

ME: *I'm impressed, that was a pretty sexy goal, sir.*

ME: *Would I be too much of a bunny if I sent you a dirty picture as a reward for that spectacular showcase of athleticism?*

As I slipped my phone into my pocket, I actually thought about sending him the real thing and not a picture of our used pizza napkins. I made a silent deal with myself. Mark would get his naughty pic, but only if they won the game.

Ray's loud "whoop" lifted my eyes to the screen.

Tampa had scored another goal.

MARK

When you scored first in a game, played two periods without letting the other team sink one shot, you'd think your team could hold their shit together for one more period. My ass hit the leather of the plane seat and I groaned. Every single muscle hurt. I'd have fared better if I'd been run through a meat grinder. I had a bruise the size of fucking Alaska forming on my hip from a hit I'd taken by a mean-as-hell blue liner who'd had his eye on me all night. The moment I'd stolen that first goal, I had a target on my back. But for all their aggression, Vegas couldn't get the W. We had, thank Christ. Three to two in overtime. Vegas had pulled a penalty leaving them shorthanded. Slashing. At the time, I'd thought Bryson was milking his "injury." But afterward in the locker room, he'd held up his mangled and bruised looking thumb like a trophy. The trainer had said he'd only jammed it, but it'd won us a power play and the game.

I ran a hand through my hair as I pulled my phone from my bag and switched it on. Mandatory post-game media, shower, and a quick turnaround left no time for phone calls. We were on our way to California to play San Jose tomorrow night, and as banged up as we were, I wondered what the morning skate would predict.

My phone was powering up too slowly. It hadn't mattered how shitfaced tired I'd felt, the moment the final buzzer rang, Stevie had been the first thing I'd thought of. She'd told me this morning she might not have a chance to watch the game because she was having dinner at her mom's. Call me superstitious, but I'd let a ribbon of worry tangle with my laces tonight. The last time she'd watched I'd scored a hatty. I kind of liked her eyes on my ice, whether it was at home or on the road. It was stupid, yet no more stupid than Karlsson's special brand of tape he had to use every game, or Vasiliev's blue laces. We all had our kinks.

My smile crawled across my face as Stevie's missed messages popped up. I heard Bryson snicker from the row in front of me, and I raised my head and laughed at his shirtless chest.

"Always late to the bus and to the plane," I said.

He shrugged and then slipped his right arm into a crisp white button-down. "Whatever." He lifted his chin. "Did she watch?"

Bryson was the only guy on the team who knew about my new Stevie superstition.

I opened up her messages, my eyes going wide before I quickly clicked out of the app.

Holy God.

"Was that—"

"Sit the fuck down already, Jensen. Shit." I almost growled, but it held no real irritation. My smile was too big, my cheeks and neck too hot.

She'd sent me a dirty picture, and I wished to God I was alone. I wanted to stare at it and...

"I'm thinking she watched." Bryson chuckled before he finally turned around to finish buttoning up his shirt.

I glanced around to make sure no other eyes were watching before I opened her messages again.

Stevie: *CONGRATS!*

Stevie: *I'm impressed, that was a pretty sexy goal, sir.*

Stevie: *Would I be too much of a bunny if I sent you a dirty picture as a reward for that spectacular showcase of athleticism?*

Stevie: *For a minute there I thought I'd be off the hook... I guess I owe you a congratulatory porn pic...*

Stevie: *If this ends up on the Internet, I'll tell anyone who will listen that you have a small penis.*

Stevie: *Not really.*

Stevie: *Well... yeah, really.*

I laughed out loud, but the guys were either too busy shit talking about Vegas or bugging the stewardess to pay me any mind. Another quick glance around the cabin told me I was safe to scroll up for my *reward*. And holy fuck, she did not disappoint. She'd sent the picture about thirty minutes after her last text, and I was grateful I hadn't opened this in the locker room. One thing you never want to do—sport wood when you're about to soap up with a pack of dudes. I had to shift in my seat and readjust my slacks as the fabric got tighter by the second. The picture was a little blurry, as if her hand was shaking when she'd taken it. Stevie's head was tipped down, but I could still see the blush in the high arch of her cheek. She must've held the phone above her head with her right arm. The angle gave me a view all the way down her naked body. Her hair obscured the top of her tits, but I could still see the slope, the shape of them and the tight nipples peeking through.

The fingers of her left hand rested on her hip. Her skin was cream, and I wanted to be the one touching her. My mouth went dry as I thought about how much I wanted to taste the curves of her stomach and thighs again. I stared at the picture probably longer than I should have in public, on a plane, with a bunch of meatheads nearby. Jesus, Stevie's body was unbelievable. Her full figure made me think of those old pin-up girls my best friend in high school had been obsessed with. The Marilyn Monroe types, but curvier. My eyes stayed glued to the screen for a few more seconds as I lost myself inside all of that soft skin. I couldn't believe she'd actually sent me a picture. This was definitely a great way to rally my confidence for every game.

I licked my lips as I typed out a response.

ME: *Sexiest. Picture. I. Have. Ever. Seen.*

I figured she'd be sleeping, so it surprised me when a text came through.

Stevie: *You should know, I've been sitting here, panicking, wishing that picture back, or out of existence.*

I laughed again as I typed.

ME: *No way. It's mine now, and I'm thinking home screen wallpaper.*

Stevie: *Not Funny.*

ME: *I'm serious. I never thought I'd be rocking a boner on a plane full of men. Good job.*

Stevie: *I'm laughing now, but seriously, delete it.*

I would delete it. After I got to my hotel room.

ME: *I will.*

Stevie: *Now.*

ME: *I think I'm gonna wait till I get to my room. You know, for further inspection...*

Stevie: *Mark!*

This time my laughter garnered some attention. I did the right thing and internally protested with a quiet groan as I deleted the picture.

ME: *Done.*

I sent a screenshot of the message thread proving I'd deleted the picture.

ME: *That would've kept me warm this whole trip.*

Stevie: *Keep winning and I promise to send more.*

Stevie: *As long as you delete them.*

I chuckled.

ME: *As you wish.*

The plane jerked into motion, and the pilot's voice filtered through the overhead speaker, "Flight crew, prepare the cabin for takeoff."

I wasn't ready to let her go though.

ME: *The plane is starting to taxi.*

Stevie: *You looked good out there tonight.*

ME: *Thanks for watching the game.*

Stevie: *I like watching you play.*

I wanted to break the FAA rules and call her. Hear her sleepy voice. Steal its sound and take it to bed with me tonight.

ME: *I'll try to call tomorrow.*

Stevie: *K, I'm falling asleep...*

ME: *Dream with me.*

Stevie: *Dream of that picture because I'm not sure I'll have the nerve to ever do it again.*

ME: *You promised. That's a solid contractual obligation.*

Stevie: *Goodnight, Mark.*

A sly grin lifted the left corner of my mouth.

ME: *Night, babe.*

I turned my phone off and threw it back i' o the small duffle on the floor. I bent down to zip it up and when I raised my head, Bryson slipped into the seat next to me.

"Well? Did she watch the game or not?" he asked, and I exhaled an annoyed breath.

"Yes." He smiled, and I couldn't help but do the same.

"Melo has a new lucky charm." He rubbed his hands together and I almost rolled my eyes. "I think, as your captain, I should get a better look at the picture she sent."

"She's my girlfriend, dick."

"The girlfriend thing... that's your problem... just make sure she watches the games from now on," he demanded, his face deadpan and serious.

"I thought Canadians were supposed to be nice, eh?" I joked and he smiled again.

"I am nice," he argued. "If you have a good rack."

My head fell back against the seat as I laughed. "One of these days, Jensen, some girl is going to burst your bubble..."

He chuffed. "Not likely."

I ignored him. "You never know..."

"No, thank you." He stretched his injured hand and winced.

"That looks bad."

"Hurts like a motherfucker..."

I smirked. "Good."

"Now who's being a dick?"

"You gonna be able to hold your stick tomorrow?" I asked.

His thumb looked jacked, but knowing Bryson, he'd downplay it.

"I'm fine. But what about you? I thought you were gonna start crying on the bench after that hit."

I avoided his eyes as I regurgitated his words. "I'm fine. It's not like I've never been hit hard before."

"About that picture..."

He snickered and gave me a goofy-ass grin.

"Bryson, I swear to God, go back to your seat, I want to try to sleep off some of this pain."

His smile fell. "You gonna be able to play tomorrow?"

My lips settled into a flat line. "What the hell do you think?"

He stood and moved to the seat in front of me. He tapped his fist lightly on the headrest, and before he sat down he said, "Hardcore, Melo, always have been. It's why I like you."

"I thought you liked me for my rack." I waggled my brows and he frowned.

"Go to sleep, idiot."

Bryson was rattling off stats about San Jose to our left winger when I finally closed my eyes. My stomach dropped as the plane climbed to its cruising altitude, and when I began to doze off, it wasn't the image Stevie had sent me that occupied my thoughts. It was what the picture represented. I was thinking about it all too hard, but I liked how she'd made herself vulnerable for me. Did something totally out of her comfort zone to make me happy. And that was pretty fucking cool in my book.

The noise of the cabin faded, and the last thing I remembered before I fell asleep was how, for the first time in months, I felt totally content.

STEVIE

The next morning I was still reeling from the previous night's text messages from Mark. I'd never been a girl to strip down naked and take a picture, let alone send it in a text. The Internet was forever, but he'd deleted it, like I'd figured, or more like hoped he would. I trusted Mark. You didn't have to know a guy for months or years to know if they were a good person. That's one thing I'd inherited from my mom, the ability to read people and see through bullshit. A trait that had saved Ben and me a few times back when we'd been building our clientele at the firm in Richmond. Shady people, they were shifty, tight-spined, and gave off the impression the world owed them something. Entitlement stunk, and I could smell it from at least a mile away.

Mark wasn't entitled. He was laid back, fun, and open. A guy like him, a successful, professional athlete, had a lot to lose when it came to his image. He hadn't held back with me. He wasn't hiding me behind some velvet VIP rope where no one would see us, and the fact he trusted me already made it much easier for me to give into the feelings I was developing. He was a good guy. Mark made me want to "live a little" like Reagan had suggested when I'd told her that I'd planned to send him a "not suitable for work" picture. And when I'd taken the picture, when I'd hit send with shaking fingers, it was confirmation enough that I was ready to explore this new side of myself. The side that was dating a younger, tattooed, and way too good with his hands, hockey player.

It wasn't until after lunch that I finally stopped overanalyzing everything and fell into my usual work-day routine. Alec had stepped back, allowing me to work on the Bruin Brothers account with hardly any supervision. I'd been nosing through their tax–deductible purchases all morning. Income tax season was fast approaching, and after Christmas, Alec had assured me I'd be so busy I'd start to dream about credits and write offs. I'd dream in numerical sequence every night if I had to. I was ecstatic to finally have a chance to prove to myself I could do this on my own.

"When you come up for air, you might want to take a look at this." David's sing-song voice made me smile as I lifted my eyes from the spreadsheet I'd been staring at for the past thirty minutes.

He was standing in my doorway, impeccably dressed in tailored Burberry slacks and a light beige V-neck sweater, waving what looked like an air-express mail envelope in his hand.

"Looks important," he quipped, his light eyes twinkling at the corners.

I used the interruption to stand and stretch my legs. "Bruin Brothers?" I asked, eyeing the envelope as he walked toward me.

"Nope," he said with a sly grin, and I was distracted by the sound of my phone vibrating against the top of my desk.

I looked at the lit lock screen and Mark's name flashed in bold. I didn't want it to go to voicemail. He'd told me his time was limited on road trips, and I liked that he saved some of it for me. David leaned over my desk. "Answer it."

"Thanks, give me a second?" I asked with a wave of my hand. A not-so-subtle dismissal.

I picked up my phone as David dropped the express mail down in front of me. "I want all the details..." He darted his gaze to the envelope and then to the phone in my hand. "You know where to find me." His smile was devious as he turned to leave.

Once David had closed my office door, I answered the call.

"Hey."

"I was worried I'd get your voicemail." Mark's voice was warm and gruff and a little breathless. "We just finished with practice, and I only have a few minutes before Maddox hauls us in to watch game tape."

"What time do you play tonight?"

"Puck drops at seven. Ten your time. Kind of late for a work night. If you can't watch—"

My laugh was soft as I said, "I'd watch if the game started at one in the morning. I'm addicted and it's all your fault."

His chuckle heated my cheeks and stirred the butterflies in my stomach. "Addicted enough to fly out on a plane and watch me play in L.A.?"

I wished.

I'd never been west of the Mississippi river. If it wasn't for my brand new mortgage payment, I'd jump on the first jet out of here. Unfortunately, being a single adult sucked and was damn expensive, too.

"Sure. Let me crack open my piggy bank," I teased, keeping a smile in my tone, hiding my disappointment. His lifestyle wasn't something I'd ever be able to afford.

"How about you open your mail instead?"

My eyes fell to the air express envelope sitting on my desk. "Mark?" I paused as I lifted it and read the sender's information. "What did you do?"

"Open it." As I pulled the strip open on the back of the package, he said, "I'll be busy, Stevie, but if you fly out Saturday morning, by the time you get here, practice and shit will be over. We can run around town if you want, sightsee, have dinner with the team, and then we'd have the whole night to chill."

My heart was beating all the way to the tips of my fingers as I pulled out a plane ticket along with a pass to his game on Sunday night against Los Angeles.

"Mark..." I stumbled over his name. "This is too much, I can't—"

Mark's voice dropped to a velvet calm. "That plane ticket is pocket change for me. I know for most people it's hard to believe, but it's the truth." I almost snorted. A nonstop, first-class flight. Pocket change. "I can hear you freaking out... stop. It's not a big deal."

"It's a big deal."

"It'll be fun."

I shook my head, my smile spreading at his nonchalant tone. "I won't be a distraction?"

"Only the good kind." He laughed, and I exhaled the breath I was holding. "It's only a weekend. That ticket will have your fine ass safely back on the plane in time for work Tuesday morning."

Tuesday.

"I'll have to ask Trent if I can have Monday off, I hope the ticket is refundable because it's busy and—"

"You have Monday off," he said matter-of-fact. "Trent is a reasonable guy when you bribe him with a few rink-side seats."

I choked on an inhale. "What?"

Mark's laughter was distant as if he pulled the phone away. I heard him mumble, "Give me a second" to someone. Meanwhile, my pulse had spiked to an all-time high. He took a deep breath. "That picture you sent last night... I want the real thing."

"You know you could've saved yourself the trouble and just Skyped me."

My laugh was more of the nervous variety and he keyed in on it as he assured me, "It's just a weekend."

I'd gone from wading in the kiddy pool to deep-sea-diving overnight. It was only a weekend, but in comparison to how long we've known each other, a weekend was a lot. We hadn't even slept together yet, literally and sexually speaking.

"I've been told I'm a bed hog." I added to my list of cons.

"I hope so," he answered with another chuckle.

"Just a weekend?"

"Melo, come the fuck on already, we don't have all goddamn day," another booming male voice yelled, and I heard Mark exhale noisily into the phone before he said, "I have to go. If staying the weekend makes you uncomfortable, I can refund the ticket, alright, but think about it, if I was home this weekend, where would you be?"

His confidence was remarkable. I couldn't predict the future, but if I thought about it, if he was here, I'd want to spend as much time with him as possible. And, he was right, if I was sitting in his apartment this weekend, I'd be hoping for a repeat of our last date, and possibly more. Los Angeles was just a zip code change.

And a pricey flight without a way to head home at the end of the night...

In truth, I hadn't wanted to go home the other night anyway.

"Should I pack something nice to wear for this team dinner?" I surrendered.

"Yeah?"

I nodded to no one in particular, a slow smile spreading across my cheeks. "Pocket change, right?"

He chuckled again. "Right." He was quiet for a few seconds and I let this crazy idea steep. "I'll text you specifics when I get back to the hotel tonight."

"You have to win tonight. I don't want to fly all the way out to Los Angeles and get stuck spending the weekend with a bunch of grumpy guys."

"Grumpy guy," he amended. "I'm only subjecting you to these idiots for a couple hours. And if we lose, I'll let you lick my wounds."

A laugh tipped my head back. "You'll let me, huh?"

He whispered, "I'm at your mercy, babe."

When it came to Mark, I was like Alice, falling fast and hard down the rabbit hole. My eyes fell to the tickets in my hand. It seemed I was at his mercy, too. "Play hard, kick some ass or whatever hockey players like to hear, I'll be here cheering, either way."

"Play hard works." He laughed. "Saturday..."

I closed my eyes allowing honest words to part my lips as I whispered, "Can't wait to see you."

"You have no idea."

Indeed, hockey was going to be the death of me. I was *not* a puck aficionado and even I could tell both teams had played sloppy last night. The final score, five to six. Mark's team had won by the skin of their teeth. Their coach had pulled the goalie in the second period after he'd allowed three goals into his net, and as much as I hated to admit it, if it wasn't for the backup guy, they might've lost the game. At lunch, Trent and Alec had been arguing over whether hockey was more of a mental or physical game, and I'd rallied on the side with Trent. Hockey relied on both. Last night, Mark's goalie had lost his mental battle, or it had appeared that way, at least. Alec ranted about how Karlsson "couldn't shut his five hole to save his own damn life" and how he was "outmatched against the San Jose lines." I'd sat there quietly eating my turkey sandwich, feeling out of my depth but grateful they'd won. I couldn't imagine what that guy Karlsson was feeling today. When Mark's team was on the ice, if I didn't pop a blood vessel cheering I'd probably die by anxious asphyxiation, if that was even a thing, and I wasn't even a player.

After a night like that, this day crawled, dragging me behind with it. The excitement had died down and the wait had begun. It was three o'clock, and I wished it was tomorrow morning already. Mark had promised to try and finish up with practice in enough time to pick me up himself at LAX, but assured me he'd send a car if he couldn't.

Every second that ticked by equated to one hour. I was too preoccupied by all the possibilities—the outcomes—this weekend had to offer. Combing through the latest batch of Bruin Brothers purchases was the last thing I wanted to do. I was mindlessly tapping my pen on the desk when my boss walked into my office.

"You all set for this weekend?" he asked with his signature charming smile.

His blond hair ruffled through his fingers as he plopped down into the chair across from me with a long, exaggerated exhale.

"I am. Thank you, Trent, for letting Mark bully you into giving me Monday off."

His smile didn't reach his eyes. "Not a problem. I'll let him bully me for hockey tickets any day."

He ran his hand through his hair again and I raised my eyebrows. "What's up? You seem frazzled."

His tie was askew, his hair mussed and not in an on purpose sort of way, and I might've gasped at the wrinkles in his shirt if it wouldn't have been overly dramatic to do so. Trent was a put together kind of guy. Pressed and starched and handsome as hell. Never a hair out of place.

He stared at me as if gauging whether or not he was going to trust me with an answer. His shoulders sagged. "Remember that account I was telling you about..."

"The big audit?"

He nodded. "I'm in crisis mode, Stevie. This is one of our biggest clients, and this audit, it makes us look bad. Their finance guy was recently fired after they found out he'd been screwing with their books, maybe even taking a little off the top. Fake purchases, falsified documentation. Daniel is worried we might be in a shit load of hot water. Maybe we didn't pay enough attention. Either way, they're depending on us to keep the IRS off their backs." Daniel Elm was Trent's partner here at the firm. He was a surly older guy who never spoke much and I was okay with that. He was always frowning and ordering people around. I stuck with David mostly, but Trent and Alec were closer to my age and much less intimidating. Elm had partnered with Trent after Mr. Byron, Trent's father, passed away a few years ago.

He leaned forward in the chair resting his elbows on his knees. He raised tentative eyes to mine. "I had our lawyer come in and assess the damage, looks like we're going to need a lot more help than I previously thought to work through this crap show."

"Put me to work, I'm ready Trent."

He swallowed and shifted his gaze to the floor. "I know, and I'm happy to have your capable hands on deck, Stevie, but I'm thinking we need to look outside the firm, get some fresh eyes. Daniel has a few associates coming in to help, and I've..." He sat up straight and squared his shoulders, his eyes finding mine. "I've asked Ben if he'd be willing to help."

My lips were numb, the first sign I'd stopped breathing. The light of the room had tunneled in around Trent, making everything seem fuzzy at the edges. Dread seeped into my stomach. Ben... that was a horrible idea. No, horrible was not a sufficient enough word for how bad this was... how about catastrophically freaking awkward.

I took a few short breaths through my nose before I asked, "What did he say?"

Surely he would be too busy, his firm was small, but always busy, especially during this time of year.

"He said yes."

Yes.

The air in my office was impenetrable as I tried to pull in a breath.

"We're obviously going to compensate him for his time, match the wages he'd usually earn, as well as a pretty sweet housing set up."

"H-housing," I stuttered. "How long will he be here?"

Panic beaded across my forehead in the form of sweat. I didn't hate Ben, he'd once been my best friend, but when we divorced, I'd expected a clean break. Having him here complicated so many things. I was finally starting to get my feet wet and having my ex-husband around, hovering, wasn't ideal. I wanted my own life, I'd given him thirteen years, and I'd thought I was getting a new beginning.

"He's set to come the week before Christmas. Ben said he could give us three months. That gives us plenty of time to get all of our ducks in a tidy row. The apartment building Daniel owns will have an opening then, as well. So it all works out nicely, I think."

Nicely for you.

Three months was an eternity.

Trent gave me a meek smile and guilt soured inside my stomach. I was being a selfish brat. Trent had brought me in, under Ben's advisement, and I was sulking like a tween. Three months wasn't that long, and I wouldn't necessarily be working one-on-one with him anyway.

"I know this isn't ideal, considering..." He held up his hand gesturing in my direction. "You should know, Ben was worried about how you'd feel."

Suddenly my throat felt hot and tight. "He was?"

Trent leaned to the edge of his chair. "He really was, he almost told me no. He said you'd wanted time, and he didn't want to throw a wrench in that." He chuckled. "But then I told him you'd already started dating, and he didn't have to worry about time. After that, he agreed to everything right away."

Ben knew I was dating, and he didn't care. Maybe this wouldn't be awkward after all.

"Okay."

"Okay?" he asked.

"This has the potential to be a train wreck," I conceded.

"I'll keep you busy with current accounts while we work on the audit. Would that work?"

I exhaled and sank against the back of my chair. "I think it's the only way to make it work."

I would've loved the experience of a large-scale audit like this, but giving me a few current accounts was undeniably a great way for me to show my skills, as well as show Trent and Daniel I was a good investment. I wanted them to look at me as a valuable colleague and not the accountant they'd taken on as a favor to a friend.

Trent's smile pulled to his ears as he stood. "This went better than I'd anticipated."

"What were you expecting? A tantrum?"

He shrugged, a sheepish grin on his face. "Maybe some tears? A little more resistance. I practiced a counter speech with David before I came in here."

I giggled. "Can I hear it?"

"No," he said waving both of his arms. "I've never been good at conflict, it's why I chose accounting over the law." He tucked his hands into his pockets. "If you had put up a fight, I probably would've recruited David to bail me out."

"He *is* oddly persuasive."

He took a step toward the door, his laugh lingering when he looked at me again. It could have been the set of my shoulders, or the trace of worry that furrowed my brow that made him pause. His smile was soft, understanding when he spoke, "You're an asset to this firm, Stevie. We want this to be a home for you. Have fun this weekend."

I nodded, unable to speak around the lump in my throat. He gave me a quick tilt of the head as a goodbye. The door shut and my eyes burned as I held back the emotion his words had spurred inside of me. I pulled my own weight. I was an asset to this firm. This was my home, and Ben was just visiting.

I raised my gaze to the clock. At this time tomorrow I'd be in Los Angeles, wrapped up in the strong, inked arms of my boyfriend.

My boyfriend.

Three months.

I could handle that.

MARK

A balled up piece of paper hit the side of my head and I turned to catch Bryson staring at me with a scowl.

"The fuck?" he whispered, and I shrugged, not sure what the hell his problem was.

My teammates and I had been huddled on the floor watching game tape for an hour, and as important as this was, I couldn't stop my foot from tapping, or my mind from worrying about how late I would be getting back to the hotel. Stevie had landed about thirty minutes ago, and she'd texted to let me know she'd heard my voicemail, and to not stress out. I was stressed regardless. I'd called Stevie during a break and left her a message. I told her practice had run late, and we hadn't watched game tape yet, but I'd sent a car to pick her up at the terminal. I'd given her instructions on how to obtain a key at the concierge and to make herself comfortable. I debated on slipping out for a second to call her, tell her I planned on bringing a late lunch, see if she'd wanted anything, and maybe tell her comfortable meant naked, but I didn't want to sound like a presumptuous asshole.

Bryson scooted closer to where I was sitting and knocked his shoulder into mine, pushing me off balance. He spoke in a low, irritated tone, "Are you even watching this shit?"

My eyes flicked to the wide screen. Coach had pressed pause and listed off stats on L.A.'s special teams. Maddox hadn't been impressed with my line this morning, and he definitely wasn't thrilled with our penalty kill percentages from the last game against San Jose. I shifted my gaze back to Bryson once Coach pressed play again. I should be paying attention, but my head was already between Stevie's legs and not in the game.

"Please tell me you're getting laid tonight so you can fucking focus?" he asked, quiet enough only I could hear.

My shoulders stretched into a rigid line. Fucker was too intrusive sometimes, even if he hit the nail on the head, he should mind his own damn business. "Shut the fuck up, Jensen. I'm focused."

"You're not, man." He dipped his head. "I get it, but don't let your lucky charm turn into a crutch."

I narrowed my eyes as a few of the guys turned to look at us over their shoulders. My voice was clipped and low as I said, "I told her I'd pick her up, and I didn't want to be late. This is the first of many promises I'll inevitably break, and I guess I didn't want it to be this soon."

"This is fucking hockey, shit happens." He turned to face the screen. "She's a chick, Melo... she could be here today and gone tomorrow."

The muscle in my jaw twitched as I lifted my eyes to watch the tape. He hadn't the faintest idea about what it was like to have a relationship. Maybe I had let Stevie into my head today at practice, but when game day came rolling around, I always shut that shit down. The only exception had been Mia and Tyler, and I swore I'd never let that happen again.

"She's not going anywhere, Bryson. Shit... you're right, okay, my head was up my ass this morning. I'll keep myself in check."

He nodded his head at the screen. "Number twenty-eight, his footspeed is sick as fuck."

"Yeah, but I'm faster."

He chuckled. "Damn straight." Bryson turned again and whispered, "I know you like her... you wouldn't have brought her all the way out here if you didn't, and I get you don't want to break promises, but don't break the promises you've made to your teammates either."

I swallowed down my smart-ass remark because this was Bryson at his best. The leader. He led by example, and if he was on his game, in his mind, we all would follow suit. Last night, when Maddox pulled Karlsson from the net he blamed himself. He'd said it was his fault, by his logic, he played sloppy, and therefore we all played sloppy. In reality, we were all fucking beat from the back-to-back schedule, and playing in San Jose had never been an easy win for us. But that was who he was, and the logic may be flawed, but there was truth to it. When he played to win, we usually did. It also helped if one of us was falling out of line, he'd always made sure to set us right again, like he was with me on the media room floor.

"I won't." Letting my teammates down wasn't an option.

"I know. I was just reminding you." Bryson gave me a smirk before he gave his full attention to the screen.

I'd always been good at balancing my real life and my hockey life. Stevie was different. I fucking loved having her in my headspace. I loved that she wasn't a part of the *hockey world*, it was refreshing. But, this was my job, and I owed my teammates better. I owed myself better. I wouldn't fall short again because I couldn't compartmentalize my life like I should have. I pulled my phone from my pocket and powered it down. I'd see Stevie as soon as I could. She'd told me not to stress and I needed to listen. I let my eyes wander to the clock one last time. I took a deep breath, turning in time to watch L.A.'s goalie smother a blistering slap shot like it was a walk in the park.

My team migrated into the hotel lobby about thirty minutes after I'd sent a text to Stevie letting her know I'd finished up at the rink and that we could grab some lunch when I got there. It had gone unanswered. We were staying only a couple of miles from the arena, but downtown L.A. traffic was a bitch. Once we were all inside, the guys dispersed, some heading to grab lunch at the hotel's bar and grill, while the rest of us said our goodbyes until dinner. A few of us wanted to check out this wine cellar-themed restaurant about three blocks from the hotel and had planned to meet there around six, giving me a little less than five hours of one-on-one time with Stevie.

My anxiety about tomorrow's game dissolved as I thought about all the possibilities this afternoon had to offer. Being away from home ice was mentally fucking taxing, but I'd always promised myself when I stepped out of the rink and out of my skates, even when we played road games, I had to clear my head. Remember the real world. Today and tonight, I'd make Stevie the center of it.

Immediately, I was assaulted with the sound of loud guitars as I unlocked and opened the door to my room. Was that... Stevie? She was singing along to some punked-out version of *I Melt with You,* and as I followed the sound of her sexy voice to the back of the suite, my lips spread into a broad, goofy smile.

I'd upgraded my room once she'd agreed to stay with me. We were on the fifteenth floor, and as I walked into the large bedroom, sunlight flooded through the floor-to-ceiling windows and across the crisp white down comforter. The Los Angeles skyline stretched and yawned toward the horizon. Stevie stopped singing and it pulled me from the view, leading me to the attached bathroom. As I neared the entry, her distinct fruity smell hung heavy in the damp air.

The music was almost too loud as I opened the door fully, but I couldn't give a shit. Stevie stood in front of a fogged-up mirror, wrapped in a white cotton towel, swaying her hips in a little dance as she bent over the sink brushing her teeth. I was paralyzed in the doorway watching her. Her hair was piled on top of her head, and a few loose strands spilled down the creamy skin of her neck. The glass enclosure beaded with the remnants of her shower, and I wanted to kick myself for not getting here sooner. I would've loved to join her, all that skin, wet and hot under my fingers. I swore under my breath but it was loud enough to get her attention.

She jumped, dropping her toothbrush to the counter and spun toward me. Stevie's hand shot to the hem of her towel as she tried to draw it closed. Her eyes were big and alarmed as her round cheeks stained with pink. It took her a second to catch a breath, to realize it was only me, and she exhaled. A slow smile worked its way to her dimples.

"Hey," I managed to say as I swallowed.

My worries about being late, about not meeting her at the airport, faded as my gaze indulged in a deliberate perusal of her body. She obviously didn't mind, standing here in a towel, too small to cover her full hips. She licked her lips. The pupils of her eyes blown wide as she silenced the music playing from her phone.

"You seriously almost gave me a heart attack."

"I'd say I was sorry, but..." I took a step into the bathroom, and then another, closing the distance.

"But you're not." My fingers spread the towel open a little more. Her breath stuttered as my hands slid along her bare rib cage and down to her hips. "Your hands are cold."

"Mmm." I hummed as I brought my lips to her cheek, her jaw, and as she tilted her head to the side, I placed open-mouthed kisses to the decadent dip of her neck. "I'm glad you're here."

"I hope it's okay I showered? Five hours on a plane—"

I kissed her lips not meaning to interrupt her, but I was greedy, enjoying the taste of mint and something just Stevie. Her flesh puckered under my fingertips as my hands explored her curves. She wrapped her arm around my neck and the towel fell to the floor. Lucky me. My hand trekked a path up and down her back before I palmed her ass. Her quiet moan sent a pulse down to my groin, my hips driven by need, seeking friction, pressed against her.

She leaned back with a deep breath, her eyes centering me as she said, "I'm kind of nervous."

I cupped her cheeks with my palms and her hands trailed down my chest, resting above my thundering heart. "Don't be." My thumbs brushed along the satin skin of her jaw. "This weekend... I wanted you here with me, I wanted time with you, but we don't have to—"

"I want to." She laughed, a deep blush rising in her cheeks. "We practically did the last time. I guess, I'm worried that if it's not what you expect, or.... It's not like I can head home after." She dipped her eyes to my mouth, gravity building, pulling, feeding that light feeling in my stomach.

"All I want to do is take care of *you*, make you feel good. Stevie, I'm a guy, and fuck, just looking at you is doing it for me, I'm easy."

She pressed her forehead into my chest, her hands slipping under the hem of my shirt. Her fingers exploring the ridges of my stomach, and when she leaned back, her kissable lips parted into a shaky smile. "You have on way too many clothes."

I dropped the hold I had on her and grasped the collar of my shirt at the back of my neck, pulling it over my head. Stevie's eyes skated over every inch of my chest and my arms. My smile was cocky as she reached for the waistband of my joggers. I clutched her waist, drawing her in for a deep kiss, only breaking the rhythm to utter a low and breathless command, "Bedroom."

Without hesitation, I took her mouth, our lips seeking and fighting and tasting as I lifted her effortlessly by the hips. She squeaked out a giggle as her thighs gripped my hips, and I walked us both, our mouths fused as one, to the bed. Her fingers were tangled in my hair as she lowered her legs. Stevie's feet found the floor and her hands were desperate as they fell down my neck, past my chest, and under my waistband. I growled as she touched the tip of my dick with her fingers. She raked my bottom lip through her teeth as the pad of her thumb swept across the head. My fingers dug into the flesh of her hips, breaking my hold long enough to shrug down my pants and underwear.

Seconds later, my clothes were kicked to the side along with my shoes. I let my gaze fall between us. The hard edges of my body seemed to fit along the soft curves of hers. Taking her wrist, I lifted her hand and let her arm fall to the side. I tickled a path of goose bumps along the length of both of her arms before I backed her into the edge of the mattress. She tried to reach up and touch me, but I had other ideas.

"Lie down for me."

I admired the marked way her chest had begun to rise and fall as she raised her hands and pulled the black elastic from her hair. Chocolate waves fell over her shoulders as she sat on the bed. She slowly moved to the center, and holy fuck, she watched me with dark eyes, her lip pinned in her teeth, wanting. *Want.* I had the urge to grab my dick and stroke away the ache she'd easily created inside me. She was fucking perfect, cream against the white of the blanket, and I wanted to feel the solid plane of my stomach sink into the curve of hers. I crawled over her body, pushing my knee between her legs. I held my weight, placing both hands on either side of her head. I tipped my lips to hers and her hot breath washed over me as her tongue swept across the seam of my mouth. Drinking her in, we kissed like there was no end to this day, like the sun would never set, and tomorrow's game wasn't looming. I ignored my sore muscles from my grueling practice. She made all that shit disappear as she lifted her hips, the skin of her belly brushing against mine.

"Fuck, you're so soft." I bit the tender skin of her ear lobe. I moved my mouth down her body, leaving kisses until I'd found what I'd been craving since I'd left Tampa. Desire pulled and pushed and I couldn't help but bury my tongue between her legs with hurried licks. Stevie's fingers twisted into the curled strands of my hair as she moaned my name. "Oh God, Mark, I'm—"

She went off like the firecracker she was, panting, and writing under my touch. Watching her come, feeling her body give itself over to me, she was loose limbs and quaking breaths, and I questioned how any man could've denied her this. I kissed her and she licked the taste of herself from my lips. My jaw clenched as she whispered a quiet and satisfied little sound into my ear.

I fell onto my left forearm, my right hand walking the length of her body down to her shaking thigh and grasped the back of it. I wasn't gentle as I hiked her leg up, allowing my body to fall into hers. She whimpered as I pressed against her. The length of my dick riding the bow of her pubic bone, the stickiness of her arousal brushing along my flesh. I groaned as her nails pulled down my back, our lips wet and sloppy as we both gave ourselves over to the pulsing need between us. Every breath I took was filled with her scent, and I was transported to the night I'd met her. The smell of the ocean in her hair and I was home.

STEVIE

I couldn't stop shaking. Every touch Mark gave me was a shock to my system. I'd never climaxed that fast, and my orgasm lingered over the surface of my skin. I panted as he laid big, bottomless kisses against my lips. His body was a blanket of heat, his soapy, masculine scent covering me. I wanted to bathe in it. I indulged in the weight of his body as he pushed his hips down. The sensation of his hard length pressing between my legs sent shivers over my skin in waves, and I whimpered as his hand brushed across the taut peak of my nipple.

"Mark," I said his name and his light brown eyes fixed on mine.

Gravity and all its principles wouldn't have been able to pull me from his gaze. It was thoughtful, serious, and dark as he scanned my face. Anticipation wound around my fluttering heart.

"I love to watch you come." He spoke in a rich, husky tone that curled my toes. He rolled his thumb over my nipple again and my hips bucked involuntarily. A rumble sounded in his throat as he took the pebbled skin between his lips and sucked. My fingers twisted into his hair as I arched my back, seeking, needing his mouth on my skin. I'd never been so responsive to touch, but with Mark, under his gaze, his fingers, and his lips, I was lit with millions of tiny lights. Everything with him felt multiplied, exponential, like every nerve ending belonged to him. I was the negative to his positive, and when we connected, sparks and feeling linked us together. He placed soft kisses between my breasts as his hand slipped between my legs.

"Mmm," he mumbled against my belly. "So fucking wet."

Two fingers pushed inside me and I rolled my hips, working myself against his hand. I was reaching the edge again, and the muscle in his jaw ticked as I contracted around his fingers.

"Oh God... God... please..." I didn't recognize the lust-filled, almost painful moan that echoed in the room as goose bumps broke across my body.

My fingers gripped his shoulders, my bottom lip trapped between my teeth as my head fell back. Another moan pleaded past my lips when he moved his hand from between my legs. He hovered over me, his lips swollen from our kisses, and even though his cheeks were splotched with pink, he was the epitome of control as he asked, "Please what? Tell me what you want."

Mark skimmed his thumb across my jaw, sweeping a strand of hair from my face, and the words I'd kept narrating inside my head, the sentence I would've never in a hundred years said out loud, tumbled from my needy lips, "I want to feel you inside me."

Mark's pupils flared as he stared at me with heavily hooded brown eyes. He kissed me, his lips moving in sensual waves against mine. After a few seconds, he rested his forehead on my shoulder. He took a few slow breaths and nipped my neck before he rolled off the bed without a word. I watched as his perfectly muscled backside disappeared into the bathroom. Confused I sat up, my heart banging against the confines of my chest. I'd been as vulnerable as I'd ever allowed myself to be...

I heard the tell-tale sound of a condom wrapper being torn open and my stomach dropped. This was happening. This was really freaking happening. It was absurd that I felt like I was losing my virginity for the first time all over again. Mark reappeared from the bathroom with an opened foil packet in his fingers. I had an IUD, but I didn't feel like breaking the mood any more than necessary by discussing bloodwork and birth control.

He knelt in front of me on the bed. His tattoos danced under the light of the sun, the warm buttered yellow glow creating even deeper shadows on his defined abs. I had the urge to run my fingers along the ink, trail them down to the etched V of his hips, and as if he could tell what I was thinking, he lifted my hand.

The room was quiet as I moved to my knees and placed my hand on his chest. I could feel the drum of his heart under my palm, and he closed his eyes as I ran the tips of my fingers down to the sequence of numbers, the coordinates for Manchester. My heart squeezed as I remembered its significance. Mark was becoming more than just the physical fire I'd needed all this time. I really liked him, and this weekend, I was taking a risk, putting myself out there, and as his eyes opened, Mark allowed his steadfast confidence to slip. Vulnerability reflected inside the amber of his irises. I wasn't the only one risking their heart. My stomach danced as he kissed me. His free hand palming the back of my head. Tender lips found their way to my cheek, to my jaw, completing his usual circuit until his mouth was on mine again. His kisses were slow as he teased me with feather light fingertips along my stomach, hips, and thighs. He groaned as I wrapped my hand around his length. He was heavy and hard, and his gentle kisses morphed into deliciously brutal bites and growls. I wanted the aggression. I wanted the Mark who fought his way across the ice. The Mark who came into this hotel room and practically cavemanned me onto the bed.

He grabbed my hips, his hands gliding to the backs of my thighs, kneading the muscle until the limbs around his neck went weak. In one swift movement, he lifted me, and I fell backward into the pillows. I watched without shame, in the bright midafternoon sun, as he rolled the condom over the thick head of his dick. My tongue darted over my bottom lip, and I found myself opening my legs for him. I'd spent too much time in the doll house, the sleepy recesses, allowing myself to think I wasn't worth the effort, worth the heat and flames. But as Mark's lips tipped into a crooked smile, his eyes appraising my body like it was a gift, I remembered what it was like to really feel free.

Mark placed his hands on my knees as he spread my thighs farther apart. His gaze kissed my skin, my breast, his regard scorching every surface as he leaned toward me. Our mouths met as he aligned our bodies. His tongue dipped into my mouth as he pushed the tip of his dick inside me. My fingers gripped his hips and I sucked in a breath.

His lips found my ear as he whispered, "Like this?"

He pushed hard and fast and I cried out as he filled me completely. He groaned and grit his teeth, his jaw pulsing as his eyes locked on mine. I was overflowing. He slid his body slowly from mine, repeating the hard thrust. My thighs ached as he continued his slow assault again and again. I felt every decadent inch of him, and when my eyes closed of their own accord, a flash of heat spilled over my body.

His hot breath was against my ear. "Want me to fuck you like this?" Mark tilted his hips and pushed himself even deeper inside me. "Christ, you feel... too good."

My eyes opened and were met with his desire-addled gaze. His movements came quicker, harder. His rhythm no longer under his control, but driven by the way my body made him feel. Empowered... by the way his eyes begged mine, my legs curled around his hips, my heels digging into the flesh of his ass. He gripped the pillows on either side of my head, the tendons in his neck stretching as the sound of my moans, his grunts, saturated the air. A sheen of perspiration coated our skin as I met each of his strokes with a rock of my hips. His tongue plunged past my lips as we found a disjointed beat. My heart spun as he kissed me once and then again, his head falling to my shoulder, his whispers incoherent as he found his way to the ledge.

Mark's body stilled and he grasped my waist, rolling our bodies as one. I was dizzy and my legs were shaking as I straddled him. For a flash of a second, insecurity cooled my pulse. My belly was on full display, every dimple, every...

"Fuck, babe, don't stop." Mark's voice was desperate as he wrapped a strong hand around my hip, urging me to move with a less-than-delicate touch. His eyes devoured me as he murmured, "So perfect." I tilted forward once and then back again. He groaned, "Shit... just like that."

My hips started to rock and his free hand gently folded around my neck before it slid to my breast. His thumb dusted across the sensitive skin sending a jolt all the way down my body. He lowered his hand, his thumb circling, teasing me between my legs, and when he finally brushed against the right spot, I came undone. My hands fell to his chest, the full feeling inside me—overwhelming as I rode my climax. Mark sat up and kissed me as if he had no other choice, as if I owned his last breath. His hips jerked and he pulled our bodies together by gripping my calves and wrapping my legs around his waist.

My breasts were pressed against his chest, my belly against his stomach as he growled into my mouth. My hands were in his hair, there wasn't an inch separating us when he came. Mark sucked in two erratic breaths, his voice gravel as he groaned, "Stevie..." His fingers pressed roughly into the rounded curve of my backside as he panted curses against my lips, guiding my body, working me against him, he pulled my bottom lip through his teeth. A shuddered pulse of electricity spread through my arms and legs. My lips were trembling when he pulled away. His forehead was creased, his eyes glossed over as he found my gaze. The pad of his thumb traced my upper lip and he kissed the imaginary line he'd drawn with eyes wide open. His kiss soothed the frantic butterflies in my stomach. His hands framed my face as he watched me come down from the high of him. He held us motionless, our bodies connected until our breathing synchronized.

His thumbs ran trails over my cheeks, my jaw, his fingers following suit down my arms, over my thighs and calves, massaging the muscles. When I shivered, he chuckled and planted another sweet kiss on my lips. I let my eyes fall from his, my nose nuzzling in the crook of his neck, inhaling the heady scent of soap, sweat, and sex.

His hand tickled up and down my spine, and I was content to stay like this for the remainder of the day. But the silence was broken by a growl of his stomach, and I laughed into his shoulder.

"You need sustenance?" I asked as I raised my head.

"I don't want to leave this room." His smile was playful. "Fucking ever." He slapped my ass and I jumped. His jaw went tight, his spine rigid. "Holy shit, Stevie, you move like that again, and I'll never let you leave this bed."

"Promise?"

His smirk was boyish as he easily moved me onto my back, pinning me to the mattress. His eyes flicked to the clock on the nightstand. "I still have four hours."

I laughed, but he kissed me quiet. The playful mood evaporated into the smoothed curve of his lips, and for the third time today, I found myself surrendering to the way his mouth commanded my body. Mark drifted the tip of his nose along my collarbone before rolling onto his left forearm. His right palm splayed across my belly as his eyes appraised me. "You are..." His cheeks filled with color. "Fuck, Stevie, I think you've ruined me for other women." I shoved him in the chest and he laughed. "I'm not kidding." His brows dipped and his eyes exposed me. "I'll never say shit I don't mean."

"Okay." I swallowed and brought my fingers to his lips. He kissed them and I rested my palm against the bristled scruff of his jaw. He leaned into my touch as I said, "I've never had sex like that before."

I lowered my hand from his face and raised up onto my elbows as he asked, "What do you mean?"

"Hard... " I swallowed around the weirdly timed lump in my throat. "Eyes open. It felt..." I struggled for the right word. Raw. Gritty. Unhinged. "Real."

His fingers painted circles around my belly button. "Real." He chewed on the word, a frown forming on his lips. "Can I say, I fucking hate that you've ever felt less than real? You're beyond real. I know you were with him for a hell of a long time, but Stevie, you should get to feel everything, to *have* everything you want."

I fought the ache forming in my throat as I whispered, "I'm finally seeing that now."

Mark leaned down, his lips touching mine. "Good, because it's the truth."

He kissed me until the ache in my throat subsided, and the only burn I felt was from the stubble of his chin. He kissed me until I forgot that I'd ever felt like a paper doll, his lips showing me how "beyond real" I was. Mark kissed me until we'd both forgotten to breathe, until our stomachs reminded us that there were needs beyond this bed, until we could no longer overlook the red numbers ticking away on the nightstand clock.

STEVIE

The restaurant host led Stevie and I through the soberly lit main dining room. My hands hadn't left Stevie's body since I'd walked in on her getting out of the shower. I loved touching her, having her heat my skin. Maybe it was the fact I hadn't eaten since breakfast, played hard during practice, and fucked the afternoon away, but I was feeling pretty damn high as heads turned watching us retreat to the private room in the back where my team was sitting.

"They're staring..." she whispered.

"I know." My laugh was low and graveled as I dipped my head. "They're staring at you though."

She met my gaze with big, amber-colored eyes. Stevie looked phenomenal in dark blue, curve-hugging jeans, and a black sweater. The fabric hung low on her left shoulder, exposing smooth porcelain skin. I knew exactly what it was like to taste that skin, how silky she felt against my lips. I wanted to leave a trail of hot kisses along the line of her neck, slip my hand under her sweater, and feel her soft stomach below my fingertips. The blood in my veins sang and pulsed toward my groin. I released her hand only to wrap my arm around her waist, needing to be that much closer to her, and whispered, "You look fucking hot tonight, I don't think I'm gonna make it through this dinner."

She laughed quietly, her delicate chin tipping forward, long chocolate strands of her hair fell with the movement and shielded her face. She pushed the pieces behind her ear and said with a confident smile, "I'm thinking you almost passed out in the shower, you need carbs more than you need me."

She might've been on to something, but I shrugged. "I did not almost pass out." She gave me incredulous eyes, the distinct blue burst flaring as my lips spread into a smirk. "I slipped. It was worth it, though, that angle..."

She slapped my chest, and I heard Bryson's deep laugh over the raucous sounds of my teammates as we entered the back room.

"Finally!" he bellowed.

Some of the guys lifted their eyes, giving me a knowing smile or a nod of the chin. It didn't take them long to avert their attention to the sexy woman on my arm. A few of them furrowed their brows, but the majority of them gave her smiles. Their eager stares lingered over her body more than I would've liked, but it was my favorite assistant coach who greeted us, showing me and Stevie to our seats.

"You brought a guest?" Meyers asked, his smile reaching his eyes.

"I did." I held out my hand and he shook it with a firm grip. "Mitch, this is my girlfriend, Stevie. Stevie, this pain in the ass is in charge of our defense."

Meyers laughed and shook Stevie's hand. "Amongst other things, but no shop talk tonight.... It's nice to meet you." He angled his head to the right, indicating the only other woman in the room. "That's my wife, Carrie, she'll be happy to have a comrade-in-arms for once."

Mitch's wife had been diagnosed with breast cancer a couple of years ago. Once they'd given her the all-clear, and she'd gone into remission, the woman was at every game, road or not. They never had children, and she'd sort of become our road mother in a lot of ways. She was there for me when all the shit went down with Mia, and it shouldn't be my favorite thing about her, but she hated Mia maybe more than I did. She'd told me, "Women who cheat, especially on their hardworking men, deserve a special place in Hades."

Stevie's smile was sweet as she said with a laugh, "Glad to get the chance to meet her, all these men, I'm a little intimidated."

"Don't be, half of these idiots are already salivating over you, they're lambs to be slaughtered," Mitch joked as he led us deeper into the room.

Four long tables hosted the majority of my teammates and were covered with drinks and appetizers. After a quick scan of the room, I noticed not everyone was here, but this didn't surprise me, a lot of the guys preferred peace and quiet before a game. Bryson, who usually preferred the exact opposite, shot me a smart-ass smile from where he sat between Maddox and Rasmussen at the farthest table to the right. The same table Mitch's wife Carrie occupied, and the only table with empty seats. I was proud of my team, my friends. But Bryson could be a dick if he wanted. He was protective of the team, of his friends. Of me. And because I've played alongside him for so long, I saw that edge, the way his eyes played at friendly, but in a faceoff, he'd unravel your game with one glare.

Carrie stood and offered Stevie her signature broad, honest smile introducing herself immediately as Mitch pulled out her chair. Stevie sat down to the left of Carrie, and as I pulled out my own chair, Mitch's mouth split into another smile.

"She's..." Amazing, I wanted to say for him, but didn't because I was sitting across from my line mates and they eyed me like a hawk waiting for me to give them a reason to embarrass the hell out of me. "Nice," Mitch finally said, his eyes tracking a line to where Stevie was now engrossed in conversation with his wife.

I nodded as I took my seat, watching Stevie's cheeks light up in shades of pink. She laughed at something Carrie had said, and knowing Carrie, it must have been something dirty. You couldn't hang out with a bunch of hockey players all the damn time and not have us influence you in some ways.

"Mark," Maddox said by way of greeting, lifting his water glass to his mouth.

"What took you so long?" Bryson asked, knowing damn well what took us so long.

I ignored Rasmussen's snort, and Bryson's dumb fucking smirk and turned my attention to the now silent woman sitting next to me. I reached for her hand under the table, and when she laced her fingers through mine, I exhaled a long, tension-soaked breath. I gave Stevie a crooked grin and started the introductions. She'd already met Bryson at the bar the other night, and when Stevie leveled Rasmussen with her sexy smile, I watched, somewhat shocked, as his bravado fell away. For the first time since arriving in Tampa, Jasper Rasmussen looked his age. Barely over nineteen, the kid talked mad shit, but Stevie apparently had his number.

"Jesus Christ, Jazz, did you just come in your pants?" Bryson asked and I pinched the bridge of my nose.

Coach coughed and Carrie laughed so hard I thought wine would come out of her nose. The room was packed with adults, adults with the maturity level of a raunchy high schooler. It was the giggle that escaped Stevie's lips, the sound like fingers kneading away the knots in my shoulder muscles that had me chuckling as well. Her eyes were open and bright, taking everything in. The rust-colored light of the room made the smooth surface of her face glow. She looked fucking beautiful. I couldn't stop myself from leaning in and kissing her on the cheek, in front of every asshole in this room, I whispered with a smile on my lips a mile wide, "I apologize for nothing."

She turned her head an inch and smiled back at me. "Good, because I won't need one." Stevie scanned the room, her gaze falling to Bryson. "It takes a lot to offend me."

"Thank fuck," Bryson barked, lifting his beer. His smile was genuine when he said, "Welcome to the team."

All the guys sitting at my table pounded their fists on the wood like they would've pounded their blades to the boards for a goal. I thought the attention would've made Stevie shrink, but she sat up straighter, her smile popping into a dimple. She lifted her water glass, reached across the table, and tapped the rim of her glass into Bryson's. I chuckled as I caught Karlsson shake his head with a laugh. "Welcome to the team" was classic Jensen, Captain Showmanship. Bryson's amused eyes met mine, and though it had receded some, a protective shadow hovered. He was giving her a chance. And for him, that was a big step.

The conversations around the table resumed again, and I settled back into my seat as I overheard Carrie whispering to Stevie about the perils of surrounding yourself with hockey players. Stevie let go of my hand, resting her palm on my thigh above my knee. Her fingertips skated figure eights against the denim as she chatted up the assistant coach's wife like she'd known her forever. Stevie fit, seamless, at my side and with my team. The cynic in me argued about *too soon*, and *slow down*, and *stop thinking with your dick*. Valid points or not, I felt better than I had in months. I draped my arm across the back of her chair, letting my fingertips graze her neck every once in a while as I talked plays and strategies with my line mates, loving how she leaned into the touch every time.

After the servers took our order, I'd won Stevie's attention back with a soft kiss to her cheek, and I whispered for about the hundredth time today, "I'm glad you're here."

She pressed her lips together, a shy smile forming as she said, "So it seems."

L.A. had shown up to their house ready to win, and win wasn't even the best word to describe what happened on the ice tonight. Demolish, destroy, they fucking owned our asses. We were shit against the boards, spending more time behind our own blue line than we had all damn season. The few quality scoring chances we'd had were smothered and saved by their impressive display at net minding. After the second period, L.A. had managed three goals while we managed to stay scoreless.

Maddox had paced the locker room during that last intermission, trying hard to keep his cool as he told us we had to be more aggressive on the forecheck, push harder on the boards, get to the net. He'd tried to encourage us, ensuring us we still had twenty minutes of hockey to play, and we were fucking capable of earning back the win. But after the first face-off of the third period, all hell broke loose. Rasmussen allowed himself to get goaded into a fight when one of L.A.'s D-men pancaked him to the plexi. He'd taken the first swing, gotten a minor penalty for roughing, and not more than two minutes into the period, they scored again. Coach's advice had gone in one ear and gotten lost somewhere on the other side. L.A. outmatched us, played a better mental game. Our game? It fell apart. Irritation—desperation—ate its way from our forward line back to the net. They'd shut us out, and we had no one to blame but ourselves.

"What a fucking nightmare," Karlsson groaned and chucked his helmet into the cubby next to mine. He whipped his jersey over his head and threw it violently down onto the floor.

I leaned down to untie my laces, ignoring his tantrum. I'd like to say he'd done the best that he could, but none of us had. Blood dripped down my face from the half-inch-long gash marring my left cheekbone. I'd taken a high stick to the face, and of course, the ref hadn't noticed when it happened. Every damn penalty *we* pulled though...

"Bullshit." I heard someone mutter but kept my eyes trained to the floor as I removed my skates.

I shuffled through my bag looking for my phone. I needed to send my obligatory, "I'll call you later, we lost" text to my sister, and let Stevie know I would head out soon, but the battery had died. Realizing my charger was at the hotel, I zipped up my bag with more force than was necessary as I heard the coaching staff grumbling to one another. Coach would save his speeches for tomorrow, like always, once we were back home. He was a huge proponent of putting a loss behind you as quick as possible, move on, and learn from your mistakes. Maddox had a great mental game, only losing his shit on rare occasions. He and Bryson were a lot alike in that aspect.

"Take this." Bryson handed me a towel. "You're bleeding."

He sank down onto the bench next to me and I stared at the towel. "I'd like to blame your girl for this..." I shot him a warning glare and he laughed. "Calm down, asshole. I was gonna say, *I'd like to*, but we lost this shit all on our own. If anything, you played your best game tonight."

I ran my hand through my sweat-soaked hair and leaned back against the wall. I was still wearing my pads, exhausted, I closed my eyes and sucked in a deep breath. I hadn't thought about Stevie since L.A. scored their first goal. I'd effectively compartmentalized like I always did. And without sounding like an arrogant prick, what Bryson said was true. I had played my best game tonight. I was all over the place, picking up slack when I could, but...

"It doesn't matter when you lose the points, though, does it?" I asked.

Bryson punched my shoulder and I opened my eyes. "It doesn't, but we won two out of three on this trip, and maybe Maddox was on to something at practice this morning with those suggested line changes. I should've listened. I like you as a line mate, we're fucking epic, man, but maybe if he split us up, gave us our own lines like he wanted to try, we'd get more depth."

"You think?"

"Shit, I don't know. Maybe it'll mess everything up, but I think we should at least give it a try. We'll never make it to the playoffs if we can't find a consistency that works."

I wiped the towel across my face and winced as the rough, dry, fabric pulled across the cut. My head pounded, and all I wanted to do was shower and fall asleep next to Stevie's naked body. Our next game wasn't until Tuesday, instead of our normal late-night flight home, we were taking off at the ass crack of dawn.

"That looks like it needs stitches," he said as he stood and removed his shirt.

"I'll see the trainer." I shrugged my shoulders. I'd had worse.

I pressed the fabric firmly against my cheek trying to dull the sting, feeling more aggravated than anything by the delay the small injury would cause. If I had my way, I'd be in the cab riding back to the hotel instead of hanging in a smelly-as-fuck locker room with a bunch of pissed-off dudes.

"Good game tonight, Melo," Bryson said, his tone loaded with sarcasm. I lifted my tired eyes to his. "You deserve a conciliatory blow job."

I choked on my laugh as I threw my bloody towel at his feet. "Christ," was all I could mutter as I stood. Every muscle in my body twisted in the wrong direction, begging for hot water.

"What?" He smirked. "That's what I'm gonna do. I think blow jobs are pretty much a cure-all for everything."

"I thought you said pussy was a cure-all for everything."

Bryson's brows pinched together as his smirk lifted into a smile. "Well, yeah... that, too."

I shook my head even though the thought of being buried inside Stevie had me thinking I could skip the stitches.

Turned out I couldn't skip the stitches. I walked into my hotel room around midnight with four stitches sewn into my cheek, every muscle and bone in my body ached as I let my duffle fall to the floor right by the front door. I moved through the suite with silent steps as I followed the path of light creeping from the bedroom door. The only sound I heard as I carefully pushed it open were even, soft breaths. Stevie was sprawled across the bed wearing absolutely nothing. A groan caught in my throat as I approached her. Slipping off my suit jacket I admired the velvet surfaces of her skin and how the sheet had tangled itself exposing her full tits. The light from the bathroom was on, illuminating the dusky pink of her nipples. My mouth went dry, and I loosened my tie, tonight's game officially forgotten.

I stripped down, leaving a pile of clothes on the floor, and crawled onto the bed. I pressed her back to my chest, my dick—hard—pushed against her ass. A breathy moan, a quiet hmm, and she wiggled against me.

"It's late," I whispered, pressing kisses below her ear.

She rolled her head to the side and gazed up at me with sleepy eyes. "I texted you."

"My phone died." I kissed her mouth and she arched her back.

A muted growl formed in my throat and I bit her upper lip. She wrapped her arm around the back of my neck, her fingers running up the nape and twisting my hair as she opened her kiss. Her tongue tasted like mint and it swept and moved in languid strokes. I cupped her breast, and I smiled against her mouth when she shivered.

I lowered my hand to her belly, pressing her hips back into mine. She broke our kiss, breathing heavy, and covered my hand with hers. She guided it between her legs and, holy fuck, she was wet and warm, and exactly where I wanted to be. She was slick against my fingertips as I teased her clit. A long, needy breath passed her lips when I slipped my fingers out from between her legs.

I palmed her knee, sliding my hand down a few inches. Not a word was said as she bent her knee, feeling my touch, knowing what I wanted, she lifted her leg. Her back to my chest, I reached down between us, aligning myself with her body. The muscles in my stomach contracted as I slid inside her. She was hot against my skin, her arousal pouring over me, dragging me in deeper and, without thinking, my body sought what it needed.

I dropped my lips to her neck, my teeth taking small purchases of her flesh as she ground herself against my every thrust, tight grunts of praise shuddered past my lips as I fucked her, lost myself inside her. My right arm was wrapped under her, around her, holding her in place. My left hand and its fingers occupied again with the sweet sensitive flesh between her legs. She exploded around me, her climax coaxing mine. It started at the base of my spine. My jaw clenched, my forehead falling onto her shoulder as I fought it, trying to hold on. Her body was too good, and I didn't want to stop. I slowed each thrust until she begged me to fuck her, to move faster, to go harder, until I could no longer take my self-imposed torture.

"Fuck, I'm gonna come," I growled into the crook of her neck as my hips lost their rhythm, as my mind cleared, and all I could feel was the heat of my release as I let go inside her.

We were both catching our breath, sweat beading on my brow as I kissed her shoulder. Being skin-to-skin with Stevie in every way was heaven. Yesterday, after she'd told me she had an IUD, we both decided condoms were no longer necessary. Feeling Stevie come, without any barriers, I was fucking hooked.

I leaned back, reluctantly breaking away from her body. She rolled to her other side, facing me. We kissed slow and deep, and when I felt myself getting hard again, I nipped her lip and chuckled.

I took her hand in mine and lowered it to my burgeoning erection. "See what you do to me."

She stroked me once and buried her face in my chest.

She lifted her hand to my heart as she tipped her head, bringing her eyes to mine. She gasped and raised her brows. "Oh my God, what happened to your face?"

Stevie raised her trembling fingers as if to touch my stitches and then thought better of it, letting them fall below the gash.

"It's nothing," I assured her and kissed the tips of her fingers.

"Mark, that's not nothing." She elevated her weight onto her elbow and my eyes trailed down to the sweeping slopes of her breasts. She playfully pushed my chest. "Can you concentrate for a second and tell me what happened?"

"Hockey happened." She rolled her eyes and I smiled. "The game was shit, their guys were rougher than we were, we lost, and I got stitches... overall, these last twenty minutes, highlight of my night."

"Getting laid being the highlight of your night over a horrible loss isn't really a compliment."

I placed another kiss, unable to help myself, between her furrowed brows. Tiny creases around her eyes formed as she smiled. Instead of aging her, the laugh lines made her look younger.

"Horrible loss? We've had worse."

"Will it get easier watching you lose?" she asked, tracing her nails along the ridges of my stomach and back up to my chest.

My lips found hers as I tried to persuade her away from this line of conversation. Her fingers fisted in my hair and I guided her down onto the mattress.

"Don't want to talk about it, huh?"

I shook my head with a flippant smile as I let her thighs box in my hips. "Talk about what?"

She narrowed her eyes, her mouth tipping into a smirk, her hands gliding down my ribcage and over the solid curve of my ass. "The game."

My lips surrounded the tight peak of her nipple, my tongue tasting the tip. The silk of her skin grazed my taste buds and my mouth watered. I watched her lids fall and hood her eyes as I asked, "What game?"

STEVIE

The water I'd set to boil on the stove was about to brim over the edge of the pot when I heard three hard and familiar knocks on my front door. I turned the heat down to medium and set the box of bowtie pasta on the kitchen island. I'd only gotten home from work about twenty minutes ago, enough time to pour myself a glass of wine and decide that I was going to stress eat an entire box of pasta. My heels clicked across the hardwood floor of my living room as I made my way to the door. Seeing his face, having his hands on my body, even if it was only for five minutes, made the carbs I'd planned to over consume almost unnecessary.

He was everything that was sexy and masculine standing in his gray tailored travel suit. His shoulders filled the doorway, his clean scent mixed with the humid, slightly chilled Florida winter air and, as I inhaled it, the stress of what I had to face next week vanished.

"Hey," he said with the smile that always seemed to send the butterflies in my stomach into a whirling frenzied flight. He stepped over the threshold and into the house, leaning down, kissing my lips gently, pulling away, and then dipping in again for another. We probably would've stood in the entryway, door slung open and making out if Atlas hadn't whined. A reminder of why I was lucky to have Mark stop by before catching his flight to Buffalo.

I laughed, scrubbing my hand over the top of Atlas's huge head. "He misses you already."

Mark shut the door before he dropped the leash to the floor and Atlas trotted toward the kitchen dragging it behind him, most likely, looking for the food and water dishes I set out for him on occasions such as this.

"Thanks for watching him." Mark's fingers threaded into my hair as he cradled the back of my head, his thumbs resting on my jaw.

"I don't mind. You should know that by now. I've got the little fella handled."

Mark's mouth broke into a crooked smile. "You know, he told me he hates it when you call him, Little Fella."

I puffed out a laugh. "Oh, he did?"

"Yeah, I think he prefers Big Guy, Stud, something less emasculating." I tried to argue, to tell him I was being ironical by calling his Great Dane "Little Fella," but he kissed me instead. He kissed me until he groaned again. "I hate long road trips."

After Mark and I had gotten back from our L.A. weekend in October, we'd been able to balance our relationship pretty well. The road trips sucked and, the longer we were together, the harder it got to say goodbye. I loved watching Atlas because it was like I had a piece of Mark with me while he was gone.

"Me too, but we still have New Hampshire." I pressed my mouth to his, softly dragging out the moment, and he lowered his hands to my hips. "Do you think it will snow?" I asked.

He hummed against my lips. "My mom said she's already got a foot or more this past week."

His mom. I licked my lips, my nerves bubbling in my stomach. Mark invited me to go home with him for Christmas, and as excited as I was, I was also teetering on the brink of panic with a side dish of scared-as-hell. Meeting the parents was big. "Monumental" according to Reagan. His sister Molly and I were almost the same age. I'd gotten over my insecurities about our seven-year age difference after I realized Mark and I, when it came to maturity levels, were right on par. He was smart and had a great head on his shoulders. He ran his career impeccably, worked hard, and treated me like a queen. But I worried what his mother thought about the age difference, if she was protective over her son after what Mia had done to him, if she'd think I was dating him because of his money, or if she wanted grandkids I'd never provide. We'd only been dating since October, and Christmas was almost two weeks away. We hadn't been together long enough for her to be thinking about grandkids, right?

Mark's chuckle pulled me from my downward spiral. "Stop overthinking."

He squeezed his grip on my hips, and I ran my hands up his chest, the smooth fabric of his shirt fit snug across the muscles. "You don't even know what I was thinking about."

He lifted one incredulous brow in challenge. A challenge he won every time. Mark knew what I was thinking. He always did. I'd fallen for the fact the man read me like an open book. Ben never had... My smile dimmed. *Ben.* He'd be here on Tuesday. Suddenly, I was craving carbs again and the opened bottle of wine on my kitchen counter.

He tipped my chin up with his finger. His light brown eyes were serious as he said, "My family is harmless. I promise."

He was talking about his family, but my mood had digressed for other reasons. Reasons he hated to talk about. It was after the same trip to L.A. when I'd told Mark about Ben coming to town to help out with the audit. At first, he was understanding. I'd told him I didn't have to work with Ben one-on-one. I think it helped that Mark had sensed how much I really didn't want Ben here, but after I'd mentioned he'd be here for three whole months, he'd gone silent. I'd watched with anxiety as the emotions moved across his features. Irritation, anger, jealousy.

We'd been at his place, standing in his kitchen, when I'd wrapped my arms around his waist, set my cheek on his chest and said, "Ben is my past." He'd rested one of his big palms on the middle of my back, the other holding my head. I knew Mark better now, and his silence that night was his way of processing. We've had a few disagreements since then, and I'd seen him get into it with Bryson enough to know, when Mark went quiet, it meant he needed a minute. He wasn't a guy who went off on a yelling spree, and he wasn't like Ben, analytically deconstructing every possible reason for why the argument happened in the first place. No, Mark was purely passionate, in everything, so when he went inside himself, he was really pissed off. Looking back, though, he'd handled it well, even if he never mentioned it again.

Right before a road trip probably wasn't the best time to remind him that my ex-husband would be here next week, but I wanted to always be honest with him. He deserved that, and maybe my distaste for the entire situation could give him some peace of mind while he was away. I sucked in a breath for strength as I met his cinnamon-colored eyes.

"I'm nervous to meet your family, but I'm excited to spend some time with you, away from here, away from *work*." Mark didn't miss the way I emphasized the word work, the pulse in his jaw was almost undetectable. But having spent almost all of my free time with him, his tells had become more apparent. In any other situation, I might've smiled. I was able to read him as well as he was able to read me. "Ben will be here Tuesday. That's four days. How is it already that time?"

Time sped by too quickly when I was tangled in Mark's arms. My life before, my time with my ex, it had been an eternity. Being with Mark was like riding in a speeding car. Every moment, every curve was fast. Touch, and kisses, and feeling. We had to fight for our minutes. We used each second we were gifted with to the max. We owned the furious sound of the clock because we had no other choice. Our time together was limited, so we made it precious.

"Tuesday." He sighed, dropping his hands and pushing them into his pockets.

I nodded. "Hurry home, alright?"

I slipped my arms around his neck and kissed him. The firm set of his lips gave way to the softness of my own. He'd recently trimmed his beard, and when I kissed the smooth dip of his bottom lip, he relaxed completely. The hands I craved rested on either side of my neck, and I tipped my head back, letting him deepen our kiss. A quiet beep sounded and a growl rumbled in his throat. I recognized the sound of the alarm he'd set on his watch so he'd never be late to the bus or to a flight.

He rested his forehead against mine, tugging a strand of my hair between his thumb and fingers. "I hate that he's going to see you more than I get to."

His honesty hung in the air between us and my heart beat twice, hard and slow, before it dropped into my stomach. Mark pressed a kiss between my furrowed brow and my throat clogged. Our relationship had settled into a comfortable pattern, like a pair of brand-new shoes, we'd begun to wear each other in. Sure, I didn't like it when he was gone, but I usually dealt with it and moved on. But there was no mistaking the way my throat ached and tapered as the heat of his kiss evaporated from my skin. I didn't want to spend more time with Ben than I did with Mark. Ben had already stolen enough of my heartbeats. I hated that Mark wasn't going to be home until late Tuesday night, and I'd have to deal with my first day with the ex on my own. I hated that Ben was swooping into my new life and screwing everything up. My nostrils flared as I fought the sudden wave of sadness.

"I have to go," he said, and I wanted to pull myself against him, keep him here with me.

My arms fell to my sides and the need to reach out to him sent a weird tingling sensation to my fingertips. "For the record..." I forced a smile. "I hate it, too."

The front door had shut with a slow click after he'd kissed me goodbye one last time, the feel of him lingered on my lips, the sound of Atlas's nails clack, clack, clacking on the hardwood did nothing to slow my breathing. Each breath was painful, scorching my lungs as I pressed my back to the front door, and for the first time since Mark and I had become a couple, I cried. Hot tears spilled down my cheeks as Atlas licked my hand. I sputtered out a watery laugh and sank to the floor. I was usually so good about not missing him too much.

Atlas plopped his large body on top of my thighs. "We can do this," I declared as I wiped my fingers over my cheeks. Atlas's tail thumped back and forth against the floor. "We do it all the time." I assured myself and it was true.

I'd actually told my mom the other day I thought the road trips were a good thing. We hadn't even been together three months, and maybe the distance was healthy, and the whole "absence makes the heart grow fonder business" worked for us. When Mark and I were together, we never stopped touching, and when we were apart, his absence became an exposed nerve.

I allowed myself and Atlas the right to mope for five more minutes before I stood up. Atlas yawned as I pulled my arms behind my back, stretching out my muscles. "Should we eat our feelings, Little Fella?"

His expression was eager, and I thought to myself, Mark had it all wrong. Atlas loved his nickname. "Come on."

I'd settled into my third glass of wine, a belly full of food and happiness when my phone rang. The name on the screen surprised me. I accepted the call and his voice turned the two bowls of pasta I'd eaten into a brick inside my stomach.

"Hello," I said and wished I'd spoken with a bit more strength.

"It's good to hear your voice."

We hadn't spoken at all after Ben had gone back to Richmond, and I didn't know how to respond. His voice was familiar and yet awkward in so many ways. The silence was only interrupted by the sound of his breathing. My words caught in my throat.

"How are you?" he asked.

"Good…" I found my voice. "Really good, and you?"

"I'm…" His stiff chuckle had guilt vining its way around my lungs. "I'm okay."

He exhaled a rough sigh, the sound spilled memories through the phone, and I closed my eyes. I could picture him in our old kitchen, sitting on the metal bar stool, his thick brows creased with frustration as I told him I was leaving, told him I didn't know him anymore, told him I felt so alone. Was he finally feeling it too, the emptiness I'd worn for so long?

"Listen… I wanted to call… I wanted to let you know I was flying in Monday night."

"Monday," I said, more to myself than as a confirmation.

"Yeah, and I was wondering, if you wanted to get dinner?"

"Ben, I—"

"I don't want…" Another painful-sounding sigh. "We used to be… Stevie, I don't want to avoid you for three months. Friends, right? Isn't that what you said?"

Friends who never spoke. Friends who felt like strangers now.

I opened my eyes and tried to infuse a smile into my tone. "You don't have to avoid me, Ben."

"Okay."

"This is hard for me, too."

"I know," he said, the two words as coarse as gravel. "I almost told Trent no."

"He told me."

"He did?" Ben laughed, and the tension unlatched its hold on my muscles.

"Yeah, I think he likes me better than you. I bring him donuts on Wednesdays," I teased.

"I'll have to remember that." Silence fell again, and I heard him swallow before he asked, "Have dinner with me... for old times' sake?"

"I'm seeing someone."

"The hockey guy?"

"His name is Mark."

"It's not a date, *Stevie*." The way he said my name, like I was a five-year-old, dredged up the past and left a sour taste on my tongue.

"I know, but maybe another time. It's an adjustment... having you here. Things are... different."

"Different," he repeated.

I rested my palm against my forehead and took a deep breath. "Let's get through Tuesday and we'll see."

I tried not to feel guilty for saying, *get through*, but I had to be real, had to set the boundaries. Ben had always been good at managing my feelings away like they didn't matter. I wouldn't let him do that to me again.

"I'll see you Tuesday, then."

We both hung up without saying goodbye and I stared at my phone. Atlas nudged my elbow with his cold nose. Bulldozing his massive head onto my lap. I opened my text messages, Ben's call withering away my good mood, and typed out a message to the only person who could make me smile right now. His phone was most likely turned off, his flight to Buffalo had left an hour ago, but I swiped my fingers across the screen anyway.

ME: *I miss you.*

ME: *A lot.*

I wasn't needy by nature, and I hoped my messages didn't make him feel bad. Being away was part of his job, and I was on board for the ride. On some nights, though, especially tonight, it was harder to find my inner cheerleader. Pulling up my big girl pants, I typed out one last text, my lips breaking into the first genuine smile I'd had since Mark had walked out my front door today.

ME: *One more thing...*

ME: *Atlas said you're a liar, he loves his nickname.*

STEVIE

The office had all gotten together to show Ben a warm welcome Monday night, even though he didn't officially start until Tuesday. I, of course, had declined Trent's invitation to dinner just as quick as I'd said no to Ben when he'd called and asked. I'd opted to stay in and mope instead, wishing Mark could've been here to make Ben's first day more bearable. Needless to say, I'd only successfully dodged one bullet, to step right in front of another one this morning. I was running late, which never happens, and I was forced to pile my damp hair on top of my head. I'd attempted a messy bun with my favorite red chopsticks, but looked more like a spinster than Mark's idea of a sexy librarian. The navy blue polka dot blouse I had on had come untucked on the drive over to the office, and to make matters worse, I hadn't slept well. There hadn't even been enough time to cover my dark circles with a quick dusting of powder.

A deep sigh parted my lips. I shouldn't care what Ben thought of me anymore, but there was some weird, superficial recess of my personality that had hoped to stroll into the office today, shoulders rolled back like "look what you threw away." Unfortunately, all I had to work with was disheveled, frumpy, and slightly wrinkled. At least my coffee was hot, I thought, as I walked into the lobby. I waved to David who smiled at me like a cat, his fingers tented under his chin. Poised and ready for all the interoffice drama Ben and I might cause. I pursed my lips and gave him the finger.

"Stevie!" he gasped and I giggled, waving over my shoulder as I headed to my office door.

I balanced my coffee in my left hand, the same hand that held my chocolate croissant. My head was down when I walked into my office, my right hand busy digging into the bag and grabbing my breakfast. I smiled once I'd managed to snatch it between my two fingers, carefully removing the heated pastry. I lifted it to my lips, the sting of the hot melted chocolate causing me to hiss and curse under my breath. A quiet laugh, one I knew very well, had my eyes darting to my desk.

"Didn't mean to scare you," Ben said as he unfolded his long legs and stood.

I could feel the heat of the chocolate dripping down my fingers as I stared a few seconds longer than I would've liked. "You didn't," I finally managed to articulate.

His calm smile was unsettling. He didn't look much different, except that his face had thinned, his cheeks and jaw were sharper than I remembered, and his eyes a bit more tired. The gray color of his irises assessed me, as well. His mouth twitched as if he was about to say something as he watched me fumble the few things I had in my hand.

I breezed past him before he had a chance to speak, ignoring his familiar cedar scent and how it conjured nostalgia and tension at the same time. I set my coffee on my desk, almost spilling it. My purse and the bag I carried my laptop in slid down my right shoulder and onto the floor by my desk chair. I held the croissant between my teeth, aware I had no dignity left, and fished the napkins from the bag. I used one to wipe the gooey mess off my fingers and the other I laid out on my desk, taking a big bite of the pastry before setting it down on my makeshift plate.

"You still hate mornings?" he asked, and the smile in his voice drew my eyes to his.

"Am I that obvious?"

He swallowed. "You always did."

Ben's eyes swept over my hectic appearance, his smile growing wider, and I didn't like how he appraised me, like he had the right to, like he thought he still knew me. He may have had the histories of my smaller details, but he'd forgotten who *I* was a long time ago.

He slid his hands into the pockets of his black slacks. The color of his suit reflected in his cold eyes as he said, "You look good."

I averted my gaze and shifted, uncomfortable under his scrutiny. I held my hand steady as I pulled at the untucked portion of my blouse, instilling as much humor in my tone as I could around the growing ache in my throat. "Oh, yeah, I'm channeling my inner supermodel today."

A movement in my peripheral vision caught my attention. He was running his hand through his sandy blond mop of hair, his mouth curling at the corners.

"Did you need something?" I asked and my curt tone dropped his smile.

He slowly shook his head, his hands deep in his pockets again. "No... I—"

My phone started to ring and I bent down to grab it from inside my bag. Mark's name was on the caller ID. My eyes shifted to Ben and then back to the phone. "I need to take this."

"Give me five minutes, Stevie."

The bite I'd taken of my croissant churned inside my stomach as my phone went silent. That might've been the only chance I would have to talk to Mark today until after his game. Frowning, I exhaled and gently tossed my phone onto the desk.

"I'm going to be here for three months."

"I'm aware."

I didn't miss the irritated noise that rumbled in Ben's throat. "I want us to be civil, a chance to be friends again."

I wanted to tell him we hadn't really been friends since college. I raised an eyebrow. "Now you want to be friends?"

"I've always been a friend to you."

"You haven't, you weren't there for—"

"I was building our business." He raised his voice.

My eyes started to sting, my throat contracted painfully as I said, "*Your* business, it was never mine."

"Stevie, damn it, I..." Voices of the office staff sailed in through my open door from somewhere close by and Ben lowered his voice, took a tentative step, rubbing the back of his neck. "I don't want to fight."

Those resigned eyes only made it harder for me to hold back my own tears. I stared at him, two, three, four seconds, until I found my nerve and the air I needed to speak. "I don't want to fight either."

He cleared his throat, his smile small and sad. "Can we do this?"

My heart stuttered.

He'd asked me that same question on our wedding day. The officiant had said, "I now pronounce you husband and wife," and Ben had leaned in and asked me, "Can we do this?" I'd replied, "It's too late." Back then Ben had been my whole world, and his smile, everything a nineteen-year-old girl could've ever wanted. Today, the sentiment hurt, and made me angry I'd wasted so much time on a man who only ever loved himself.

"It's three months..." I gave him a steady smile even though I was feeling like a cracked branch in a thunderstorm. "I can be a professional, if you can."

Ben's stature seemed to wither. "Of course, I can."

"Then everything should be fine."

He nodded, taking a step backward.

"If you'll excuse me..." I lifted my cell phone. "I have to return this call."

He hesitated, his lips tipping up on one side. "You'll be at the meeting?"

I exhaled a shaky breath. "Yup." My smile was genuine when I said, "You'll want a double shot of espresso. Mr. Elm loves to hear himself talk."

"Thanks for the tip."

He turned to leave and his back was facing me when my phone rang in my hand. Ben hadn't made his way completely out of my office, but I didn't want to chance missing the call. With nervous fingers, I hit accept and breathed in the rich, calming tone of Mark's voice. "Hey."

Maybe it was the overwhelming morning I'd already had, but a lump formed in my throat, my voice scratchy and worn as I whispered, "God, I really wish you were here today, Mark."

I raised my eyes and found Ben's still form in the doorway. A seed of guilt sprouted, but died just as quickly when he walked away. This was good, I told myself. I had moved on, and he needed to see me living my life—without him.

Tuesday turned into Wednesday without any more awkward incidents. True to Trent's word, I'd seen very little of Ben so far. Except for the office meeting, and the weird run-in inside my office, I'd not seen Ben at all. It was almost one, and I was trying my best to tick off the last few things on my to-do list so I could get out of here early. Mark was due back in town today, and I needed to go grocery shopping for the dinner I'd planned to make for him tonight. It had sort of become my way of welcoming him back from the road. A home-cooked meal, wine, and hopefully lots of sex. Sometimes sex came first, but I wasn't complaining.

I'd finished emailing an invoice to one of my clients when my boss and Ben trailed into my office.

"Gotta second?" Trent asked, laying two large folders down onto my desk.

Ben nodded his head in a silent hello. My gaze hastily slid to Trent as I asked, "What's up?"

It was Ben who answered, "If you have time this week, I could really use your help going through these expense reports our client sent over today."

"Apparently," Trent shot Ben an irritated look, his voice more authoritative than normal as he continued, "There were four files sent, Mr. Elm thinks our team is moving too slowly, and I thought—"

"*I thought* you'd get some great experience working on this portion of the audit," Ben interrupted and Trent rolled his eyes.

"I know you're loaded down already, Stevie, but..." Trent wet his lips and it made me antsy. "I think Ben's right..." He winced when I frowned. "We could really use your help."

I wanted the experience, and I could work on this and maintain a healthy distance from my ex. Honestly, having him here hadn't been as bad as I'd thought, and Ben was at least trying to be a friend to me by offering me this opportunity. Maybe this was his white flag.

"Sure."

"Really?" Trent asked.

He was so conscious of Ben. On Tuesday, he'd asked me if everything was going okay. He'd called me at home to make sure I'd felt comfortable, stating that David had told him I'd been quiet at lunch. It was good to know Trent was looking out for me.

"I don't mind at all. Leave the files, and I'll get started on them first thing tomorrow."

"You're a lifesaver." Trent's smile was less anxious as it stretched across his face.

Ben's smirk was smug as he fit his hands into his pockets. "I told you she'd say yes."

"Say yes to what?" His deep voice cut through the room and I could've sworn my heart had grown wings.

Mark leaned on the frame of the door, his dark hair falling over his forehead. His t-shirt snug on his biceps and pulled tight over his shoulders as he crossed his inked arms over his chest. Trent and Ben turned at the same time I stood, my smile like a reel of film, unwinding itself in slow clicks until it met my eyes.

"You're here?" My voice was a gauzy whisper.

Mark's full lips tipped into sexy dimples as he ignored everyone else in the room and locked his eyes on mine. "I didn't want to wait till tonight."

It was a private moment with public eyes and I suddenly felt raw. Mark pushed off the door frame and held out his hand to Trent. "Good to see you again."

"Great game last night, Toronto is a tough club to beat." My boss still had moon eyes for Mark whenever he came to the office.

I made my way around the desk as Mark said, "It got pretty greasy in the final period, but we got the win." Mark's friendly gaze clouded into a stoic mask as he held out his hand to my ex-husband. "It's Ben, if I remember correctly?"

My ribcage squeezed against my lungs as Ben said, "Yeah." The word was clipped and Ben's spine went stiff as he took Mark's hand and shook it. "Stevie introduced us back in October, you're the guy who plays games for a living."

Oh God. *Games for a living?* I wanted to crawl into a hole with how rude his statement was. I sidled in next to Mark and he draped his arm around my waist. His hand firmly gripping my hip. Ben's gaze fell to the connection and his eyes narrowed.

Mark released Ben's hand with a chuckle. The sound of it was off, and because I knew him so well, I was the only one who noticed. "Game," he corrected. "And it's the best fucking one there is."

Ben's mouth pursed, never a fan of swearing, in general. "I suppose that's a matter of opinion. I've always found hockey to be overly violent."

"It's not for the weak-hearted, that's for sure." Mark tilted his head, his crooked grin giving me goose bumps as he set the full weight of his gaze on me. "I've turned Stevie into quite the fan."

Mark leaned down, his mouth hovering over mine for a half of a second, his eyes asking for forgiveness before he brushed his lips against me. My body warred against what it wanted and what was right. Ben wasn't my husband anymore, but I didn't want to hurt him, and this... this kiss was like parading my joy down his side street of misery. Mark's mouth pressed against mine for the shortest of kisses, and when I looked at Ben again, I saw something in his eyes I'd never seen before. Jealous anger brewed inside the gray storm of his irises.

Trent coughed before he said, "Good to see you again as always, Mark."

Mark nodded his chin. "Yeah..." He let go of my hip to thread his fingers through mine. "You, too."

"Come find me if you need help with those expense reports," Ben said to me with a tight jaw, before walking out of my office without a second glance at Mark.

Once the door was securely shut, I spun on my heel and smacked Mark in the chest. "What the hell was that?"

He laughed and the sound untied my nerves. "He was being a dick."

"Still." I couldn't help the smile that tugged on my lips. Mark was here, and I'd missed him so much, more than I was used to. He pulled me into his body, his arms snaking around me. I exhaled and relaxed into his touch. "We should take the higher road. Ignore him, Mark, because all that matters to me is you."

Mark pressed his lips to the top of my forehead, his nose burying itself in my hair. I smiled as he inhaled. "I missed this," he whispered against my skin.

"Me, too." I placed my hands on his chest and felt the hard and fast beat of his heart.

Desire poured down my limbs as his hands gripped my waist. He pulled back, his eyes consuming me from head to toe. "You look hot in this dress... like a pin-up girl."

I never knew how to take his compliments. They set me on fire, made me feel more confident than I ever had in my life, but speechless all the same. I was wearing a forest green dress I'd found at a vintage store in Ybor. It was short sleeved, the neck line dipped to show a little cleavage, but nothing too saucy. The material flowed out into an A-line from the thin, black patent leather belt that cinched in my waist. It was cute and simple, definitely not sexy, but Mark was eating it up. "You're thinking about your weird librarian fantasy right now, aren't you?"

He raised his hand and unlatched the clip that held up my hair and put it in his pocket. The waved strands tickled my neck as they fell around my shoulders. "Maybe," was all he said as he walked me backward until my butt hit the desk.

"Mark," I warned, but I could admit it was a thin threat.

"Hmm?" His hands framed my face, his eyes hooded with lust and five nights' worth of distance. "I need to kiss you."

His lips lowered and dusted my cheek, my chin, his lips pressing to the hollow below my lower lip. A soft moan fell from my lips at the rough touch of his stubble. His hands slid down my hips, turning me abruptly. My back hit his chest as he inched the fabric of my dress into his fingers. I felt the cool air of the office on my legs and the warmth of his breath on my neck as I grasped the edge of my desk. His left hand held my hip, his right holding the hem of my dress in his fist. He pushed against me, the wood of the desk digging into the top of my upper thighs.

"This desk," he mumbled, his lips brushing gently down my jaw, his teeth at my ear. "I want to fuck you, right here."

His hand slipped under my dress and I grabbed his wrist. This didn't feel right. I wanted to turn around, face him, feel his gentle eyes on mine, feel the slow heat of his gaze and let it drown me like it always did. "We... can't."

His hot breath coated my skin and I shivered as he spoke. His voice was unraveled, "Let me touch you."

My cheeks stained with need and I let go of his wrist. I twisted my body, wanting to face him. My eyes flicked to my unlocked door and a fearful excitement hammered my heart against my sternum. Insecurity peaked and mixed with adrenaline. I wanted his hands on me, but not here. I wanted to be back at my place.

Mark's thumb slid below the seam of my underwear, and he groaned as my arousal wet the tip of it. "Christ," he whispered and nipped the lobe of my ear.

His hand was between my legs, my fingers twisted in his shirt as he melted our mouths together in lazy strokes. The kiss heightened from his familiar sweet, to smoke and cinders. Voices in the hall stilled my lips and Mark smiled against them as he dipped his fingers beneath the cotton of my underwear. I moaned involuntarily and the voices in the hall went silent.

"Oh my God," I whispered and grabbed his wrist, pulling it away. Mark's grin was salacious and it pissed me off. "Do you think they heard me?"

He chuckled as he lifted his big hands to my hips. "I hope so."

"Why would you say that?" I tried to wriggle out of his hold but he pulled me closer.

His laugh was gentle. "I'm sorry. I guess I got carried away."

My cheeks were hot with aggravation and embarrassment. "What if that was Trent... oh my God, or worse Mr. Elm. I could lose my job, Mark."

His mouth broke into a smile. "You're fired up."

My eyes narrowed into what I hoped was a serious-looking glower. This wasn't funny.

His smile faded and he scrubbed his palm along his jaw. "Shit, I'm sorry, I..." The long line of his throat bobbed. "I fucking missed you, and I wanted to surprise you, and *he's* in your office, and I guess... it fucked with my head a little."

"A little?"

His chest rose and fell with a long sigh. "I wasn't trying to piss a circle around you, if that's what you're thinking." He lowered his chin, kissed the tip of my nose, and my anger abated.

"Good, because that would be really uncalled for. I'm yours, remember."

"Mine?"

I shook my head, my smile growing slowly. "All yours."

"Can you leave early?" he asked, a little breathless.

I nodded, eager to get home, eager to be with him alone. "I need to grab a few things from the store on the way."

"What are you making?" His light eyes beamed.

I loved that he got excited about his homecoming meals. "Your favorite."

"Grilled cheese?" His brows dipped with disappointment.

I laughed and raised onto my tiptoes, my mouth an inch from his. "Lasagna."

"Fuck yeah."

Mark's mouth fell against my lips, and when he kissed me this time, it felt like him, like a thousand feathers were touching my skin, like always, like home.

MARK

The bar erupted into loud hoots and hollers as the five large-screen televisions played the highlight reel from tonight's game. My teammates were rowdy enough as it was, when you added the cheers of the fans, it was like you were back in the arena all over again. I'd wanted to head back to my place after the game with Stevie, we had an early morning flight to catch, but Bryson had always been a persuasive fucker. He never went home for the holidays, and tomorrow was Christmas Eve. I couldn't help but feel bad for the guy. His mother had passed away when he was little, and his dad, all that man cared about was how much money Bryson made. So when I'd told him I was taking off early, he'd razzed me about being pussy-whipped, but I'd known him long enough I hadn't missed the sad flicker that had crossed his eyes. I'd faltered and now I was sitting at a table with my girl watching Bryson be a drunk asshole.

"Lord, he's a sexy idiot," Reagan said as she set her beer on the table and slid into her seat.

I chuckled. "The idiot part I get."

Stevie giggled and I squeezed her thigh under the table. She was wearing skin tight jeans and the jersey I'd gotten her last week. My jersey. My number. The blue color made her skin glow, and my last name scrolled across her back spoke to the primal rumblings inside my chest. I'd been unsettled ever since Ben had rolled into town and back into Stevie's life. When she'd first told me he was coming, I'd tried to not let it bother me. But it did. It bothered the hell out of me. The green monster Mia had kept well-fed for so long had woken up again, and I was angry with myself for letting the idea of Ben get the better of me. Stevie wasn't Mia.

Stevie's phone vibrated against the table, and as if I summoned him by the mere thought, I watched as the color drained from Stevie's face.

She groaned. "I have to take this."

"What? All the important people you know are at this table," Reagan said with a sarcastic smirk.

Stevie exhaled an irritated breath. "It's Ben. It's probably about the expense reports I gave him to work on while I was gone." She eyed me warily. "Two minutes." She kissed my cheek, and my stiff shoulders relaxed enough I was able to fake my way through a smile.

I winced at the timid way she said, "Hello," before walking toward the back hallway of the bar. Ben changed her. Insecurity fell off her in waves, and it drove me nuts he could make her feel that way with a simple phone call.

"Don't let him get to you," Reagan said, and I turned to look at her.

"That's what Bryson's been saying." I chugged down the rest of my beer and placed the glass onto the table.

"Well, maybe Bryson is smart after all." She gave me a big smile. "Ben's an asshole, has always been an asshole, and will always be an asshole."

"You think?"

"I know." She twirled a piece of her pink hair between her thumb and forefinger. "Stevie has always been... bold ... audacious... and she never knew how gorgeous she was either. I remember in high school, the guys we'd go to punk shows with, they practically drooled all over her dyed red hair and green chucks. She never noticed, always stayed in the friend zone, and then one day, this jerk, some rich prick in her AP math class, asks her out on a date, and she thinks she's struck gold."

"Ben?" I asked even though I already knew this story. Stevie told me she'd met him in high school.

"He was everything she wasn't and I think it's why she fell hard for him. Her mom... well, you've met her."

I had met Stevie's mom last month, briefly, after she'd brought her to a home game instead of Reagan. It was easy to see where Stevie had gotten her looks. Her mom was beautiful for an older woman, a touch on the hippy side like Stevie had mentioned. I remembered she'd actually woven flowers into her braid.

"Her mom went through men like I go through Oreos, I think Ben became an out."

I knew all of this. Ben had been a security blanket. She'd told me everything Reagan was saying, but it still didn't make me feel any less unsettled about her white knight being back in town.

"She's different around him."

Reagan nodded and took a long drag of her beer. "He wanted a wife, not Stevie. He wanted the ideal, not the awesome girl she was. He cut her down inch by inch, year by year, until she lost who she was. He tried to change her. And he had for a while, until she finally woke up. Thanks for that, by the way."

"I didn't do anything."

"The night you guys first met, you gave her a push. You just didn't know it."

"Nothing happened."

"Oh, I know, but I think you gave her back the fight." She smiled at me. "You gave her back the bold."

My heart was a hammer. The bass of the music blaring overhead made the rhythm of my pulse disorganized. I'd allowed jealousy to wind its way around my ribs and spine, and for what? I was pissed he got to spend more time with her than me. I'd hated how he'd looked at me last week in her office, like I wasn't good enough for her. How he'd attempted to cut me down with his snide ass remark about my job. How his eyes had challenged me as if to say "you think you've won." But maybe I had won after all. Stevie was with me.

Mia was with you, too.

The voice inside my head leaked through my confidence and my lips set into a line.

"I think he realizes what he lost. I think he wants her back." My voice was stone and Reagan's gaze softened at the corners.

"Mark..." She stared at me for a few seconds. "Don't be that guy."

I couldn't help it but I laughed without humor. "What guy?"

"The jealous boyfriend. Ben is a fucking tool, trust me, Stevie is all about your ass."

The grim line of my lips parted into a real and genuine laugh. "My ass?"

Reagan snorted. "You have nothing to worry about. Give Stevie some credit."

My laugh quieted. I wasn't giving Stevie any credit at all. Trust was something I struggled with, but that wasn't Stevie's fault. "I trust her."

"Good." She sipped her beer. "When are you going to give me your blessing?"

"Oh God, here we go." Stevie's voice made my heart jump, but it was the warmth of her hands, her fingers kneading into my stiff shoulders that made me melt a little.

"What am I missing?" I asked as Stevie lowered her hands and slipped into her seat.

I wrapped my arm around her waist and pulled her in for a quick kiss.

Reagan scoffed. "Bryson."

I pulled away from Stevie's lips dazed. "What about him?"

I was a jerk for thinking it, but I was more interested in asking Stevie what Ben had wanted.

"I'd like to know him better." Reagan's tone matched the coy grin growing on her face.

"Oh, hell no. Absolutely not." I shook my head, and Stevie's soft laugh made me smile.

"Why not?" Reagan whined.

"Are you serious?" I scratched my fingers along the bristle of my bearded jaw. "He's a love `em and leave `em kind of guy, Ray. I wouldn't want you to—"

"Get hurt? I'm a big girl." She picked up her beer and stood. "Now if you'll excuse me... there's a hockey player I'd like to meet."

"You warned her." Stevie laughed softly, and I watched as Reagan eased her way into the pack of wolves.

I chuckled when Bryson painted on his million-dollar smile, pullin' Reagan in for a hug instead of a handshake. It was his M. O. He was a good guy when he wasn't thinking with his dic'. He'd told me the same shit Reagan had told me. He'd said to trust my woman and to trust myself. I didn't want to listen to the guy who'd never been in a real relationship, so it was nice to hear Reagan echo his sentiments.

"It's bizarre." Stevie leaned into me and I draped my arm behind her chair. "They look kind of cute together."

"Don't get any ideas. That man is only after one thing."

"So is Ray." She let out a long breath. "When she's not with Pete."

"I gotta meet this Pete guy."

"You will."

I shifted in my chair, my heart beating its way up my throat, as I asked as nonchalantly as possible, "So, what did Ben want?"

She yawned. "I messed up some of the figures."

Her eyes met mine and I found a few specks of defeat muting the blue burst around her irises. I pushed a piece of her hair behind her ear. "That bad?"

She shrugged, and I wondered if I imagined the glassy appearance glittering behind her lashes.

"He was a jerk about it. Said I added more work for him." Her voice was tight. "I told him I'd fix it on the plane tomorrow and send him the spreadsheet when I was finished, but he told me he didn't want me to mess it up even more." My jaw clenched as I watched her fight her emotion. "Then he said, 'have a great time in New Hampshire' and hung up on me. Everyone at the office is stressed. I get it. But I'm not the only one taking off for the holiday."

It wasn't the time off. It was that she was with me. Maybe I was jumping to conclusions, but I didn't give a shit. Stevie looked like she was about to fucking cry, and all I wanted to do was drive over to her office and teach that prick some goddamn manners.

I took a few even breaths and lifted her chin with my thumb. "Mistakes happen."

"It's a quick fix, I don't understand why he's..." She let the statement fade and exhaled. "It doesn't matter." She smiled up at me and the space between my lungs and heart contracted. It ached as I witnessed her confidence fall away again. "I'm tired, ready to go?"

"Yeah, baby, let's go home."

The plane passed through the clouds slowly as we reached cruising altitude. Stevie took a sip from her mimosa, and I pressed my lips together, hiding my growing smile. Her hair was tied into a knot on the top of her head, her face was clean of makeup, and her eyes were bright as she stared out the window. She looked so beautiful, and as much as I wanted to blame the pressurized air of the cabin for my difficulty breathing, I couldn't. She took my breath away.

"Nervous?" I asked and she turned to face me.

"A little." She chewed the inside of her cheek.

I laced her fingers with mine. "Molly, my sister, she loves all that punk shit you listen to."

She laughed and bumped me with her shoulder. "It's not shit. It's... classic."

I grinned at the crinkle between her brows. "It sounds like shit, classic or not." Instead of another bump on the shoulder, she squeezed my hand and I chuckled. "Is that supposed to hurt?"

"Maybe."

I leaned down and kissed the back of the hand I was holding. "You'll never overpower me," I teased.

Her cheeks heated and she gave me a shy smile as she whispered, "What about this morning?"

I swallowed as I thought about how good it had felt to have her lips on me. After we'd gotten home last night, we were exhausted enough we'd both passed out. I was so tired I'd slept through my alarm, but Stevie had found a better way of waking me up. I'd thought I was dreaming, when I'd opened my eyes, the view in itself was enough to make me come. Stevie with her dark hair spilling over my thighs, her mouth—those lips surrounding the head of my...

"Looks like we're going to hit some weather up ahead, please keep your seatbelts fastened at all times until further notice." The pilot's voice pulled me from the memory.

"You can wake me up like that tomorrow, too, if you want."

"No thanks, I'd like for your mom to think I'm not a total slut."

"And why would she think that?" I laughed at her serious expression. "My room is in the basement. We can have all the loud sex we want."

Stevie's eyes darted to the seats in front of us and she squeezed my hand again. She spoke so quietly I had to lean in to hear her. "There will be no... shenanigans happening in your parents' house."

"Then we'll stay at a hotel."

"Mark."

"Stevie."

She bit her lip, holding back a smile as my lips separated into a winning grin.

"Don't be impossible. It's disrespectful and—"

"My family is fucking crazy, Stevie. You'll see. My mom will try to ply you with chocolate, my dad will talk your ear off about cider and his innovations in tree grafting, while my niece will most likely make you cry at least once because she has no filter and is as honest as they come." Stevie's lips gradually pulled into a face-splitting smile as I rattled on about all the inadequacies of what she was about to face. "I'm not joking, Stevie, sex will be the only way you'll make it through three days with them."

Her head rolled back and she laughed. "You mean the only way you'll make it."

"That's exactly what I said."

She leaned over the armrest and pressed her lips to my cheek. The tension that had hidden itself inside my stomach untwisted and I cupped her face with my palm.

"They're gonna love you." I placed a kiss to her forehead.

She exhaled a shaky breath as I pulled away and she whispered mostly to herself, "Sure."

I was about to tell her to stop worrying when a flight attendant placed her hand on the back of my seat and said, "Excuse me." Her smile was nervous. "I'm not supposed to do this sort of thing, but..." she whispered, her eyes flicking over my shoulder to Stevie and then back to me. "But I'm a huge fan." She blushed and I gave her a friendly smile.

"Not a problem," I said and offered to shake her hand.

She took my hand in hers and shook it awkwardly a few times as she gushed, "My husband is gonna die when I tell him Mark Carmelo was on my flight." Her formal tone slipped into a southern drawl. She reached over me and held out her hand to Stevie. "And can I say, the pictures do not do you justice. You are just as pretty as a peach in person."

The color of Stevie's cheeks matched that of the flight attendant's. "Umm... thank you."

"That article last month in *Hockey Hunks,* the one about the hockey wives and girlfriends, I thought you were the prettiest."

Stevie gave me a blank look and I shrugged.

"Well, don't let me bother you, but if you wouldn't mind..." She released Stevie's hand and reached into her pocket, handing me a small slip of paper. "Would you sign this?"

"Of course."

She looked over my shoulder nervously as she handed me a pen. "My name's Penelope."

I scribbled a personalized thank you with my name across the slip of paper and attempted to hand it back to her.

"You too, sweetheart." She smiled down at Stevie.

Humor lit her eyes as I handed her the pen and piece of paper. She signed her initials under mine and something I didn't have a name for settled inside my chest as I looked at our names together on the strip of paper. Proud. Warm. Unsteady.

The attendant practically squealed as she said thank you, and once she was well out of earshot, Stevie sank into her chair. "That was surreal."

"I don't think I'll ever get used to strangers getting excited about my signature. I mean, I understand they admire the talent I have, the game, but who cares if I sign some random piece of paper."

She tilted her head to the side. "It's a piece of you, Mark, and they get to keep it forever."

Her words sucked the air out of my lungs, or maybe it was the thoughtful look inside her eyes, either way, the way she was looking at me... I wanted to keep that feeling forever.

She raised her gaze to the ceiling and puffed out a laugh. "I don't understand why she wanted me to sign something. That was weird. Famous by association, I guess."

"You're prettier than a peach, that's why."

She rolled her eyes. "Ugh, I'll have to look up that article when we land."

"I never read anything I didn't commission myself through my agent. It's why I don't parade my life on social media. I'll give answers when I want, on my time, and anything else they choose to say about me or you, it's all speculation, don't bark up that tree, babe."

A few weeks ago Bryson had shown me a thread in some forum where a bunch of women were discussing whether or not Stevie was considered "plus-sized." I didn't even know what that meant, and from the few comments I'd read, most were negative. It pissed me off. I couldn't imagine what Stevie would've thought if she read that shit, or any woman, for that matter. Size was a number, and whether Stevie was plus or not, she was sexy as fuck. Bryson had boiled it down, though, when he'd said the women in that feed were envious trolls.

I rested my palm on her thigh and I liked how perfect it fit there.

"It's something I'm adjusting to. Ray tells me the same thing, ignore it."

"Have I told you how much I like Reagan?"

She gasped as she sat up, giving me a megawatt smile. "*I almost forgot*. She texted me." Stevie tapped the top of my hands with her fingers. "Bryson shared a cab with her, and when she invited him in to her place... get this... he said no."

"He said no?" The surprise in my voice made her giggle.

"He took her home, walked her to the door, kissed her on the cheek, and sent her packing. Crazy, right?"

"I'm speechless."

And grateful.

I definitely needed to thank him for not fucking around with my girlfriend's best friend.

"You're gonna give him crap, aren't you?"

"So much shit."

STEVIE

The frozen earth crunched under the rental car tires as we pulled up the long driveway to Mark's family's home. The bent tree branches hovered over the car, and the weight of the snow burdened the damp wood as we drove underneath them. My stomach was jumping rope, and my heart pounded as the first glimpse of the house came into view. It was smaller than I'd expected and incredibly quaint. White vinyl siding covered the majority of the box-shaped, two-story farmhouse. Black shutters hung alongside the front windows that were adorned with pine garland and red bows for Christmas.

"This is it." Mark's husky voice pulled my eyes to his.

He was smiling, and it could've been the bright white of the snow that blanketed the ground reflecting in his gaze, but he was absolutely beaming. Mark was home, and the way the corners of his mouth reached and stretched into his eyes, my heart squeezed and sighed with something I wasn't ready for.

My lips parted in reaction to the handsome spectacle sitting next to me. "It's beautiful."

He reached across the console, his fingers toying with a piece of my hair. "It's small, but it never felt like that to me growing up. My mom was really good at making everything seem larger than life."

I took in the wide expanse of land on either side of his home. I could see another structure to the left sitting far back from the main house. "What's that?" I asked.

"It's the cider house and..." he pointed to the left and then to the right, "All of that behind it is our orchard."

Trees stretched for what seemed like a mile or more behind the cider house. "Wow."

He chuckled. "It's a shitload of work, but my dad is good at what he does. I always felt guilty growing up. Farming isn't known for its big salaries, and with a daughter in figure skating and a son in hockey, he worked hard for us." Mark stared at the house. The lights were on and the clouds rolled in making the noon sun disappear. The yellow glow from the windows seemed to invite us in. "I helped pay off the mortgage after my first two years with the NHL."

"You did?" I asked in disbelief, letting my eyes roam all that land, it must have cost a small fortune.

"It was the least I could do." He swallowed and his mouth tipped into my favorite crooked smile. "Wait till you see the rink out back, my dad built it when I was little and the fucking thing still stands. Poppy loves coming here to skate when it's cold enough to have ice."

His warm timbre soothed away my anxiety, and the way he spoke about his family, he made me want to know them, to be a part of something like that. I'd never had what he did, but I wanted it. Wanted them. "Should we go inside?"

"You ready?"

I nodded. "I think I am."

Mark cut the engine. "Wait here," he said and opened the driver side door. The cold blast of air made the hair on my arms stand at attention, and I watched as he walked around the car. He opened my door and held out his hand. "This driveway gets icy as hell. I'll have my dad help with our bags later."

I was wearing skinny jeans, a thin green sweater, and Converse. Looking at the piled snow on either side of the drive, I immediately realized I hadn't packed appropriately. "This Florida girl is not prepared." I laughed as I took his hand in a death grip and stepped out of the car.

"I probably should've given you a heads up on how cold it gets here."

"I'll be okay."

"I'm sure my mom or my sister has a pair of boots and a coat you can borrow if you need it." He kissed my cold cheek. "It's only three days, I don't plan on doing much more than relaxing on the couch and stuffing my face with food."

"And no shenanigans?" I asked dryly.

"I make no promises."

I took a deep breath as we moved toward the house.

Ignoring, or more like pretending my heart wasn't spazzing out, I flashed Mark a smile as he reached for the door knob.

"Don't say I didn't warn you."

Warm, spiced air pooled inside my lungs as we stepped inside. Laughter filtered into the small foyer from the back of the house. The living room, colored in earth tones and dark wood, was empty. The television was on, the volume low, playing hockey highlights. Mark released my hand long enough to pull off his jacket and hang it on the coat rack installed into the wall next to the front door.

He laced his fingers through mine again and yelled, "Mom? Dad?" It made me jump and he laughed under his breath. "Easy, girl."

I smacked his shoulder, giving him my "definitely no damn shenanigans for you" glare.

"I'm sure he deserved that." A woman who looked about my age stood by the couch, a wide grin on her round face. She was shorter than me, but not petite by any means. Her athletic shape was apparent in her black leggings and tight, long-sleeved thermal. "The prodigal son returns."

"More like Mom's favorite. Get your ass over here, Mol."

Her soft features became almost childlike as her smile grew beyond broad. She hopped in place before bounding toward Mark. He swallowed her into his arms, a deep laugh, and... was she crying?

She sniffed as he set her onto her feet. A laugh mixed with a sob barked from her full lips as she wiped under her eyes. "It's been too long." She hugged him again and he ruffled her long chestnut-colored hair.

Mark tugged on her sleeve. "You guys went skating without me?"

"You know how Poppy is." She glanced at me, and then back at Mark, biting back a smile. "My brother has the worst manners, you can thank all the years he spent on a bus with a bunch of hooligan hockey players." She held out her hand. "I'm Molly."

"Shit, sorry. This is my sister and Molly; this is my girlfriend, Stevie."

I took her hand and she pulled me into a hug. My spine straightened for the briefest of seconds and she whispered, "Don't let us scare you, Mark is a keeper."

I relaxed as she released me and gave her a shy smile. "It's nice to meet you."

"Where's Dax?" Mark asked and Molly groaned.

"He's stuck in Denver, nothing is flying out with the storm."

"Work?" Mark asked and Molly nodded.

Mark had told me Dax sold farming equipment and traveled a lot for work. He'd said it was hard for his sister that her husband was gone all the time.

"Will he miss Christmas?" I found myself asking and watched as Molly's smile wavered.

"His first," she said.

An annoyed grunt sounded in the back of Mark's throat. "You'd think Denver would have their shit together when it comes to snow."

"That's what I said." Molly laughed and she ran her hand through her hair. "Oh well, he docs what he docs so I can stay at home with Poppy. Sacrifice, it's part of life."

"Where is Poppy anyway?"

"In the kitchen... Dad's driving Mom crazy, hovering over the damn turkey, as per usual. Poppy is trying to distract him with Boston stats." Molly smirked.

"Oh, yeah? What year?" Mark asked.

"Nineteen-seventy-nine."

"Nice." Mark leaned down and kissed my cheek. "My niece is a walking hockey encyclopedia. I tease her that she should work at the hockey hall of fame."

"And she promptly reminds Mark that she's only eight."

"Almost nine."

I laughed and any remaining weariness I had about meeting the family faded. Molly smiled at me and it was the real deal. Her eyes were curious, but open and friendly. Mark beamed again as he lowered his eyes to mine.

"I'm excited to meet her," I admitted.

Molly snorted, but there was humor in her eyes when she said, "I'll remind you of that very statement after she offends you the first time." She waved her thumb over her shoulder. "Come on, they're all probably in there eavesdropping anyway."

She turned first and Mark leaned down to kiss me with tender lips, leaving me a bit light in the knees.

"Hey," I whispered.

He kissed me again, but this time his free hand cupped the back of my head, pulling me into the warmth of his body. When I opened my eyes, his sister was gone. "Thanks for braving this."

I curled the fingers of my right hand into the fabric of his shirt. "So far I feel like you've oversold the crazy." I grinned.

Mark tipped his chin, his lips brushing my forehead as the heat of his breath washed over me making me shiver. "I care about you, and they know it, they'll be on their best behavior."

I care about you.

I knew he cared about me, and I cared about him, more than I thought possible, but he'd never said it outright.

He chuckled as he leaned back and considered me. "Don't look so freaked. I promise, my family is harmless, I like messing with you."

"I know." I breathed in and out letting those four words feed my pulse.

"Come on."

Mark had been truthful in his assessment of his family. They were completely harmless. And pretty damn cute, if

I was being honest. His mother made the word jolly seem sweeter in person. She had dark brown hair cut to her chin and was about the same height as her daughter but softer in the hips. She'd accosted me with hugs when we'd walked into the kitchen an hour ago. His dad, a bear of man, and the spitting image of his son, had given me the same reception as his wife. His hug had practically crushed me, and it hadn't been until Mark cleared his throat, twice, that his father set me back on my feet.

The only person who hadn't yet warmed up to me was Poppy. She'd given me a wave, a once over, and had been quiet while Mark's parents and sister asked me about my life over sandwiches and cider. Poppy's dark eyes had followed my every move and I'd been too nervous, spewing all the details about my hippy mother, to get a chance to engage her in conversation. She sat on the breakfast nook bench, lacing up her skates, eyeing me from under her black lashes. Mark and his sister were upstairs digging through a trunk filled with Molly's old skates in hopes to match me with a pair. His mother had lent me a coat and I fiddled anxiously with the zipper, trying to listen to Mark's parents talk in the other room. Their words were muffled and I laughed to myself when I heard his mother grumble about the amount of sage her husband put in the stuffing for tomorrow.

"It's every year." Poppy's stoic voice commanded attention.

I turned and fell into the gaze of the little girl. "Christmas?" I asked and her features crumbled into a scowl that made me feel stupid.

"The Great Turkey Debate. Grand Dad always puts too much sage in the stuffing. And Grandma always makes a separate batch." She blinks a few times. "Do not eat Grand Dad's stuffing."

I wait for a smile that never comes, giving her one of my own. "Thanks for the advice."

"Do you know how to skate?" I shook my head. "Mia knew how to skate."

My heart fell to the floor and I almost looked down at the mess. Mark had warned me Poppy was implacable when it came to facts, truths, and honesty.

"Maybe you could teach me?" I asked.

Her mouth twitched. "That is a feasible option. But, my mother is a coach. That would benefit you better." She leaned back and I flicked my eyes to her feet. She wore hockey skates with the laces tied in tight bows. "Did you know Mark was drafted at the age of nineteen?" I nodded. "He's played five hundred and forty games for the NHL and has two hundred and ten career goals."

"He's a great player."

My statement earned me a nod and a small curve of her lips as she whispered, "The best." I could hear Mark and Molly stomping down the stairs and I glanced at the doorway.

"You're much prettier than Mia."

I froze. My eyes wide, my greedy mouth pulling into an involuntary grin as I faced Poppy. "Thank you."

She lifted her shoulders. "Your face is much more symmetrical, and I like your hair. It looks soft." I unconsciously smoothed my hand over the waves I came by naturally. "Mia didn't smile as much as you."

The ache in my chest was a living, breathing thing as Poppy's words absorbed. Mark had told me how Mia had never wanted to go with him to Toronto. How she'd never wanted to help out at the special needs hockey camp he donated his time and money to every year. Mark had gotten into a fight with Mia's boyfriend this year because of the terrible name he'd called Poppy, and I wondered if Mia had been cold to Poppy when she'd visited.

I didn't like the frown that was growing on Poppy's lips. "I smile too much sometimes."

She blinked at me. "That's okay. My mom told me that you use less muscles to smile than you do to frown. This is a falsehood, but I understand her reasoning."

My light laughter was out of place in the quiet kitchen. Poppy was eight going on forty. "I think I like you, Poppy Grayson."

Her lips twitched again as she watched me, the moment only lasting two, maybe three seconds before a strong hand rested on my shoulder and a deep, familiar voice warmed my stomach. "I found a pair of skates."

"That took forever, let's go." Poppy stood, grabbing the hockey stick resting next to the back door of the kitchen.

"You're so bossy," Mark teased as he handed me the skates he'd found.

"Who do you think she learned it from?" Molly laughed as she walked into the kitchen holding two hockey sticks.

My pulse jumped as I gawked at the weapons in her hands. "Um... what are those for?" I asked, my voice taking on a high pitch.

Poppy's brows dipped deeply with confusion, and what I thought might be a bit of irritation. "They're used to hit the puck... Uncle Mark... have you not taught her the basics?"

Poppy's question was earnest and it made me like her even more.

Mark pressed his lips together. His smile only obvious in the dimples popping in his cheeks. "No, kiddo, I haven't." She glared at him and I let a laugh slip. "But I will..." He held up both of his hands. "I promise, as soon as we get her skates on."

Poppy gave a quick nod of her head and disappeared out the back door.

"She's worse than my coaches." Mark kneeled down in front of me. "Can I help?" he asked taking a skate from my lap.

Molly leaned against the door frame. "She told me she wants to play for the Bruins. I told her not to tell Grand Dad, he'd be devastated."

"He's not a fan." I surmised.

"We were born Toronto fans, didn't I tell you?" Mark asked.

Molly snickered. "She's been throwing Boston stats at him all day, I think he looked nauseous at one point. How many factoids did she hit you with while we were gone?"

I slid my foot into the skate and Mark began the process of tightening and tying as I answered, "Not too many..." I hesitated, not sure if I should mention what she'd said about Mia. "Mostly Mark facts."

He took the other skate from my lap, meeting my gaze. "Oh, yeah? Like what?"

"Something about NHL goals and games." He chuckled and held my calf as I slipped my foot into the other skate. His fingertips dug into the muscle and a puddle of heat gathered in my belly.

"Hopefully she didn't bore you too much." Molly's tone was filled with mirth. She exhaled. "You guys have fun, I'm gonna help Mom make her second bowl of stuffing for tomorrow. Tell Poppy one hour, alright, Christmas morning comes early."

"I don't think I'll make it an hour," I said.

Molly scoffed. "Just sneak away after the first ten minutes, they'll never notice."

Mark tapped his palm on the ankle of my skate before he stood. "Not true."

"You and Poppy always get lost in your own little private hockey bubble..." Molly's eyes met mine. "Seriously, Stevie, head on in after a few, and you can learn how to make the proper stuffing... there's hard cider, too."

It had started to snow again. My warm-blooded veins liked the offer she'd presented. "I might take you up on that."

Mark held out his hands and I wobbled to my feet.

"Have fun," Molly said again before leaving us alone together.

He held my face. "You can be a poor sport and leave early if you want. I won't mind at all." His lips spread into an easy grin. "Hanging in there?"

I kissed his top lip and he lowered his hands to my waist. "Your family is amazing."

"I think so, but I'm biased. Poppy is—"

"She said my face was more symmetrical than Mia's."

He cringed. "Shit, I'm sorry, she's too—"

"I really like Poppy."

His light brown eyes flared. "I heard."

"You did?" I whispered.

Mark didn't answer me with words. First, his nose touched mine, gentle and soft. He leaned his head to the side, his eyes on me. His kiss was sweet and my arms slid around his neck, and I didn't care my ankles were starting to hurt, or that I was going to have to hold a stick and try to hit a small disc, all while trying not to fall on my butt. Mark's tongue swept across my lips and I opened for him.

He tasted like apple cider and longing. My heart answered to the memories his lips created with heavy thudded beats.

He kissed my bottom lip once and pulled away with a satisfied hum.

"You're about to get your ass handed to you by an eight year old."

I let my head fall into his chest as I grumbled, "Don't remind me."

MARK

Stevie was sound asleep, tousled in the sheets she'd stolen from me some time in the night. Shadows floated across the length of her body in slow motion, and when I turned to the small basement window, the snow was coming down in fat white flakes. The clock on my nightstand told me it was too damn early, but even on vacation, I couldn't shake the schedule I'd grown used to. Stevie was sweet with soft breaths escaping from her parted lips. She wore the pair of long johns I'd let her borrow. My room was freezing on most winter nights, and I savored the way the fabric clung to her breasts and hips. Stevie had enlisted the "no fucking around rule" and even snuggling, for the sake of warmth, was out of the question.

I eased myself to the edge of the bed and it shifted as I stood. The full-sized mattress was laid out on the floor, no frame, and a box-spring to give it a few inches of height. The only thing about my childhood bedroom that had changed, was the woman sprawled out and snoring in my sheets.

My Toronto Maple Leafs posters still adorned the walls, and Stevie had gotten a good laugh about the few swimsuit models I had pinned up, as well. I'd shrugged and told her every teenage kid had something they'd spanked it to. The comment had gotten me a cute and disgusted swat to the chest.

My eyes devoured her perfect form for a few more seconds before I turned toward the door. I wanted to grab the presents I'd hidden upstairs, figuring she'd rather open them before the Poppy's-The-Only-Grandchild-Christmas-Day-Massacre occurred. It wasn't hard to admit Poppy was spoiled. The girl got everything she wanted. She had doting grandparents and an uncle who couldn't tell her no to save his own damn life. The only saving grace was Poppy didn't act like a brat. She was wise beyond her years. And my favorite thing, for a girl who never showed much emotion, she had an abundance of gratitude. The smile I had on my face spread to my tired eyes as I thought about the interaction I'd witnessed between my niece and girlfriend last night. Poppy's gratitude had been out in spades, or maybe it was graciousness, as she'd taught Stevie how to hold a hockey stick. In her own way, Poppy took Stevie under her wing, and to my surprise, let her steal a few pucks and even win a goal. Stevie wasn't too bad of a player... when she wasn't on her ass.

I was lost in my thoughts as the bedroom door clicked behind me. My feelings for Stevie, seeing her with my family, she fit us, fit me more than Mia ever had in two goddamn years. My mother had pulled me to the side after dinner last night and said she liked how happy I seemed. My dad's opinion hadn't been much different. He'd told me Stevie was one of the "good ones." Mia never made me feel good, never made me smile like Stevie did. She'd always nagged about how NHL players didn't get paid like basketball players or football players. She'd freaked out when I'd injured myself the first season we were dating, and it wasn't because she was worried about me. She'd been worried about my career, what I could offer her—what she'd lose if I wasn't playing. She'd wanted to be arm candy, a hockey wife, but Stevie, she wanted to be mine. Stevie made me feel human, real—more than just the logo I wore on my jersey.

The basement stairs creaked under my feet as I ascended to the main level. The house smelled of cinnamon and sugar, and as I drew closer to the pale light of the kitchen, the scent got stronger. It was only a quarter after six, and I knew there was no way Poppy would be awake. We'd all stayed up late playing Yahtzee, and she'd fallen asleep on the couch, her head in my lap, around midnight. A long sigh poured through the kitchen doorway, but it was the quiet sob that had my feet moving faster through the living room. My sister stood in the kitchen, her face in the palms of her hands, crying.

"What's going on?" I asked in a rushed whisper. Her big, watery eyes found mine. Her lashes like wet soot speared me in the chest. My gaze fell to the phone on the counter and then back to her. "Everything alright?"

She nodded. "Yes..." She blew out a breath and croaked, "No."

Three strides had my arms wrapped around her waist, her cheek to my chest. "Jesus, you're shaking, Mol. What happened?"

She sniffled into the cotton of my shirt before she pulled away and wiped the tears from her cheeks with her fingertips.

"Dax… we got into a huge fight…" I ran my hand through my hair, letting my lungs expand. No one was hurt. "He said he couldn't get a flight out until the twenty-seventh."

"Mol, he's stuck, it's not his—"

"Fault. I know, Mark." She shot daggers in my direction. "I understand. He's stuck. It's part of his job to travel, but…" Her temper ebbed and tears trickled down her cheeks again as she spoke in a choked whisper. "I asked him to quit for me when I got pregnant with Poppy. I hated that he was away all the time. He gave up his dreams for me, took this sales job… and fast forward eight years later and here we are. He probably would've been home more if he still played for Providence."

"Molly…" I stepped toward her but she held up her hands and shook her head. "The AHL, those guys, some of them never see NHL ice. He knows that. He did what he wanted to do. He didn't give up a dream, Mol. He got a family. He loves you and Poppy, and I guarantee he'd make the same choice again, I sure as fuck would've done the same thing."

She lowered her eyes to the floor. "You can't say that… you don't know. You would never leave your team for—"

"I would if I had to be there for my family, for someone I loved. If that was my only choice, I'd always choose my family."

Molly lifted her head, a sad smile forming on her lips. "You sound just like him." She gently shoved me in the chest on her way to the coffee maker. "I know I'm crazy. I know he's paying our bills." She poured herself a cup of coffee, her chin tilted down. "I yelled at him, asked him how he could do this to me on Christmas. He told me I was being selfish and hung up."

Dax and I had always gotten along, we were cut from the same cloth. There wasn't much either of us wouldn't do for the people we loved. We would give the fucking sky if we could. Molly was stubborn like our dad, and sometimes it was hard for her to see around her own nose.

"He missed Christmas with his family, Mol. He's sitting in a shitty hotel in Denver, alone." I picked up the phone from the counter and held it out to her. "So he said the wrong thing because he's hurting... as much as you are."

She took the phone from my hand. "I hate that you're right."

I chuckled and ruffled her hair with my palm. "Give him a break, the big stuff can wait till he gets home."

She nodded, her eyes filling with tears again. "Stevie is lucky to have you."

"I think it's the other way around."

"Possibly." She cleared her throat, a smirk growing on her lips. "Mom made cinnamon rolls before she went to shower, steal a couple before Dad wakes up and eats them all."

She headed to the living room with her phone to her ear and I overheard her whispered, "I'm sorry." After I used the bathroom, and splashed some water on my face, I loaded a plate with cinnamon rolls, and grabbed the bag with Stevie's presents in it from the cupboard inside the pantry. It was heavy and I worried the paper sack wouldn't hold as I took the basement stairs two at a time.

She hadn't budged an inch, but her shirt had ridden up a little, and the smooth expanse of her stomach teased me from where I stood in the doorway. Setting the bag to the side, I locked the door and placed the plate of rolls on my dresser. I raised my hand to the back of my neck, pulling my shirt over my head. The cold air of the room tickled the hairs on my arms as I stalked toward my girl with intentions she'd probably smack me for later. Slow and quiet I crawled onto the mattress, tugging the sheets until she rolled onto her back with a light hum. The other day she'd woken me up with a blow job, and I figured this morning I'd return the favor.

Pressing kisses to her belly, my nose dusted along the line of her hip as I pulled down her pants one stealthy inch at a time. She wriggled under my touch as my lips moved lower, much lower, and finally, I was tasting her. She was warm under my tongue, the slick heat of her body inviting me in as I slid two fingers inside her. Her hand was in my hair, nails on my scalp as I kissed and nipped her clit.

"Mark…" My name was a lust and sleep-filled syllable.

She rocked her hips, urging me. My fingers pumped faster as she arched her back. She swore softly, her hands dropping from my hair, only to shield her mouth as she cried out and came on my tongue, on my fingers. She was breathing hard and heavy as I pushed down my sweats letting them fall to the floor and climbed over her. Our lips collided together as I slipped inside her, the need I had for her driving my hips brutal and quick. She grasped my shoulders, spread her legs farther apart, letting me fall into her completely. Messy kisses and a hasty rhythm, I rode her body. My chest sinking into the softness of hers, the scent of sex and Stevie clung to my sheets, making itself known and permanent in my home, in my life. My left hand fisted in her hair, my right arm cradling her lower back as I closed off any space between our connection. Tight words spilled from our lips. *Don't stop, I'm almost there, Please, and God, and Oh, fuck.*

The room, the world faded, and the painful anticipation settled at the base of my spine as I whispered, "Don't close your eyes."

All that was left was the euphoric relief I found in the amber color of her irises as I let go. Filling her, I spiraled down until our lips met. I took deep sips from her mouth, my tongue sliding alongside hers stroke for stroke. Breathless and spent, I pulled away, burying my lips inside the crook of her neck. I could feel the way her heart pounded inside her chest, and it matched my own deafening beat.

Stevie ran her fingers along the nape of my neck, through my hair, and back down again.

She was the first to speak, her tone content with a touch of humor. "You broke the rule."

I raised my head, holding the weight of my body with my arms. My hands braced against the pillow beside her head. "Merry Christmas."

She brought her fingertips to my lips and traced a line across them. My eyes closed as she cupped my cheek. I was fucking gone for this girl. "Merry Christmas."

I opened my eyes and she smiled at me, her cheeks flushed all the way down to her chest.

"Have you ever had sex in here before?" she asked and I laughed.

"No."

Her eyes widened. "We just christened your childhood bed... I feel so..."

"Good?" I offered.

"Dirty."

I dropped my lips to hers and chuckled against her mouth. "Dirty... like you'll let me fuck you on every surface of this room before breakfast kind of dirty?"

She shook her head, pushing my shoulders until I fell to the side and admonished me with mock irritation. "You broke the rule."

"I think you liked breaking the rule."

I palmed her breast and she wrenched her shirt down with an exhale. "Mark."

I lifted onto my elbow and laughed. "What? You did. You loved it. Twice."

"What if your parents heard—oh God—what if Poppy..." She glared at me and I had to bite back my smile. "I hate you right now."

"Does that mean I can't give you your presents?"

Stevie's features softened, her eyes glimmered as they appraised me. "Now?"

With the tips of my fingers, I moved a strand of hair from her forehead. "Now."

I didn't give her a chance to answer as I rolled to my side and stood. I picked up my sweats from the floor, hauling them on before grabbing the bag and the plate of rolls off my dresser. When I turned around, Stevie's smile punched me in the stomach, knocked the wind out of me like I'd been hit by a two-hundred-and-twenty-pound blue liner. Her hair was everywhere, her cheeks were splotched with pink, and she was wiggling into her pajama bottoms. Excitement danced across her face as she flipped on the bedside table lamp. She crossed her legs as I sat on the bed, leaving the bag on the side of the mattress and placing the plate on the night stand.

"My mom makes these every year." My gaze slid to the rolls. "It can get crazy up there, and I wanted some privacy," I said, mirroring her position, crossing my legs under me.

"I like that plan." She watched me with inquisitive eyes.

I was about to tell her how fucking gorgeous she was, how running into her that night after she'd moved back to Tampa had changed my game, made me happier than I ever thought I could be. I wanted her to know how good it felt to trust again, to fall for her, how easy it was to breathe again, because kissing her, being with her, was the pulse point I'd lost.

My nervous-as-hell mouth wouldn't open though, and before I got the chance she jumped up and said, "*Wait.*"

She practically hopped to her luggage and pulled out a medium-sized box wrapped in bold, royal blue paper. She set it on the floor across from my bag and settled back onto the bed.

I couldn't help the dopey ass grin forming on my face as she bounced in place. "You want to go first?" I asked.

She eyed the bag, her decision made. "No, that's okay, you can."

I lifted the two wrapped gifts from the bag and put them between us on the bed. She stared at them, her teeth pressed into her bottom lip.

"Open them."

Stevie opened the bigger package first, her eyes flitting between me and the box until the paper was torn and strewn across the bed and floor. She gasped when she realized what it was.

"A record player?" She raised a shaking hand to the large, white, vinyl nineteen—my number—I'd placed on the top of the lid. It was a small player, one she could move around the house if she wanted to.

"I haven't had a record player since I was eighteen. I sold mine when I moved to Richmond." Her mood was a mixture of sadness and surprise, and I worried I'd screwed up. I should've gone the traditional route, jewelry, or a trip somewhere fun.

"Do you like it?"

She traced the number, my number, with her fingers and then opened the lid. "I love it," she answered in a small voice. "I wish I hadn't gotten rid of all my records."

I nudged the other gift, the unopened one sitting between us. "There's more."

She removed the paper at a tortured pace. I wanted to rip it open for her, but it was the tiny squeal, the flash in her eyes when she looked up at me, that fucking sexy-as-hell grin on her face made the wait worth it.

"Holy shit." She looked down at the records in her lap, flipping through them furiously. "*Holy... shit.*" Stevie's jaw dropped. "Mark, are these—"

"Originals, yes."

"*Mark.*"

I chuckled.

"Mark, this is too much." Her lips trembled as she flipped through the records again. The Ramones, Jawbreaker, The Vandals, Dead Kennedys, The Clash, Sex Pistols, Descendents, and a couple Misfits records Molly said were a must-have.

"Molly helped me find them."

"I love Molly," Stevie crooned, hugging the records to her chest.

My head fell back with a laugh. "I looked up a lot of those bands online. How the hell do you listen to that shit?"

Her pout made me chuckle.

"Don't ruin how much I like you right now by saying stupid things."

"How much do you like me right now?"

"A lot." She set the records in her lap and leaned over the player. I met her halfway and kissed her. My palms held her face as she opened for me with greedy lips.

"Does this mean we get to break the rule again later?"

"I think it might."

I sat back, my brows raised to the ceiling. "Really?"

She laughed. "You're cute when you want sex."

"I'm cute all the damn time."

"Shh." She set the record player on the floor and grabbed the box she'd pulled out from her luggage. "Your turn."

Unlike Stevie, I tore into the paper, and when I opened the box, confusion had me lifting my eyes to hers. A Tampa Bay jersey was neatly folded inside the square of cardboard.

"I overheard you talking to Bryson about Poppy a few weeks ago." Stevie spoke, her confidence dangling from a rope as she continued, "I heard you tell him she wanted to wear the number thirteen when she got to play for the NHL."

Poppy had big dreams and why not? Everything started somewhere, and if anything, my niece reminded me of what I was like when I was a kid. I picked up the jersey and felt something hard in the middle.

"What's this?" I asked, not really expecting an answer as I parted the material, revealing a framed picture of me and Poppy when she was a year old. I'd come home on a rare weekend, my rookie year, for her birthday.

"It was on the desk in the kitchen where you keep all your important paperwork, sitting under a few envelopes. I found it your last road trip, when you asked me to pick up your mail." I gaped at the framed picture. Words clogged in my narrowed throat. "I wished I would've known she wanted to play for Boston..."

The name GRAYSON was spelled out across the back, the number thirteen stitched underneath it. Poppy's last name and favorite number. A small flame grew bigger, into a blaze, a five-alarm feeling consumed my chest.

"I know how much she means to you... the camp, helping kids reach their goals. I thought it would be cool. I don't know, it's like a piece of the future, and you could wear it and think of her." She dipped her chin, her smile fading as I sat there totally dumbstruck. "Poppy's going to—"

"Fucking love it." I found my breath and a smile crept across her face.

"Yeah?"

I held Stevie's gaze, fighting the overwhelming and strange sensation building with each thud and whoosh of my pulse. "Fuck yes." The wrapping paper crinkled and the records in her lap fell to the side as we met in the middle. "I love it," I whispered against her lips. "If I could, I'd wear it on game days."

"What about camp?"

"I'll wear it every day I'm there, Poppy will never stop smiling... I'll have to get her one of her own."

She giggled. "Maybe get her a Boston one."

I gently placed the jersey and framed picture on top of the record player, off the side of the bed, as I scoffed. "Screw that, if I get her a jersey it will be Tampa or Toronto."

"Matching jerseys would be kind of adorable."

My lips silenced her worry over team loyalty and my arms folded around her waist. She bit my bottom lip as my hands found the round curve of her ass. In one easy move, I had her on her back and the rest of her vinyl collection fell off the mattress and onto the floor. I kissed her hard and her knees gripped the sides of my hips. She didn't push me away, or spout out rules, she surrendered to my touch. Taking a breath, I held her chin between my thumb and forefinger. Her eyes searched mine and the weight of her gaze plummeted down onto my shoulders. I wanted to surrender, too. I wanted to show her how much I fucking loved her gift... loved that she was mine, loved it more than I normally allowed myself.

The hot silk of her palm caressed my face and I kissed her. I closed my eyes as her mouth melded to mine, and I let the addictive weight take me under.

STEVIE

"She hugged you?"

"Yup," I said and I switched my phone to my other ear.

"Wow, that's pretty epic." I didn't miss the sarcasm in Reagan's tone.

"It doesn't seem like a big deal, but Mark said Poppy isn't a hugger. I feel like I've been officially welcomed into the pack."

I thought about the day we'd left to come back to Florida and my lips split into a wide smile. Mark's entire family had given me bear hugs, including Poppy.

"You're in and now you can never leave." Reagan's laugh was overly dramatic with a villainess flare.

"I'd be happy to stay forever." Once the words left my mouth, there was no taking them back. "You know what I mean... the whole trip, it was perfect. I've never had the whole family dynamic thing. They treated me like they've known me forever. His mom cried when Mark came up wearing the jersey I'd gotten for him... and you should've seen Poppy's face." I laughed as I continued, "It was a mixture of excitement and horror. When Mark showed her the back of the jersey she'd smiled at first and then frowned. I asked her if she liked it and she'd said 'it's cool, but it should've been a Boston jersey.'"

"She said that?" Reagan giggled.

"Straight up, honest... she's a freaking pistol." And I love her, I wanted to say, but I'd already admitted too much out loud for one morning. "I know it's not a great idea to get too attached so soon, but I had a great time."

She exhaled a breathy sigh reading me like she always did. "Stevie... you're happy. You don't have to defend it to anyone."

I was happy, elated, lost in the haze of Mark and his family. Mark and I had flown back to Tampa on Wednesday. He had to be back to practice Thursday, and had a New Year's Eve home game this Sunday. In New Hampshire, we'd been in our own personal snow globe, life had been smooth and unhurried, and now it was just another Friday. I sat in my office alone, and everything was rush, rush, rush again. I'd give anything to go back to our Christmas morning, to be wrapped in Mark's warmth, his strong arms, looking into his smiling eyes, and running my fingers through his sleep and sex-tousled hair. Instead, I had to deal with Ben's nitpicking hissy fit as soon as I'd walked through the office doors.

"Ben makes me feel guilty. It was like he chose to be an asshole as a way to show me how much he disapproved of my smiles and contentment."

"Your happiness isn't something you should have to explain, and if Ben can't deal, then that's his problem."

"I should tell Trent I can't work on this audit." My words came out in a strangled string of worry.

"Is that what you want? I thought you needed the experience?"

I rested my forehead in the palm of my free hand. "I don't know."

"You need to talk to Trent."

"I will." I lifted my head to stare up at the ceiling, and wet my lips, letting a small smile infuse my tone as I not-so-subtly changed the subject. "You coming to the game with me Sunday?"

"Why wouldn't I? The best way to get a man out of your system is to surround yourself with opportunities to test your strength."

"And watching Bryson play hockey is testing your strength?"

"Yes, because damn, he's hot when he's sweaty, and I can't even say that from personal experience. How does the team man whore turn me down, Stevie? How?"

I giggled. "You sound insulted."

"I am."

"Mark said, and I quote 'he's probably trying to keep his dick out of the family cookie jar'."

"What if I want his—"

"Hey," I cut her off not really wanting to talk about my boyfriend's best friend's sex life, or body parts, for that matter. "You could bring Pete to the game?"

"Ugh."

"You guys love each other, and you both are stubborn asses and are too chicken to admit it."

She was quiet for a few seconds. I'd picked away at her defenses, and her silence proved I'd hit a little too deep this time.

She took a long breath. "Ask Mark for an extra ticket... just in case."

A knowing smile sprawled across my lips. "Of course."

"I'll call you later," she said, her good humor distracted and shaken.

She hung up and my guilt clouded over me. She was always throwing in her two cents about my life, and what I said wasn't really a secret. You can only be on-again, off-again with the same person so many times before someone has the guts to slap you in the face and say, "Hey, idiot, look, your chance is right there." Mark was my slap in the face and my chance. I only wanted the same thing for her.

I'd finished typing out a quick text to Mark, asking him if he could grab an extra ticket for Pete, when a knock sounded on my office door. Trent didn't wait for an answer before he walked in.

"These are for you," he said, laying three large, overstuffed folders onto my desk. "Ben needs these postal receipts put into the expenses spreadsheet."

"Good morning to you, too," I teased and Trent's frown curled up at the corners.

He lowered himself into the chair across from me without any grace, a long exhale shuffling the blond mop of bangs over his forehead.

"I know." He groaned. "I haven't had enough coffee, my manners don't take effect until after the fourth cup."

I opened one of the folders and wanted to groan as well as I milled through the receipts. "What's my deadline?"

He cringed. "Tomorrow?"

"That's impossible."

He scrubbed his palm down his face. "I know... but Ben said—"

"Trent. There are hundreds of receipts here. This will take me all weekend." I shut the folder, summoning my good grace. He was overworked, stressed out, and apparently delusional. There was no way I could get this finished by tomorrow. "The soonest I could have this finished is Monday, and that's a holiday."

"Unfortunately, it'll be a working holiday." His brows dipped deeply, anxiety crinkling and aging his handsome face. "I'll let Ben know you'll have them ready by Monday." He gave me his charming smile, the one he'd used on David when he knew he was in trouble. "You're an angel, Stevie."

"Don't you forget it." He stood to leave and my tongue stuck to the roof of my mouth as I struggled to find the right words to say. "Before you go..." Trent stilled. "I wanted to talk to you about Ben... it's been difficult working with him again."

He pushed his hands into his pockets with a resigned set to his shoulders. "I think the Mark thing is getting to him. He's not himself."

"It's too hard," I whispered and Trent's eyes met mine. I blinked past the burn and harnessed the strength I'd found inside myself the day I told Ben I was done. "I don't think we should work together on this audit."

"What if you reported to me? I need your help with this account, all hands on deck, Stevie. I'll take Ben off expenses, reallocate his experience."

"I think that's a great plan."

The air in the room seemed less thin, and I gave him a reassuring smile, lowering my shaking hands to my lap before he turned to leave. Rocking the boat wasn't my forte, but Ben and I working together was toxic for everyone.

Having him here was like opening a scab, picking at it every day until it bled, and I was out of ways to stop the bleeding.

He tipped his chin. "Consider it done."

There were several theories online about disaster premonition. People who'd reported seeing a man who looked like a moth days before a catastrophe, interviews with survivors who felt like something was off before they boarded that plane or that train. Women who had sensed danger, some special type of fear before they picked up the phone only to receive bad news. Heartbreak was supposed to come with some sort of prerequisite Spidey Sense, but in hindsight, nothing had appeared out of place when I'd woken up that morning.

I'd gotten up early enough to kiss my boyfriend goodbye before he left for practice. I walked Atlas around the block like I did every day. Mark had his own apartment, but when he was in town, we were always at my house. I loved how easily our puzzle pieces fit together. I loved waking up next to him, having his suits in my closet, his sweats in my drawer, and our dog at my side. I loved the sweet and dirty Post-it promises he'd leave on my coffee mug before he left for the rink. Today's promise still had me smiling when I'd arrived to work ten minutes earlier than usual. I loved that no matter how thick the tension between Ben and I had become, the fog of it never hindered my vision. I'd fallen in love with Mark, and this morning, when he kissed me for those few achingly perfect seconds, if I had known how the day was going to play out, I would've never let either of us get out of bed.

I'd been prepared for a bittersweet day. Mark had to leave for another road trip tonight, and after almost three months of hard work, the final meeting wrapping up the audit had been scheduled for nine this morning. It was the second week in March, and even though Ben and I hadn't been working on the account together since the New Year, he'd still been there every day, in every meeting, and the coldness he'd worn as armor weakened the closer we got to the end of his stay. He'd find reasons to pop by my office, reasons to linger after meetings, reasons to call me at least twice a week; usually, and I'd begun to think premeditatedly, when I was with Mark. If anything, Ben's silence during the meeting should have been an indicator that this day was about to go up in flames.

It was almost noon when Trent switched off his laptop, ending the meeting. Alec was the first to stand and his smile was tired as he swatted my arm with a folder. "Shit, girl, it's done."

"Congratulations," I said as I stood, fighting the urge to raise my arms over my head and stretch away the last few hours.

"We earned it. I don't think we could've gotten through this without your help." Alec wasn't one to give compliments. I found myself smiling a little bigger than necessary and he laughed. "Don't let your ego get too big, remember, I was the one who trained you."

"You're always going to remind me of that, aren't you?"

"Would you expect anything less?" He tapped his folder on my arm again, his smile sincere as he asked, "You coming to lunch with us?"

"I'm meeting Mark, he's leaving tonight."

"How long this time?"

"Ten days," I whined.

He shook his head. "I don't know how he does it. He's a better man than me."

It wasn't polite to agree, but this was Alec. "He really is."

"I'll remember that next time David asks whether or not you want a chocolate croissant."

"Hey," I protested, but Alec's smile dimmed, and the minute he spoke, I knew why.

"Can I talk to you for a second?" Ben asked, and like always, my heart jumped ship and fell into my gut.

Alec gave me a sympathetic smile before he turned to leave. I avoided Ben's eyes as I picked up the last few folders from the table.

"What's up?" I asked as the room emptied too quickly.

Ben waited for the last few stragglers to file out of the door before he said, "I'm leaving this weekend." His cool eyes grabbed my gaze, hoping, waiting for something I couldn't give him, not anymore. "I... I wanted to say I'm sorry."

"Ben..." I let out a shaky breath. "We've been through this, haven't we? It's done, there's no need."

He took a step forward taking up my personal space. "When you told me you wanted a divorce, I was angry at you. I needed time to reconcile my feelings, to figure it out... to realize what I was losing. I thought I had time, and before I knew it, everything was finalized and you were gone. And..." He closed his eyes, and the pain in his voice matched the ache in my throat.

"I'm in love with him." I hadn't even told Mark how I felt yet, but Ben's words were a last-ditch effort and I needed to be honest. He needed to understand.

His eyes opened and his nostrils flared. "He doesn't know you like I do."

"You're right. He doesn't... I've changed." I shook my head. "Actually, I didn't change, Ben, you just forgot. Mark knows the real me, the woman you never wanted."

"I'll always want you."

He took another step forward as hot tears fell down my face. Anger swelling and spilling over my lashes. "You didn't fight for me, you let me go, and I'm happy now, and you're selfish to even—"

"I know." His Adam's apple bobbed once and then again. "I fucked up." He clenched his jaw when a quiet gasp caught in my throat. "I fucked up, and I want to fix it. I've known you half my life, and I can't believe I let you walk away." Each uneven breath I took he inhaled, stealing tiny pieces of me.

His lashes were damp, his eyes earnest and he looked like the boy I'd met when I was a teenager. A sob I'd held in for over thirteen years worked its way past the confines of my chest. "You did, you let me walk away."

The heat of Ben's hand on my cheek was foreign as he gathered away the tears with his thumb. "I can fix this, fix us..." He leaned in, framing my face with his other hand, his eyes falling to my mouth as he whispered his ammunition, "Can we do this?"

Panic stole my breath, fattened my tongue, and before I could tell him no, tell him nothing he could do or say would fix what he had broken, tell him I belonged to someone else, Mark's angered and wounded words shattered the weighted silence into sharp and dangerous pieces. "Fuck this shit."

MARK

She said my name, but her voice was in a tunnel of red, and all I could see at the end of it were his hands on her face, her head tipped back, waiting. Waiting for what? For him to fucking kiss her? To tell her he still loves her? I was sick. Nausea roiled and bile crept up my throat as I thought about how fucking stupid I'd been to think our five months mattered compared to the thirteen years of their history. A familiar feeling rolled my fists as her betrayal gorged itself on my heart. A flash of desperation in her eyes held my feet steady and my pride kept my fist from Ben's face. I wouldn't give him the satisfaction, wouldn't let him know how much she fucking meant to me, how much I just lost.

Two, three steps backward and I relaxed my fists and walked away.

"Wait!"

I heard her plea as I stalked through the lobby and out into the hot, muggy air. It usually suffocated me, but today it offered me relief. How was this shit happening to me again? I shoved my hand into my pocket, grabbing my keys, and hit the automatic lock.

A frantic sob broke through my rage. "*Please, don't leave, nothing happened.*" But I couldn't stop my feet from their forward progression. Déjà vu settled over me like a noose. I've heard this all before. "Listen! Please, Ben."

I jerked to a stop, her slip like a slap across my goddamn face. My lungs were on fire, my voice like sharp glass, "That's not my fucking name."

Terror filled her eyes. "Oh God... I-I didn't mean—"

My laugh was humorless. "But you did... you did mean it. I'm glad I found out now and didn't waste another two years."

Her hands trembled as she wiped under her eyes. Her cheeks were stained with tears, new ones pouring down over her pale skin. I didn't recognize her. Stevie's lips were swollen and they shook as she tried to explain, "Mark... I..." The fresh tears brimmed, trickled down her cheeks, and over her quivering lips as she choked back another sob, and something inside my chest splintered. The pain of it begged me to touch her, to hold her, to pull her into me. Bury my nose in her hair and take away the hurt that bled from her eyes. "I'm upset... I didn't mean to call you that. I-I'm losing my mind."

The muscle in my jaw was ready to snap as I stared at her, fighting myself, fighting what I saw, and what I thought I knew.

"Nothing happened, I swear to you." Her promise rang shallow.

She was married the night I'd first met her, and she'd let me hold her face like he had in that goddamn office.

"It almost happened," I corrected.

"No," she answered quickly and shook her head. "I wouldn't have—"

I stepped closer, torturing myself with her scent. "He was touching you." My tone simmered. "You let him fucking touch you."

"It's not like that—"

"Isn't it, though?" I ran a rough hand through my hair.

"He caught me off guard, you walked in and nothing was going to happen. I was about to push him away, tell him I didn't care about him anymore. I told him he needed to move on, Mark, and he made a desperate move." Her voice broke on the last word and the strangled sound of it dulled my anger.

"You still care about him." I laid my fear at her feet.

Her eyes glittered as she sucked down a breath. "I don't love Ben. I don't want Ben. I want you, us. It was a mistake to let him get that close, but I promise you, I was one second away from leaving."

Trust and truth were a luxury I'd lost when Mia screwed me over.

Stevie approached me with cautious eyes, moving slowly with her hands raised as if she was afraid I'd bolt like a feral animal. The heat of her palms soaked through my shirt as she rested them on my chest, and it wasn't until her fingers curled into the fabric, that I realized how much I wanted to run. I wanted to believe her, hell, I wanted to rewind this day and show up a little earlier and put my knuckles through that asshole's teeth. I wanted to believe the feelings I had for Stevie were real, that I hadn't fallen in love with someone who'd only used me to send a message to her ex.

"Maybe it's good I'll be gone for a while." I held her gaze, but kept my arms at my sides.

The weight of her fingers seeped into my skin, and I couldn't decide whether her touch was a taunt or a gift.

"What does that mean?"

"It means I need to distance myself from this."

"From me?" Her lashes gave way to the damp heat of her tears.

I was making her cry. I was letting her go. Two sentences I'd never thought I would have to process.

"When I'm home with you..." I swallowed and the gravel in my throat cut me. I allowed myself to raise my hand and push a piece of her hair behind her ears. The soft strands fell through my fingertips, enabling the vacancy in my chest to spread. "It's everything I've ever wanted."

"I'm right here, Mark." Her whispered declaration did nothing to stave off the old ghosts of my insecurity.

I couldn't face her, my eyes fixed into the distance. His hands had branded her cheeks and I needed time. "I can't go into this road trip worried about you and... every road game has been a fucking battle since December. My game is inconsistent and I'm letting my team down. It's my fault. My head was here with you, worrying about him, and how he was weeding his way back into your life."

"You're not listening." She gripped my shirt tighter. "Look at me." My jaw pulsed as our eyes met. "It's done, Mark. He's leaving."

"When?"

"This weekend." She pressed her palms flat on my chest and I hoped she could feel how hard my heart was punching against my sternum, how much this was killing me. "I care about Ben, but not like you think. He's a part of who I am in a lot of ways, but I don't love him, I—"

"You have to give me time." I couldn't talk about it anymore. She cared about him, and maybe she needed time to sort through that shit, because I sure as hell did. I was over Mia, I'd been ready to give all I had to Stevie. I'd brought her home to my family, I'd opened up again, and, in one swift knee to the groin, she took it all away. She could deny it all she wanted, but Ben was rooted in her heart and I wasn't going to be the idiot who got blindsided again. I took a deep breath and stepped away from the hold she had on me.

"Don't leave like this," she begged and the sound of it made the keys in my hand feel like knives.

"I'll be back in ten days."

She swallowed deeply, her gaze finding mine, and the hurt I'd seen seconds ago paled. Hope colored her amber irises. "If time is what you need, take it, and then come back to me."

It hurt to fucking breathe and it was almost impossible to take the steps I needed to reach my SUV. *Come back to me.* It was all I wanted, and everything I was afraid of. Mia's betrayal had been a paper cut, but losing Stevie to Ben, to any man, I don't think I'd survive it. Maybe letting go, before it was too late, could save us both. Standing two strides away, she was so close. The distance singed my fingertips as I took in her cheeks and wet lips. I wasn't ready. I didn't want my anger to blind me, my past to push me into something I couldn't take back. These ten days would either be a curse or a blessing.

Throwing down a white flag, I asked, "You got Atlas?"

"Of course." She opened her mouth as if to say more, but pressed her teeth into her bottom lip.

The awkward silence only fueled my need to put miles between me and what happened today, and as I reached for the door, I repeated the last thing I'd said to her the night we'd met, "Take care of yourself, Stevie."

But unlike the first night, when I pulled away, there was no regret in her eyes, only tears, and I couldn't help but wonder, if like last time, she'd end up going home to Ben.

We'd lost the first three of the five games we were slated to play on our road trip. The chemistry between me and Bryson was off and it had begun to spread through the lines like a fucking disease. The guys had been out for blood in the locker room before we'd even hit the ice. Our defense had hit harder, pulled more penalty minutes than we had all season. Even Bryson sat in the sin bin for a total of six minutes. We'd wanted to win badly enough we were willing to break bones for it. Instead of smart play, we used brute strength and all that had done was serve us up an overtime loss.

There was dissension brewing as my teammates stewed over the cause of our losing streak. I could feel the blame all the way in the back of the plane as we took off. Usually, I sat somewhere in the middle with Bryson, but this trip I'd banished myself to the tail, making friends with the chip on my shoulder. I'd played like shit in all three games, and Coach threatened to scratch me if I didn't show improvement in the next practice. I'd never been scratched without an injury, never been benched for having my head up my ass. I'd hoped the space I'd put between me and Stevie would be enough to keep me in the right mindset, keep me in the game, but the distance only made the truth harder to find and made it easier to hold onto the anger.

"When the hell are you gonna turn on your phone," Bryson balked before he roughly fell into the seat next to mine.

My lack of an answer earned me a hard punch to the shoulder. "The fuck, dude."

"You should call her."

"You should mind your own goddamn business." I turned away from his accusing glare and stared at the blue leather seat in front of me.

"This team is my goddamn business and you're sinking our fucking ship, man."

The ache in my jaw extended to my temples as I clenched my teeth.

"It starts with one, and we all feel it... you're not here. You don't have this shit handled, and you're gonna get yourself benched for the trip. Is that what you want?"

"Fuck no," I grit from behind clenched teeth.

"Then call her, work this shit out. Get her out of your head and get back on the ice." He knocked his knuckles on the top of my head. "You hearing me?"

I pushed his hand away. "Do you want me to beat your ass?"

"Hey, if it will help..." His smirk almost made me smile. "She didn't actually kiss him, right?" he asked, lowering his voice.

"No, man, she didn't."

"But you don't trust her?"

I'd been over this with him already. I'd told him everything.

"I don't know, I can't tell how much of this is about Mia, or about what I saw with her and Ben."

"You want my opinion?"

"Not really."

He grabbed my bottle of water and took a swig from it before he said, "Too bad." He kicked my carry-on bag with his foot. "I think this is about Mia. From what you told me, that dick Ben threw down the gauntlet and you walked in at the wrong time. I believe her, I've seen how she looks at you, all starry-eyed and shit. She's ready, Melo, she loves you."

I huffed out an incredulous laugh. "You're talking out of your ass."

"And I thought I was the idiot. Ask me why I sent that Reagan chick packing?" I ignored him, my hand balling into a fist at my side. "Because girls like Stevie and Reagan, they're forever, bro, and I'm not about that life right now. Stevie fucking lives for you and you're going to let Mia destroy that, you're going to let her fuck you over again."

Guilt washed down my spine, weakening the foundation of my anger, fracturing its base as I exhaled the last six days into the cabin air.

Bryson stood. "Get yourself handled... show up and fucking play."

I didn't miss his point. The seeds of doubt were slowly dying. Stevie wasn't the problem... I was. I never wanted to feel like I had when I walked in on her and Ben ever again. I had to decide if forever was worth the risk.

"And call your damn sister, she's been blowing up my phone since you turned yours off."

Bryson's large frame squeezed down the narrow aisle, smacking heads as he went, stirring the nest and laughing the whole way to his seat. I'd never seen him torn up over a chick, maybe "not being about that life" was the better way to be.

The flight to Raleigh wasn't long, but it was after midnight by the time my ass hit the mattress in my hotel room. I was mentally and physically exhausted. All I cared about at this point was sleep, but as I dug through my bag, looking for my sweats, I spotted my phone. My pulse quickened as I thought about turning it on. Had she called? Could I handle hearing her voice? I stared at my cell deciding to stick to my vow of silence. I was about to hit the bathroom when the phone on the bedside table rang. I figured it was Bryson, and when I said hello, I didn't expect to hear my sister's voice.

"What the hell is going on?"

I chuckled. "Hi."

"Mark, we always talk when you lose."

"I don't deserve your pick-me-ups." I dropped unceremoniously onto the bed.

"Why is your phone off? Is it broken?"

"I turned it off."

"O-kay." She drew out the word.

I let out a harsh sigh. "Shit's a little messed up right now, big sis."

"I gathered... want to talk about it?"

"Nope."

"I was about to call Stevie to see if you were alive."

Silence.

"Ahh."

"What?" I clipped.

"Did something happen?"

My sister was a bloodhound.

"We're working through something..." I ran the palm of my hand down my face. "I... I don't know if I'm ready, and—"

"You're scared?" she asked. Her voice was gentle and warm like always, and I was homesick and alone.

"Yeah... I love her, and it scares me how much I could lose when things go wrong."

I could hear the sound of her sheets rustling through the phone, and when she spoke again, her voice was clear as if she'd sat up to say what she had to say.

"I got to see a side of my brother this Christmas I never knew existed. She makes you shine. She amplifies everything that is good about you, and seeing you as happy as you were, God, Mark, you guys lit the whole damn house."

My nostrils flared as I tried to breathe back the burn in my eyes, and with a thick voice I said, "That's what I'm afraid of, Mol. Look how far I'll have to fall, there are some heights you can't come back from."

"You're stronger than that. You told me you'd give up your career with the NHL for someone you loved... That Mark, he'd dive off the cliff, every single time."

That Mark was a glutton for punishment.

"I'm working it out."

She hummed. "Seems like it, how many minutes were you in the box tonight."

I laughed. "Don't worry, Coach and Bryson are on my ass. I'll be in top form in twenty-four hours."

"I hope so, otherwise, you're gonna get yourself hurt." Seconds ticked by. "You going to be okay?"

"Yeah, I got this."

I tried not to let her anxious goodbye rattle me. I set the phone on its receiver and fell back onto the pillow. Still wearing my dress shirt and slacks, I let the fatigue of the last few days flood me. My sister's advice twisted and snarled inside my stomach as I closed my eyes, hoping, when I opened them again, I'd feel like less of a coward.

STEVIE

The dark circles under my eyes had deepened overnight and there wasn't enough make-up in the world to keep my mother's all-knowing glare from solving the riddle. Her long, drawn-out breath alone was evidence that she'd figured out I wasn't getting much sleep at night. Over the past eight days, I'd gotten good at evading her questions, using her couch to drown myself every time he played. Being alone, with pieces of him scattered throughout my house, it was too much. If I could, I'd sleep at my mom's too, but I wasn't a teenager who'd broken up with her high school sweetheart. I was a grown woman who'd had her heart handed to her in a parking lot. I suppose the grown-up thing required me to make nice with my dignity and show up to work looking partially human.

Atlas whined, his nose nudging my hand, reminding me all was not lost. My mother's stare felt like a pinch on the cheek, but I ignored her, keeping my eyes fixed to the television screen. It was the only link I had to him. Ray leaned over, shifting her weight on the couch to grab her giant thirty-two ounce Diet Coke from the coffee table. Atlas pranced over to her, laying his head in her lap. She nuzzled her fingers behind his ears and glanced up at me. Her smile small, weary, and because I'd known her my whole life, I could see the dash of fear. Like all good best friends, she'd learned very quickly this week to avoid the subject of Mark. His name was like the bell for Pavlov's dog, bringing on the same reaction—crying, in my case— every time. I guess she didn't want to feel responsible anymore for cutting me open again and again.

Exhausted and drained, I watched as the Tampa Bay players skated onto the ice. And there he was, his number coming to the surface in the sea of blue, a small stab with every beat of my pulse. The only thing keeping me from completely shutting down this week had been the small flame of anger blooming in my belly. He'd closed me out, slammed the door in my face, turned off his phone, and made the space he put between us unbearably vast. I never knew it could be this hard to breathe.

I knew what Mark had seen, and I knew how stupid I'd been for not kicking Ben in the balls the minute he'd touched me. All I'd wanted was to cut my ties, give him closure, and it wasn't in my nature to be a jerk about it. It didn't matter, because Ben was gone now, and by the way he'd left the office Friday evening, it was clear he was gone for good. His contrite "everything will work out" had been his way of saying have a nice life, sorry I messed everything up. His leaving was the check in the box I'd hoped would make Mark understand we could move on, but I hadn't had the chance to tell him. I'd called him a hundred times. I'd left at least twenty messages. But there were some things too intimate to leave on a voicemail. I wanted to tell him I loved him, the one thing he hadn't let me say the day he left. He'd interrupted me, told me he'd needed a break, and I hadn't been about to drop the L word if he was jumping overboard. Hadn't I proven to him I wasn't her, that I cared about him, that he could trust me?

The sound of the ref's whistle pulled me back to reality, and I realized my fingers were balled into fists and my nails were digging into the palm of my hand.

"Stevie? Are you going to answer me?" Mom's lips were set into a grim line.

My eyes swept to the television, and the clock ticking down on the screen alarmed me. The game had already been on for seven minutes and I'd completely zoned out.

"What was the question?" I asked, faking a smile.

"When was the last time you slept?"

My shoulders drooped and Reagan heaved a sigh. "I've been busy at work."

Mom turned her head to the screen and I followed her gaze. There was a fight happening behind Tampa's net. Mark stood out like a beacon on the outskirts of all the mayhem as he tried to wrap his arms around a player, number twenty-two from the opposing team, in what looked like an attempt to hold him back. The referees broke it up as my mother asked, "How long have the two of you been fighting?"

Tears crept to the surface and stung the corners of my eyes. "I think it's more than a fight."

A sob kicked inside my chest, but I gulped it down with a ragged breath.

My mom's face fell and she glanced at Reagan, who nodded so carefully I figured she was trying to hide it from me.

"You think it's over?" I accused her.

She exhaled, a frown working its way over her lips. I didn't like the pity in her eyes. "He hasn't called."

"That doesn't mean anything."

"What happened?" My mom's voice was tinted with the same shade of anger I'd used as a life rope this week.

Mom sat there with soft eyes, listening to me fall apart as I told her how my world had been turned upside down. I'd told her everything about Mia, and Ben, about how Mark didn't trust me, and how all I wanted was to shake him, kiss him, and tell him he was so dumb and had everything all wrong.

"You're not going to like what I have to say," she announced as I brushed away the tears from my lashes.

"But you're going to say it anyway." I surmised.

"He's not ready, Stevie. He's got a monkey on his back, and what he saw between you and Ben isn't going to help. He's gotta work through it and you have to let him."

"And what if after he's *worked through it...*" She narrowed her eyes at my irritation. "He decides he doesn't want me in his life?"

It was Reagan who answered, "You don't need a man to have self-worth, to be whole. You have to let yourself be okay with being alone. If he ends it, he ends it, it isn't the end of you."

The rational part of my brain accepted the truth in her statement, but my heart, it was hung up on the feel of his lips, how his touch felt like home. It needed the smell of his soap, and the way he'd look at me with eyes that said my heart beats for you.

"He left Atlas with you, that's a good sign." My mother's smile reached her eyes, and every muscle in my body begged me to hold on to that little offering of happiness.

"Or..." Reagan hedged. "Worst-case scenario, he breaks up with you, and you guilt him into letting you keep the dog."

One of those, hysterical, overtired, and definitely needed, barks of laughter bubbled up my throat.

I was laughing when I turned my attention back to the game. There were only two minutes left of the first period and Tampa must have scored a goal, because they were up by one. They needed a win. Their playoff spot was in jeopardy after the three losses they'd had this trip, and I couldn't help but notice Mark's game had become sloppy and brutish. He was off, and on top of everything else, I worried he'd take the burden of each loss personally. The ache in my cheeks subsided as my smile waned. Mark was in his own zone with the puck and was about to take it behind the net when a Carolina player, number twenty-two, crushed Mark so hard into the boards the entire arena gasped. The sound of it lifted the hairs on the back of my neck. The loud crunch reverberated in my ears and the next breath I needed to take jammed in my throat. Mark's body, like a rag doll, crumpled, while the arena erupted in cheers. His helmet hit the ice and flew off as it bounced, skidding into the back of the net.

"Holy shit," Reagan's voice was like the soft tin of an old radio, distant and choppy.

My vision failed and everything around me splotched in black. All I was able to focus on was the way Mark's arms were splayed to the side and not moving. I didn't hear the whistle blow, and as the camera zoomed in, I'd only had a second to see Mark's face before his entire team surrounded him. His eyes were closed.

I hadn't eaten much today, but the small amount I'd managed to put into my stomach threatened to find its way back up. I took two steps and fell onto my knees in front of the television. I felt someone's hand on my shoulder as they replayed what had happened over and over again, at all different angles, and in slow motion. I watched with horror, hoping when they showed the ice again, he'd be sitting up.

He wasn't.

Get up.

Get up.

Get up. Get up. Get up.

The emergency medical staff moved slowly across the ice with a stretcher and my entire body went numb.

Get up.

Stand.

Oh God, let him stand.

When the network went to a commercial break, the fear I'd kept on a leash snapped.

"Stevie... calm down..." Reagan's soothing voice was like nails on a chalkboard.

I stood too fast and glittered specs of light exploded in my periphery. I grabbed my phone from the coffee table, and my fingers sprinted across the keypad, but like it had been all week long, his number sent me directly to voicemail. He wasn't going to answer, but I dialed it anyway. I needed to hear his familiar voice telling me he would call me back as soon as he was able. The promise I planned to hold onto until I got answers.

"It's back on!" my mother shouted, and I dropped my phone to the floor.

They had him on the stretcher, affixing some type of collar around his neck. Too many people hovered over him, too many speculations coming from the commentators, but the dark locks of his hair stood out between the gaps.

His teammates were a blur of blue and white as the medics lifted the stretcher and moved toward the exit.

"*He's not moving. Why isn't he moving?*" Tears boiled over into sobs as dread wrapped its fingers around my throat.

A commercial blared from the speaker, stealing my last glance. Trapped in my own skin, I began to pace, blocking out the false reassurances my best friend was trying to give me, and calculating the flight time between Tampa and Raleigh. How fast could I get from the airport to the arena? I hit a wall. The game would be long over, his team, flying to the next city. Mark was only one player. Games would still be played, even if he was unconscious and alone in a hospital bed. They had trainers and medical staff, and stuff like this happened all the time, didn't it? That loud crunch, the way his strength dissolved onto the rink floor, his body a pile of bones and dust. I'd get a flight, I'd go to him and...

My mother's warm hands grabbed the tops of my arms. "You're going to pass out," she warned. "Ray, grab her some water." She shook me lightly. "Sit down, sweetheart, you need to breathe."

The sound of the game was white noise in the background. They hadn't stopped the play, they'd put him aside and kept going.

My tongue was heavy in my mouth as I found my mother's eyes and she asked, "Who can you call?"

"What?" Confusion addled my senses.

"Who could you call, Stevie, to find out what happened?"

"He won't answer."

"I know, sweetie." Mom had reverted back to the days when I was five and I'd needed her to chase away invisible boogie men.

"Bryson," Reagan whispered.

I moved past my mom without a word, bending down I picked up my phone. He was playing, but he could call me during the intermission. Tears began to flow again, but I'd left him a coherent enough message, and when the horn signaling the end of the period sounded, I'd never been so grateful and terrified in my entire life.

"We're all praying for him," the coach had said to the nameless faces of the media.

And when asked for comment on his way out to the bus, Bryson waved off the camera, and for a half a second, his haunted eyes caught the lens and the desolation almost gutted me entirely. That moment was on a loop inside my head as I lie in my bed with my phone clutched in my hand. Sometime after ten, I'd convinced Reagan and my mom, not without promising to call them as soon as I got home, being alone was the best option.

Bryson never called. Anxiety and fear had settled inside the muscles of my shoulders, weaved into the striations with anger. It was after eleven, the team would be on a plane by now. I'd left several messages for Bryson, for Mark. I'd watched the post-game interviews hoping for information. The only explanation the coach had given was that Mark was at a local hospital being treated for an upper body injury and a possible concussion. A small brick of worry had been removed from my shoulder when he'd said Mark had regained consciousness before EMS had carried him off the ice, but there was nothing to keep the numbness at bay. It was the only way I could keep a hold on myself.

I turned my head on my pillow to check the clock again when my phone vibrated in my hand... I almost dropped it. I flew into an upright position, my shaking fingers swiping manically at the lock screen.

"Stevie?"

"Oh God, Molly." I choked. "P-please tell me he's okay, I can't get a hold of—"

"He's okay..." Her voice cracked. "I think."

The dam of panic inside my chest ruptured and poured out of me in waves. Tears cascaded down my cheeks as I asked, "What happened?"

"The trainer called Mom about five minutes ago, said he might have a mild concussion, broke some ribs, but the good news, they ruled out a spinal injury. They'll keep him overnight for observation. We'll know more in the morning."

Relief slowed the rhythm of my heart.

He's conscious. He's alive. He's okay.

"Did you talk to him?"

"No. Mom did, though. Said he sounded like he was in a lot of pain."

He was in pain and all by himself. I needed to be there for him, touch the heat of his skin, hold his hand, let his fingers lace with mine, and anchor me to his side.

"I'm a mess..." I admitted through my tears. "I saw it happen, and..."

The sureness in her voice faded. "I know... I've seen him get hurt, but for a second, I thought this... this is it."

I worked a swallow past the lump in my throat as I said, "Thank you... thank you so much for calling me."

"I'm sorry I didn't think to call you right away, I was... we all were..."

I blew out a thick breath. "It's okay, Molly, he's your brother. I just wish when I switched phones a few weeks ago, I hadn't lost some of my contacts. I would have called you instead of Bryson."

"What did he have to say? Did they tell him anything?"

"He never responded, I tried Mark, too, but—"

I could hear the quiet whistle of her breathing as the silence expanded.

"He's stubborn, Stevie. I don't know what happened between you two, he wouldn't tell me, but whatever it was, don't give up. I know how much he cares about you, and I know how much Mia cost him. Give him a call tomorrow. I'm sure he'll need a friendly voice."

"I won't give up."

"Don't... he's crazy about you."

I wanted to take her words and find the first plane that would take me to him. "Call me if you hear anything?"

"I promise, and the same to you. Bryson probably had his phone off like usual, if he calls with any developments—"

"I'll let you know."

I stared at the phone in my hand after I ended the call, the news not really easing the tangled bulk of nerves in my stomach.

He's conscious. He's alive. He's okay...

For the hundredth time tonight, I lifted the phone to my ear. It rang this time, and the expectant beat of hope thrummed in my veins. Maybe he'd answer, maybe he'd let me in. Mark's voice droned, sewing itself into my pulse and it smothered my hope as quickly as it had sprouted. My eyes emptied over my lashes as I left one last voicemail.

"I'm scared ..." I exhaled a shuddered breath as the salt coated my lips. My chest was caving in. The anvil of this night pressed into my sternum and the pain of it caused me to sputter my words. "I l-love you so much... and it's so real it hurts... please... let me hear your voice."

I shut my eyes, clenching them, until the drum in my head went quiet.

MARK

It was like the flash of a camera bulb. One, two, three, and then four thousand all at once. There was so much light I couldn't see anything. The flashes repeated over and over again until my vision was carved out, hollow, and everything went black.

"Mark..." a faint voice whispered, stirred me from my dream, and when I opened my eyes, a white-washed reality flooded my senses.

Disoriented, I sat up and immediately regretted the movement. My muscles protested, the cage around my lungs faulty and broken. Each breath I took was a vicious stab. I blinked, letting my eyes adjust to my surroundings.

"Hey, there." Kristy's smile was unsure as I stared at her.

My head felt fuzzy with sleep. I'd had a long night, and I didn't think my mind or my body had caught up with the sunrise, but the smile on her face could only mean she was here to deliver good news. She was one of the team's trainers and one of my favorites. If anyone had to babysit me while my team moved on without me, I would have chosen her.

My throat was dry, like I'd swallowed sawdust. "Hey."

I pressed the button on the railing, gradually moving to an upright position, and to my surprise, it didn't hurt as much as I thought it would. Until I coughed, and then it felt like I'd been stabbed.

Holy shit.

"They cleared you for discharge."

I could handle the pain, as long as I got the hell out of this hospital bed.

"Good."

She had a large envelope in her hand, and she held it up, walking over to the small closet on the left side of the room. She opened the door, revealing the gym bag I took with me into the arena for all of my games. She must have grabbed it and brought it here before the team shipped off.

"Everything you need is in this folder, discharge instructions, scripts for pain meds, they'll dose you before we leave and you can fill these when you get home. In a few days, you'll need to meet with Maddox and the PT team so we can get a better forecast of how long you'll be out. But I'm thinking, since they ruled out the concussion, about four weeks for those ribs to heal."

Four weeks.

The burden of time pulled at my limbs. If we made it to the playoffs, would I even get to play? Would I be ready? My team was gone, playing without me. There was this bag of concrete sitting on my chest and... I didn't want to think about her right now. I didn't want to wonder if she watched last night, if she was worried, or worse, if the distance I'd put between us had been enough to push her back to him.

I attempted to suck in a breath and the pain radiated down my right side.

"Three broken ribs... I swear to God, if we hadn't won last night, if you took that hit for nothing, I would've found Paulsen and took out his knees myself." Her green eyes flared and her no-nonsense attitude I loved so much cracked my smile. "But I guess annihilation is a much better revenge than assault. Six to one and Bryson made that asshole his target for the rest of the game."

I'd been hurt before, but never like this. Paulsen was known for this shit, but the fucker always seemed to make it look like a clean check, otherwise, he'd be suspended by now.

"I'm sure Bryson will tell me *all* about it."

I hoped, for the sake of my team, they put last night behind them. They needed to stay focused if they wanted a shot at making it to the playoffs.

She pulled my bag from the closet and shut the door. "The team sends their..." She held up one hand to make quotes. "Love." I laughed and it rained knives. Fuck, this was going to be a long four weeks. "I assume everything you need to travel is in this bag?" she asked, setting it onto a chair. When I nodded, she laid the yellow envelope on top of it. "The rest of your luggage was shipped overnight back to Tampa. You should be all set to go." She turned her head to the door. "As soon as that nurse gets her ass in here. I'll be right back."

Kristy's petite frame disappeared beyond the soft click of my hospital room door. The room went still, and without her whirlwind of a presence I was forced to sit there, listening to the brash silence. And, like the tiny cracks on my ribs, Stevie's voice infiltrated my thoughts.

Come back to me...

I tested my pain tolerance and moved to the side of the bed, letting my feet fall to the floor. It was uncomfortable, but I closed my eyes and let the sting be heard. Pain was a warning, it was tangible and an ever-present reminder that you were still able to feel. I'd rather this pain than the numbness I'd forced upon myself this week.

My eyes fell to the hospital phone on my bedside table and the craving, the overwhelming need to hear her voice, the plague keeping my mind in knots, pricked at my fingertips, spread up my arms until all I wanted to do was pick up that fucking phone. My cell had been off the whole trip, sealed away in my luggage, and now on its way back to Tampa. I knew her number, it was a fingerprint. But the fear, the anger, even after all that had happened; the insecurity I'd held onto, his hands on her face, his name on her lips, distrust was a muscle memory, and I couldn't seem to find a way to retrain my heart.

I glanced back at the door before I picked up the phone and dialed. It rang twice, and my mom's voice, a kiss to my wounds, sifted through the receiver.

"How you holding up, kiddo?"

I was a child again, sitting on the back porch, the summer sun on my face, and my mother's hand on my scraped knee. My world was toppling down around me, and I wished for that summer day. I wished for it, because back then, I could let it all fall. This brave face, this mask I'd put on every day since I'd left her, was starting to crumble.

"Really good," I lied. "I get to go home."

"That's great news." Her voice carried through the phone as she yelled to my father, "He's going home!"

I laughed despite the pain. "Did you let Molly know?"

"I did, good thing Poppy was sleeping, missed everything."

"Thank God." A piece of relief snapped into place.

"You sure you're okay? You must be hurting?"

"Pain meds."

She chuckled. "Another thing to thank God for."

Kristy walked into the room with a nurse.

"Hey, Mom, the nurse walked in, I gotta go, let everyone know I'm alright."

"Love you, Mark."

"I know."

Her warm laugh made me smile.

"Call me when you get home."

My smile faded as the line went dead.

Home.

I wasn't sure where that was anymore.

"Thanks, Val." I watched as the doorman set my luggage and gym bag on my living room floor.

"Not a problem at all, Mr. Carmelo."

"It's Mark, come on now, you know that." I gave him a crooked grin.

His eyes swept over my chest, looking for some sign of injury. "That was one hell of a hit."

"Nah, nothing but a few broken ribs."

"Hope you heal up real fast, we need you on the ice."

I handed him a few bills. "I'll try my best."

"Good to see you're okay." He smiled and slipped the tip in his pocket, nodding his chin before turning to leave.

Once the door shut, I turned to face my empty apartment. Remote and unrecognizable. This apartment was a phantom limb, an extension, but not a home. My eyes scanned for a detail that felt familiar, but this place was a shell. My dog wasn't here, my stuff, my life was neatly folded in the drawers of Stevie's dresser. Calling her wasn't a choice anymore, it was an inevitability. Apprehension had a cold sweat prickling at my temples as I moved toward my luggage—my footsteps a vacant echo.

Bracing myself, I bent over and unzipped my suitcase. I dug through almost ten days' worth of laundry as I ignored the dulled sensation on my side. It was better than the nausea brewing in my stomach. I found my phone and charger at the bottom of the bag, and as I walked into the kitchen to plug it in, something cold and lonely gripped my spine. Pressing the power button, my phone exploded in my hand, vibrating with all the missed calls, texts, and voice messages.

I opened the lock screen and the first name I saw was Bryson.

Bryson: *Dude, you better call Stevie. Talked to her this morning, she's freaking out. Don't be a dick.*

She'd watched.

She'd actually watched.

I clenched my jaw, swallowing down the bitter taste in my mouth as I flipped through at least fifty text messages from her. My eyes caught on words like, *call me, are you okay, I'm a mess, freaking out, where are you, I'm so sorry.* She'd watched and I let her drown in her own panic. Fuck, for how long? I pulled up a voice message from sometime last night and the terror in her voice ruined me. It scratched out my stubborn veins, and kickstarted my heart. She was sobbing, fractured. I deserved every fissure that had found its way across my bones. I listened to the next message, and then the next, each one was reliving the hit from last night, over and over again, but through her eyes. I listened to the last message in horror as my girl came apart at the seams. My hand of silence had picked away each thread.

"I'm scared... I l-love you so much... and it's so real it hurts... please... let me hear your voice."

Fury seized my throat, clenched my fists at my side. I'd let Mia.... No, I'd done this to Stevie.

I was responsible.

She loved me. She loved me and I hadn't listened.

The fear of losing her coiled its way around each broken rib. The guilt of what I'd put her through tugged at the reins until I couldn't fucking breathe, until my legs moved quickly toward the front door regardless of how much it hurt, or how scared I was. I pulled my keys from my pocket, locking the door behind me, and not giving two shits about the no driving rule.

The throbbing in my side had reached a new level of fucked by the time I got to Stevie's house, but I welcomed it. I welcomed it because it meant I'd finally found my fight. Her car was parked in the driveway, and my heart was parked in my stomach. I didn't know how she would feel about me showing up unannounced, but I had to see her, tell her I was sorry, that I loved her, too. So damn much. Mia had taken away my ability to trust, and I'd done the same thing to Stevie. At the first sign of struggle, I'd run away like a goddamn coward.

Her front windows were open, and I heard Atlas bark as I climbed the two stairs to her front door. The humidity, or maybe the fact I was scared shitless I'd lost her for good, had my palms sweating. I pushed up the sleeves of my shirt, sucked in a breath, letting the fire burn away my nerves and knocked on the door. Atlas barked again, and I heard the scuttle of paws on wood floor before she finally opened the door.

She was devastation in the flesh. Her brown eyes were weary and wide, her skin pale. She had her dark hair piled on the top of her head, a few stray pieces had fallen from the knot and kissed the curve of her neck. She was tragically beautiful standing in her doorway. Tears instantly welled in her eyes as she took in my form. Her bottom lip quivered, and I was about to reach out to her, when she flung herself at me. Her arms, warm and perfect, cinched around my ribcage and I flinched.

"Shit." She unhooked her arms before I could tell her it didn't matter. I needed her wrapped around me, no matter how much it hurt.

Stevie took a step back, and as if she just realized who was standing in her doorway, a sudden flash of anger crossed her eyes. She smacked me in the middle of the chest, and I hissed, the muscle in my jaw working as agony rattled through me.

"Oh God, I'm so sorry." Her resentment spilled away like the tears down her cheek.

She was crying, and it was my fault. The sad set of her mouth made me take a step forward. "Can I come in?"

She wiped under her eyes and stepped to the side. My feet permanent as I walked into her living room, no empty echo—no old ghosts. This house had become a part of me, a part of us. Atlas lingered at my feet, his head down, like he sensed my discomfort. He took tentative steps until his soft fur was under my palm, his hot breath on my fingers.

"Hey, boy." I chuckled as he pushed his body against my legs. Stevie's scent surrounded me and I raised my eyes.

Her cheeks were wet and rose and the last piece I'd been missing clicked into place. "I'm—"

"An idiot," she interrupted.

Atlas left my hand cold and walked into the other room.

"I'm sorry." It wasn't good enough, and when she took another step backward, the damage I'd caused barreled down on me. The corners of my eyes stung as I looked at her. She was shaking and all I wanted to do was hold her, show her I wasn't going anywhere, tell her I fucked up, and I was here to make it right.

"Why didn't you call?"

"I didn't think you'd watched."

She scoffed, her tears coming faster.

"I-I saw everything." Her chest was rising and falling faster with each second that went by.

I chanced a step forward, and when she didn't immediately move, I stole another inch. I took each inch with grateful steps until her breath was my breath, and her scent found its way back home inside my chest.

"Your sister called me... then Bryson this morning, but not you."

Her wounded eyes fell from mine, and I feared I'd pushed things beyond repair.

"I shouldn't have shut you out." I dared another inch. "I should have called you, talked to you. I should've had the balls to tell you I loved you so much it fucking terrified me..." Her eyes, brilliant in amber and swimming in tears, locked onto mine. "I'm sorry, and I know that's not enough to fix this... it's not enough, Stevie. I can't change that I ran away, but I love you enough to know I'll never do it again." Her tears soaked the skin of my palm as I held her face. "I saw you with him, and I knew better, but it—"

"Hurt." Her throat contracted as my thumbs brushed away the tears from her cheeks.

I leaned down, letting my nose bury itself in her hair, in her sweet summer scent as I kissed the top of her forehead.

She gently gripped the fabric of my shirt in her hands, her head fitting under my chin, her cheek to my chest as she whispered through a sob, "You hurt me, too."

My body rebelled as I folded my arms around her, but I'd suffer through the pain if it meant I got to pull her closer.

"Tell me how to fix this.... Tell me what to do."

She exhaled a thick breath and leaned back. "This is a good start."

A smile gambled its way across my lips. "Yeah?"

She lightly framed my rib cage with her hands. "I watched you fall... like your body didn't belong to you anymore. In that second, everything felt so trivial. When you didn't get up..." Stevie's eyes shadowed. "It didn't matter anymore, it didn't matter as long as you were okay. As long as you came back to me." Her fingers skated slowly down my ribs to my waist. "I'm mad, Mark, but it doesn't mean I don't love you. I love you so..." she stuttered, blinking her wet lashes as she shook her head with a small smile. "So much."

I cradled her jaw with my hands, dipping my chin, bringing my mouth close enough her breath poured over my lips. "I'm such a fucking idiot."

"The biggest."

Stevie pressed her hesitant lips to mine and I didn't miss how they trembled, or how she started to cry as I deepened the kiss. I could taste the salt on her lips as she laced her fingers through my hair, turning this week into static. Her eyes met mine and then dusted down my face, and my jaw. She stepped back, her hands fixed on my hips, her appraisal sliding over my chest, her fingers moving up and feathering under my shirt and over my stomach. My skin shivered beneath her touch as I lifted my shirt over my head, letting it fall to the floor. The pain subsided, as she traced the giant bruise covering the right side of my rib cage. The tips of her fingers walked softly, exploring. "It wraps around to my back." I turned slightly and she gasped. I faced her again, hating the worry in her eyes.

"I'm fine." My palms rested on her hips as I drew her against my chest, and it was me and Stevie and the rhythm of our hearts. "As long as I have you."

EPILOGUE

MARK
TWO YEARS LATER

"Stevie, watch out!" Poppy hollered from the bench. It was too late, though, and I chuckled as Stevie took a hit into the boards. If you could really even call getting checked by an eight-year-old a hit.

Poppy let her face fall into her hand as the opposing team stole the puck from Stevie and made a goal.

"She's terrible."

I laughed, knocking my shoulder into hers. "Hey, that's my wife you're talking smack about."

"Your *wife* is terrible, you should be ashamed. Can you not teach her to keep her head up, she's always—" My smile spread across my face as I listened to my niece shit talk her aunt. "Why are you smiling?"

"Maybe I should let you coach."

She narrowed her eyes, deciding if I was being funny or serious. "I don't think this is the time for jokes. Our team is down by four."

I clenched my jaw in an attempt to hide the smile playing at the corners of my mouth. "Tell you what, I'll let you pick the teams tomorrow."

Her eyes lit up. "That's a much better idea." She gave me the side-eye. "I'm benching her."

We both turned to look at Stevie at the same time and my heart skipped two full beats. She held her stick with one hand, wobbling like a stack of bricks about to fall, her head was tipped back, and I could tell she was laughing by the way her shoulders shook. Three of the kids from the opposing team were giggling as they pushed and shoved her in an attempt to get the puck she'd trapped between the blades of her skates.

I blew my whistle as I stood and, when my skates hit the ice, she locked her eyes onto mine. As I got closer, the gorgeous smile on her face soaked her eyes with humor, and I shook my head trying to maintain a serious face, keeping up the front that I wasn't enjoying this, or that I didn't love how sexy she looked in all that gear, or how watching her with these kids didn't fucking light me up inside. I'd tell her all of this later, when we were alone, in our room.

Some would say a hockey camp for kids wasn't the best place to go on your honeymoon, and maybe they were right for the most part, but the reassuring scrape of steel on ice, the cool air of the rink, the kids laughter mixed with cheers and shouts were the things that made this place special, had made it a sanctuary for me every summer. And I wanted to share it all with her. She hadn't been able to make it up last year, and after we'd gotten married last month, we'd both decided to do this together. I might've also promised to take her on a proper honeymoon before I had to report to training camp at the end of the summer. Maybe somewhere tropical or some shit, definitely somewhere we could be alone for an entire week without any distractions.

Stevie's voice cut through my wandering thoughts. "What's the whistle for?"

She gave me a sly grin as I said, "Delay of game, two minutes in the sin bin for you, Carmelo."

Her eyes fell to my mouth. "I've gotta get used to that."

I skated closer, the rink fading away around me as I placed my hands on her hips. I was grateful she wasn't wearing a helmet with a full mask as I leaned in and pressed a soft kiss to her supple lips. The other coaches were probably staring, and I think I heard a few of the kids catcalling, but I didn't give a shit.

"Now who's delaying the game?" She pulled away and I lifted my hand to her face.

"Two minutes…" I brushed my thumb over the satin skin of her cheek before letting my hand fall to my side as I skated backward slowly. "FYI, Poppy said she might bench you."

"Thank God."

"It's not that bad," I argued.

"Hey, Coach." Simon, one of the new six-year-olds, pulled on the hem of my shirt. "Carrick isn't letting anyone else get the puck."

I ruffled his hair. "Don't worry, little man, I'll make sure everyone gets at least one shot on goal today, alright?"

He nodded, a small smile on his lips as he skated off.

I opened the penalty box for Stevie, and the smile on her face hit me right in the chest. She watched me, her eyes filled with something I could feel in every beat of my pulse. "I'm glad we decided to do this."

I risked another kiss, this time on her cheek. "Me too, baby."

This place, I'd thought, had always held the future I wanted, but it wasn't until I'd watched Stevie take the ice, watched as she left her burdens behind her and fell in love with these kids, that I realized something very important had always been missing. I turned to look at her and she waved her hockey glove-clad fist and I smiled. It was her... always her.

STEVIE

My fingers ran through his hair as he rested his cheek on my belly. The heat of his breath bathed my bare skin. We were lying naked on the world's smallest full-size mattress, in a bedroom that smelled more like a locker room than I would've preferred, and I couldn't have been any happier. I was here with him, and after spending the last two weeks witnessing my husband do what he loved best, I wouldn't have thought it was possible to fall in love with him anymore than I already had. Mark the NHL hockey player, was something to behold, but Mark the coach, it was otherworldly, next-level kind of sexy. His patience with the kids, his love for the game, the way he encouraged and loved these kids like they were his own, my heart was bursting. Having a child wasn't something either of us wanted right now, or if ever, but in this moment, if he'd asked it of me, I'd say yes. I blamed the past two weeks. Watching Mark with Poppy, with all thirty of these kids, a woman's ovaries could only handle so much.

The thought made me laugh softly and he lifted his head. His dark eyes smiling, he raised himself onto his elbows, framing my hips with his arms.

"What?" he asked.

"I was thinking about how hot it is watching you coach these kids." He raised one brow with a chuckle and I playfully swatted his shoulder. "I'm serious, you're great with them."

"I know." His voice was a combination of sleep and sex.

"So humble."

He laughed and the carefree sound of it squeezed my heart. We'd worked hard to get here. Our relationship was defined by miles and minutes, Skype and hotel rooms, adoration and honesty. Even the strongest of couples would have struggled to survive his schedule, but after our first real fight, back when we'd been barely five months into this journey, we'd gotten a taste of what life was like without the other in it. And it was in that short break, we both recognized being apart was the only un-survivable condition.

"You like my confidence..." He gripped my hips, pressing a kiss to the arch of my pubic bone.

The ache between my legs began to pulse for him. My fingers twisted through the locks of his hair as he lowered his mouth to my belly, licking and kissing and teasing. His teeth pinched the flesh of my inner thighs, and I let my head fall back onto the pillow. I moaned as he left wet kisses along the sensitive skin of my legs and stomach, following a path up to my mouth. Every kiss we shared was like our first, hungry and desperate. He held my face between his palms, capturing me in his gaze as he entered me with a long, slow stroke of his hips. His eyes fluttered closed for the briefest of seconds as he seated himself all the way inside of me. Neither of us moved, and when his eyes opened, he smiled. His nose was almost touching mine, and as the pad of his thumbs caressed the curve of my cheek, he cut the distance between our mouths. His tongue swept into my mouth, and

I was flooded with his taste, his heat, and the anticipation of his movement made me moan.

One agonizingly slow thrust of his hips had my fingers knotting in his hair. His lips found the crook of my neck, his nose tickling my skin as he whispered, "Love you."

Mark's eyes burned through mine, and it was the reflection I saw in his irises, my reflection, that always took my breath away. It was in him I was able to find myself again. Every road game, every hour we had to spend apart, made each heartbeat, each minute of this, of him, of our time wrapped up in one another, so much better.

This was us.

Together...

This was love...

THE END

ACKNOWLEDGEMENTS

To my Husband, Family and Friends, without you I would never have been able to finish this book. You were there for me, you supported me when I was sick, and when I needed to write you let me disappear into the words, you helped me get myself up and dust myself off.

To K & M, Go STANGS!!

To my editing teams, Kathleen and Elaine, as always you keep Team Johnson afloat.

To everyone who helped, had their hands on, beta read, edited, proofed, or listened to me whine and ask: is this dumb? cheesy? cliché? five hundred times, this book exists because of you.

To Bex Harper, your cover gives me life.

To Becca Z., my friend and PA, thank you for helping navigate the shit storm of my life and this book world, you are an anchor in the current, my love.

To Aaron and Tracy (in advance), you're going to make Stevie and Mark real, and I can't fucking wait!!!!

To AJ's Crew, everyone on this ship is a bad ass.

As always, if you are in my life, you know I love you.

Much love and side hugs,

Amanda~

PLAYLIST

Visit the website below to listen to the *Breakaway* playlist
https://open.spotify.com/user/12150951606/
playlist/olBJvVrXbZoee9dTFAVEwq?si=
4zQPfFQISR2eoDwFoM6QUQ

ABOUT THE AUTHOR

Amanda lives in Utah with her family where she moonlights as a nurse on the weekends. If she's not busy with her three munchkins, you'll find her buried in a book or behind the keyboard where she explores the human experience through the written word. She's obsessed with all things Austen, hockey, and Oreos, and loves to connect with readers!

Stay up to date by signing up for her newsletter here
http://bit.ly/NewsLetterAMJBooks.

Connect with her online

https://www.facebook.com/AMJOHNSONBOOKS/

Instagram @am_johnson_author

OTHER BOOKS BY A.M. JOHNSON